SAINT MIKE

SAINT MIKE

a novel by
JERRY OSTER

1817

Harper & Row, Publishers, New York
Cambridge, Philadelphia, San Francisco, Washington
London, Mexico City, São Paulo, Singapore, Sydney

This book was written in the Writers Room, among friends.

SAINT MIKE. Copyright © 1987 by Jerry Oster. All rights reserved. Printed in the United States of America. No part of this book may be used or reproduced in any manner whatsoever without written permission except in the case of brief quotations embodied in critical articles and reviews. For information address Harper & Row, Publishers, Inc., 10 East 53rd Street, New York, N.Y. 10022. Published simultaneously in Canada by Fitzhenry & Whiteside Limited, Toronto.

FIRST EDITION

Copy editor: Marjorie Horvitz
Designer: Erich Hobbing

Library of Congress Cataloging-in-Publication Data

Oster, Jerry.
  Saint Mike.

  I. Title.
PS3565.S813S25   1987   813'.54   87-45138
ISBN 0-06-015687-2

87 88 89 90 91 HC 10 9 8 7 6 5 4 3 2 1

To the memory of Nathan Fain

1

Thunder.

A quail stammered up out of the hedgerow, flushed by the din. The pale blue cloudless dawn stunned it. There was no storm; the racket was man-made.

Two mounted knights on a collision course—forty yards apart, then twenty, then ten.

The knight on the bay gelding carried an azure shield with a gold St. Andrew's cross, the knight on the roan mare a shield of sable with a scarlet eagle. The gonfalons at the ends of their lances stood straight out.

It was no contest, for the sable was clearly a beginner; he struggled to keep his mount from shying from the tilting rail, to keep his shield up, to keep his weapon from bouncing off the lance rest on his armor's breastplate. All the azure had to do to unseat him was tap his lance on the pauldron over the sable's left shoulder. The sable spun halfway round in the saddle; his feet flew free from the stirrups; his lance made crazy circles in the sky; his shield slammed down on the neck of the roan, which darted left, right, left. The knight lost his grip on the reins; he fell, clattering.

The azure knight turned the bay around the end of the rail and walked him back toward the sable knight, on his hands and knees now, panting. The azure tossed his lance to the turf and dismounted.

The sable knight sat back on his haunches and wrestled with his helmet's visor.

The azure knight drew his sword.

The sable knight got the visor open; his face was white and dry with terror; his lips moved soundlessly.

A car horn blared.

The azure knight turned, opened his visor, waved.

A white Jaguar convertible, glinted with gold from the rising sun, bucked off the road into the meadow, a blonde at the wheel, Phil Collins on the stereo.

The azure knight shook one gauntlet off, unscrewed the handle of his sword, and took out a plastic vial. He uncorked it, tapped some cocaine onto his armored hand and snorted it into his left nostril, then his right. He corked the vial and dropped it in front of the sable knight. "'Ave a toot of that, mate. Then we'll get a bit of breakfast. The lovely Rachel approaches."

2

It would have made a great photograph—one that would not have needed a caption. (There aren't many pictures that don't, notwithstanding the saw that any one of them is worth a thousand words.)

On the left, one of the city's undomiciled, a derelict, a street person, a feral man, a bum (a caption reveals a lot about its writer), squatting at the doorstep of his home, a Kenmore refrigerator box, its cardboard shell insulated with layers of newspaper (the down of the down-and-out), in the lee of a brownstone stoop on the north, the sunny side, of the street. He wore a brown trooper's hat with earflaps down; a forest green sweatshirt; the coats to two suits, one gray glen plaid, the other brown Harris tweed; two overcoats, one camel, one navy; khaki work pants over, from the padded look of his legs, at least one other pair of pants; black high-top Keds sneakers. (It was late spring, and winter had finally capitulated, but his home lacked closets and his life certainty, and it was both practical and prescient of him to always wear all he had; it *was* certain that it would one day get cold again.) He had several days' worth of beard, weathered skin, a hawk's nose, a high, narrow forehead, intelligent eyes: a face, but for the whiskers and the weathering, that wouldn't be out of place in a boardroom, or on the jacket of a book.

On the right, a golden couple, two perfectly beautiful people, embracing, framed by the fanlight window of a perfectly out-of-the-way restaurant—the sort that serves free-range chicken and sun-dried tomatoes (for which the clientele gladly—thankfully—pay high prices without being sure what the adjectives connote).

The man wore a banker's gray pin-stripe double-breasted suit, a blue shirt with white collar and white French cuffs, a maroon silk tie, a matching pocket handkerchief, black kid loafers, a gold watch. Not so tall that *tall* would do to describe him, he had a breadth of shoulder and a narrowness of hip that spoke of a particular kind of athletic prowess: that is to say, he didn't look like a former (he was in his early forties) basketball or football player; tennis, perhaps, or baseball, had been his game, or maybe something arcane—something that other athletes, especially, would recognize as demanding in rare combination strength, quickness, coordination and concentration: rowing, or pole vaulting. His dark brown hair was combed straight back from high on his forehead and curled slightly at the collar. Skin: fair but rouged with health. Eyes: teal. Nose: noble. Lips: thin but animated. Chin: narrow, with a trace of a cleft.

The woman in his arms was blond, but was to blondes as *crème fraiche* is to skim milk. Tumbling about her shoulders in waves and loops, her hair had the luxurious texture of something rare; it was a gold silk taffeta pillow on which the jewel of her face was displayed—the face of a fashion model without the vacuity, of a sovereign without the inbred debility; a face to stop traffic or launch an invasion, to silence a din or start a riot. Alabaster, Meissen, ivory, cornflower blue, violet, ruby, cherry: words like these mustered in the mind in the hope of being tapped for use in apposition to her skin, her eyes, her lips; any of them would do and none of them would do, for they were just words and she was flesh and blood.

She wore an off-white double-breasted blazer over a black silk jersey turtleneck sweater (sleeveless, we'd know if we'd been inside the restaurant, where she'd had the blazer off and hung over the back of her chair, revealing strong arms adorned with nothing at all—no bracelets, no watch, no rings) and (this was the best part, the detail that would have made the photograph, if there had been a photographer around, a classic) blue jeans that were not just faded but almost shabby, with a rip in the left knee and the right hip pocket torn off, leaving a square scar of darker blue, and on her feet, battered, scuffed, mud- and (perhaps) manure-caked pointy-toed cowboy boots....

4

They kissed, the golden couple, a kiss at once passionate and affectionate. The woman had to take one hand away from his face to keep her alligator shoulder bag from slipping down her arm. They let each other go. The man stepped into the street, an indolent arm up, like a falconer who knows his well-trained hawk will plummet to his glove, to command a taxi. The tableau melted; the critical moment ticked over and was gone.

Having materialized, the taxi stopped. The man opened the door, waved at the woman, and got in, unbuttoning his suit jacket and saying his destination into the driver's left ear as he did. He closed the door and sat back.

Suddenly, as if she *were* a goddess and could get from here to there in a wink, the woman was at the taxi window, rolled down to let in the air. She ducked to put her head in, then her shoulders, then her torso. She kissed the man again, on the lips, one hand on the side of his face. Then all at once she was back on the sidewalk, blowing yet another kiss.

The taxi sashayed eastward. The woman turned, her hands thrust partway in her blazer pockets. She turned, with a military flourish, and walked west, in her mannequin's stride a dash of cowgirl.

The bum watched her until she turned the corner at Broadway and went north. He reached a hand down inside his pants and scratched his crotch.

The cabbie *was* a classic, a peripatetic polymath:

The mayor, the Mets, arbitrage, meteorology—by Thirty-fourth street he'd discoursed on each. By Forty-second, he'd covered rap music and Russian women; by Fifty-seventh, Bill Cosby, the princesses of Wales and York, and bicycle messengers.

Children: "They're bigger today, kids, than when we were kids. My kid's got feet, I come home sometimes and see his sneakers lying in the hallway, they scare the shit out of me."

The limits of tolerance: "A couple of, uh, gays moved in down the block. Hey, whatever gets you through the night, but I don't want them running around in tutus where my kid can see them, inviting him over to see the landscapes they painted out on Fire Island, trying their quiche. My wife says, Marvin, with their creative talents and all they'll improve the neighborhood, plant flowers, put up nice drapes. I say, yeah, well, I'm sure there's a leper or two who's a hell of a guy, I don't want him living next door."

Traffic: "Some days it's so bad people coming into the city from Brooklyn, Queens, Westchester, Jersey meet themselves going home. Why's it so bad? Hey, simple. I'm no rocket scientist. It's so bad 'cause there're too many cars.

"People who live in Brooklyn, Queens, Westchester, Jersey, they come into the city, they should have to pay. Yeah, I know, they pay now. I'm talking *pay*—ten bucks, twelve, fifteen. See this Benz next to us? Cost thirty-five grand if it cost a nickel. You telling me that guy can't afford ten, twelve, fifteen bucks to drive it into the city—from Scarsdale, probably, or Greenwich, I can't see his plates?

"Crosstown. We've been here ten minutes without moving and we're going uptown—you ever try to go crosstown this time of day? Forget about it. The Convention Center. The Coliseum's too small, let's build a convention center, let's put it as far away from subways, hotels, restaurants as we can, let's not have any parking lots, people'll have to take taxis, buses, we'll have vans to run them over from the hotels, we'll have no parking, no private cars, no deliveries on Forty-ninth, Fiftieth, so the taxis, buses, vans can whip across town. Yeah, sure, you better believe it."

Free-associating now: "Jake Javits. There any Jewish senators anymore? I can't think of one. Moynihan. Hah. D'Amato. Think there'll ever be a Jewish President? I'd've liked to see Ted Kennedy take a shot at it. I fell for that Camelot shit, I guess, even with the stuff about Jack and Bobby and Marilyn Monroe and all.

"That friend of yours, now there's a looker. You're a lucky man, my friend, don't ever let anybody tell you different. People'll tell you it's compatibility or something, how you get along

6

and all. But it's not compatibility, it's whether your wife still turns you on after twenty years. Hell, after two years. Two years from now, ten years, twenty years, that friend of yours, she's still going to be a looker. She'll look better, probably. Women like that look better. Say, you don't mind my asking, is she an actress or something, a model?...

"You asleep? I should shut up, you're asleep, I didn't know you were asleep. I'm sitting here talking, you're taking a nap. I didn't know that....

"Hey, buddy...?

"Buddy...

"Jesus Christ...

"Ah, up yours. Stop honking, will ya, there's something wrong with my passenger, I got to see what's wrong with him, stop honking....

"Jesus. Oh, no. Jesus...

"Hey, Mack. Hey, you. Open the window. Open the fucking window. You got a phone in there? You got to have a phone in there—you got a Benz, you got to have a phone. You got a phone? Yeah, you got a phone. Call nine-one-one, will you, there's a dead guy in my cab. Yeah, yeah, a dead guy."

3

Not only the dead know Brooklyn.

Sitting on the wooden steps of the so-called back porch, shoeless, sockless, playing masochistic footsie with a splinter, Susan Van Meter took a reef in her holey terry robe, blew on the coffee in her mug (indisputably hers, for on it was hand-painted MOM), and surveyed her yard and her neighbor's yards, searching amid the meager winnings of one small group of gamblers at life for something, anything, familiar.

All she saw were things she'd seen so often and for so long that she needed an effort of will to see them at all: pint-size swimming pools, barbecues, hibachis, chaise longues, Adirondack chairs, gliders, picnic tables, umbrellas, awnings, tents, marquees. What an investment in taking it easy and in pretending they were doing it at the beach or in the country!

Rakes, hoes, spades, pitchforks, trowels, trellises, dowels, twine, bags of soil and fertilizer—symptoms of an agricultural urge that seized them periodically. Some blasted tomato plants and skimpy ivy were the region's only crops.

Unless you counted children: carriages, walkers, strollers, Gerry packs; rattles, pacifiers, mobiles, stuffed animals and animals not so stuffed; bicycles, tricycles, little red wagons; balls, balls and more balls, round and oblate, big and little, hard and soft, and things to hit them with, or catch them; roller skates and skateboards, swim fins, sneakers with no siblings; Slinkies, Frisbees, boomerangs; ordnance—tanks, trucks, planes, helicopters, swords (Conan broadswords and Luke Skywalker light sabers), knives, rifles, pistols, disintegrating-ray guns, tommy guns, grenades, bazookas, bows and arrows; pogo sticks, trampolines and jump ropes; turtle sandboxes and wading pools that leaked both air and water; shovels, pails, measuring cups, steam shovels, backhoes, bulldozers, road graders; plastic alligators, sharks, frogs, and ducks; swings, swings, swings.

What else? In a corner of the Webers' yard was a black mound of what looked like obstinate, filthy snow. It had a certain dignity, for everywhere else the predominant colors were the oranges and yellows that are the final certification that something is entirely man-made, that it contains no natural substances.

And the laundry. Susan knew every sock, every jockstrap, every girdle. Buy some dainty underthing and you'd better hang it in the bathroom unless you wanted Susan Van Meter to know how you got your kicks. Stained sheets? Throw them out. A new man around the house, with dirty shirts? Send him to the laundromat.

Any condoms? Susan wondered. Any bodies? Any reefer, any soda? Any semiautomatic weapons? Just the other week, Paul had told her about a raid the cops made on a crack factory in the Bronx; the alleged perps threw bags of drugs, drug paraphernalia and guns out the window; the cops, deprived of the evidence for the drug bust, arrested them for littering.

It was a funny story, nicely told, like all Paul's stories, with a compassion for the cops that not many other feds could have mustered, but Susan hadn't laughed. She'd made what Carrie used to call—back when Carrie was amused by her mother—her garglegoyle face.

Paul had read it right. "I know. I've been away."

"And who knows where? Who knew where?"

"Jamaica."

"Jamaica. You don't have a tan."

"It was night work."

"Somehow that's not reassuring."

"It wasn't my choice. Bad guys never sleep."

"Jamaica. What's funny—it's not funny; it's pathetic—is my fantasy about what you're doing when I don't hear from you for days and days at a time is that you're sitting in a crummy car in a crummy alley in the South Bronx or Bed-Stuy with a partner in as much need of a shave and a shower as you, drinking rotgut coffee and eating cold pizza and waiting for a junkie snitch who might be straight enough to remember what he has to sell you if he's straight enough to remember to show up if the people he's snitching on haven't killed him—"

Paul smiled. "You know that's usually what I *am* doing."

"—and you're in Jamaica, with that girl in the wet T-shirt and the breasts you could eat. Calypso bands and daiquiris."

"Susan, people envy me for having a wife who's been on the job too, who understands that the Jamaica I've been to isn't the one in the travel brochures."

"I'm not on the job now. I'm a secretary. A file clerk."

"I don't want to avoid talking about this, Susan, but it's impossible to talk about it if you put yourself down."

"Research specialist." She exaggerated the sibilances. "I'm a drudge."

"Barnes said your Bolivia report's one of the best he's ever read."

She did Barnes's superannuated-preppy singsong. "God, Susan. Super. Top-notch. Interesting, interesting stuff. Beautiful. Really beautiful."

"Joanna's kicked him out."

"No? Jesus. Honestly? I can't. I don't. I won't. It isn't. He'll be Director one day simply because he never speaks a complete sentence. No one knows what he really thinks about—Oh."

Paul was standing behind her, with his hands on her breasts. "I missed you."

Susan put her hands over his and encouraged them. His touch, his lips, his tongue, the fit of his body with hers reassured her. Afterwards, clothes and bedclothes everywhere, she said, "Take that, Jamaica."

Through the screen door Susan heard Imus say it was six thirty-two, twenty-eight till seven. Six thirty-two, twenty-eight till seven, and the fourth day in a row she'd woken up with Imus instead of her husband, who was on the job again—in Jamaica, in the South Bronx, in Bed-Stuy, who knew?—because bad guys never sleep.

10

She went inside and folded the comforter she'd fallen asleep under on the couch and put it in the front hall closet. The television had been on, tuned to Jimmy Swaggart, when she woke, but she couldn't remember what she'd been watching to make herself fall asleep. Or was it what she'd done to make herself stay awake?

What did those wives who hadn't been on the job, too, do when their husbands didn't come home? Did they call the shop and make a fuss? Did they snoop in their husbands' desks to see if they'd taken their passports, in their closets and dressers to see if they'd packed for warm weather or cool? When their husbands came home did they refuse to feed or fuck them until they promised they'd never go off again without saying where they were going and for how long?

It was supposed to have been different. Fifteen years ago, they were going to be Batman and Robin, the Lone Ranger and Tonto, Superman and Wonder Woman, Robin Hood and Maid Marian, Van Meter and Van Meter, Mr. and Mrs. Narc. Saint Paul and Saint Michael . . .

"Szentmihalyi?" Paul had cornered her, fifteen years ago, during a break between Pharmacology and Ballistics, or some such, and demanded to know what kind of name that was.

"Hungarian. It means Saint Michael."

"The one who killed the dragon?"

"That was George. The archangel Michael."

"Susan Van Meter's a nice name."

"Yes, it is. Is she your sister?"

"Susan Van Meter. I like it."

"I can't marry you till after lunch. Unless you're the kind of man who doesn't mind if his wife has lunch with another man."

"Depends on the man."

"John Barnes?"

"You had lunch with him just the other day."

"If you want to marry me, Van Meter, don't surveil me."

"You don't strike me as the kind of woman who'd date her teacher just to get a passing grade."

"It's not just a passing grade I want. I want to be at the top of the class."

11

"I'm going to be at the top of the class. I'm betting on you to be top woman."

"I'll take that bet."

"You'd bet against yourself?"

"No. I'll bet you that I'll be top overall."

"A kiss?"

"A Coke. I'm going to kiss you anyway."

"After lunch?"

"Saturday night."

She kissed him Saturday night and slept with him Sunday morning and lost the bet, for Paul Van Meter was top overall, and Susan Szentmihalyi was the number two woman, behind Rita Arroyo, and fifth overall. They did get married, and she called herself Susan Van Meter, and for a while they dreamed of being a team, until Susan got pregnant and Paul said it wouldn't be fair to their child for both of them to work at risk, so he would, and she could take a desk job. She had never really been on the job, just on the verge. . . .

"I'm Imus in the morning. It's six forty-six, fourteen till seven."

Time for the morning slugfest.

"Carolyn!" Never give a child a three-syllable name; there's no way to yell it without whining. "Carrie!"

The sound of serious sleeping.

Susan tapped then rapped then knocked then pounded on Carrie's door.

"What?"

"Time to get up."

"Ten more minutes."

"I'm coming in."

"No."

"Then get up."

"I'm up."

"Now."

"I'm *up*."

12

"Open the door."

"Don't come in here."

"Open the door."

The sounds of drugs and drug paraphernalia and semiautomatic weapons being thrown out the window.

Susan opened the door. Cigarettes spilled from the pack Carrie was trying to stash under her mattress.

"Hey." Alleged perps were always righteously outraged.

"That'll cost you your allowance for the rest of the week and your Saturday night out."

"You're not supposed to come in unless I ask you."

"You're not supposed to smoke."

"They're not mine, okay? They're Jennifer's."

Who had blue hair, nine earrings in her left ear and six in her right, wore fingerless black lace evening gloves, a motorcycle chain around her waist, a sleeveless blue-jean jacket over a full slip, torn fishnet stockings, one Doc Marten combat boot and one high-top black sneaker. "I'll tell Jennifer's mother." Who smoked tobacco and marijuana and had a gin and tonic for breakfast.

"Oh, rad."

"And your father." Who was who knew where.

"Is Dad coming home tonight?"

"I don't know."

"Is he all right?"

"Why shouldn't he be?"

"*Is* he?"

"I don't know."

"Don't you care?"

God damn them. You tried to set a good example and they faulted your every move. "When you're out on your own, young lady, then you can malign your mother."

"When I'm out on my own, I'm going to change my name."

"Breakfast," Susan called, and went down the hall.

Carrie followed after her. "It isn't fair to go through life with a name someone else gives you."

"Horses do. And dogs and cats. And boats and cars and towns. Most things, come to think of it."

13

"That doesn't make it fair."

"Shredded wheat, shredded wheat, or shredded wheat?"

Carrie picked up an orange from the bowl on the table and held it like a crystal ball. "I'm going to change it to Cher."

Susan laughed. She loved Cher, loved that she looked different every time you saw her, loved that she told Barbara Walters on TV once that people who didn't like the way she went through men thought of her as a vacuum cleaner with a belly button. "Cher's taken."

"All the rad names're taken. Cher. Madonna. Vanity. Fiona. Apollonia."

"Eat something, Carrie."

Carrie went to the refrigerator, but to tune the radio to Z100. She danced to something by Heart. At least Carrie wasn't a fan —or maybe she was, in her sanctum, and on the street—of Jennifer's favorite bands: the Circle Jerks and Doggy Style.

The F train was air-conditioned and not too crowded, but Susan sweated so much the woman sitting next to her told her she had a fever and to take the day off.

She didn't have a fever; she had a question. Since she'd been on the job too (almost), and knew there was nothing to be gained by calling the shop and making a fuss; since she couldn't refuse to feed or fuck Paul if he wasn't there; even though she knew that there was nothing to be learned from snooping in his desk, his closet, his dresser—he could be traveling under any fairy tale at all and would be wearing clothes that fit that fairy tale—she'd snooped anyway, and found his passport and what looked to her to be most of his clothes. She'd also found, in a manila envelope in the back of Paul's sock drawer, where nobody but an idiotic amateur would put them—or nobody who didn't want them to be found— one hundred hundred-dollar bills.

14

4

"I finally figured out," Red Sayles said, "why the heavy hitters, the Iacoccas and so on and so forth, wear dark suits."

John Barnes, in dark gray slacks and a blue blazer, tipped his head back to watch the numbers go on and off as the elevator ascended: *forty-six*—his age—*forty-seven, forty eight, forty nine;* time passed that quickly, sometimes.

"First of all, they can carry a newspaper without getting ink all over them. *And* they can dribble on their pants and it doesn't show. When they're urinating and so on and so forth."

Rita Arroyo breathed a ladylike flame through her nose.

Time didn't pass quickly at all at meetings like the one they were bound for, where he was going to have to explain to assholes from ATF, the FBI, INS, Customs, NYPD, the mayor's office, the governor's, the U.S. attorney's, the Manhattan D.A.'s, the Taxi and Limousine Commission, for Christ's sake—with Nix, jet-choppered in from Georgetown for the occasion, looking over his shoulder all the while—how come one of his agents got whacked in the back seat of a taxi in the middle of Manhattan in the middle of the afternoon.

"The heavy hitters might try to tell you they *don't* dribble on their pants. But everybody dribbles on their pants—present company excepted, of course, Rita. It's the inevitable result of the dovetailing of two flawed designs—the penis and the zippered fly."

Rita tossed her head like a fandango dancer. "It is not just the penis that is flawed; it is the entire organism."

Explain how come and then endure their smug, silent impugning. Sitting deep in their leather chairs, elbows on the

15

arms, fingertips lightly joined together, eyes hooded but looking right inside you, praying, really, but trying to look like they weren't, praying, *Dear God, don't let* me *fuck up like that*.

"So they wear dark suits—even in the summer they wear them; navy, charcoal gray and so on and so forth—so the dribbles don't *show*." Sayles checked the crotch of his beige suit (a hurried trip to the men's room had inspired his observation), straightened his tie, tucked in his shirt, patted his belly. "Plus a dark suit makes you look thinner and so on and so forth. It's not like I eat too much, though. You know what it's like? It's like that Levi's for men commercial—you ever hear it on the radio, Rita?—the commercial saying a guy gets to be a certain age he needs pants with a *scosh* more room around the seat and thigh —not 'cause he's fat or anything, just gravity, nature, doing their thing and so on and so forth. I've just got a scosh, that's all."

"You are a scosh," Rita said.

The car stopped at seventy-six and a virgin got on—a virgin in a black suit, collarless. She had dark brown hair pulled straight back and gathered in a braided elastic band at the base of her skull, just where Barnes would shoot her if he had to kill her. In front of her ears, some strands of hair hung straight down, not unkempt strays but deliberately cut and combed into sideburns, spit curls, *peyes* —he didn't know what to call them. Her neck—perhaps it was the effect of the collarless jacket—was rather thicker than he liked, but he did like the way her hair looked against it, converging to the gather, then fanning out again into a tidy brush.

She looked neither straight ahead nor up at the lighted panel nor down at her shoetops, but toward about eleven o'clock, as if waiting for him to speak. Her hands were empty—no purse, no briefcase, no papers, no coffee container—and she had them in the slash pockets of her narrow skirt, hemmed just at the knee. They were big hands, Barnes guessed, to go with her neck, with her developed calves, with her big feet in black sensible shoes; her ankles were thick but had definition.

Ponytails—the virgin's wasn't a true ponytail; it was too low on her neck—had been one of Barnes's many paternal Waterloos. He'd finally learned that you had to brush and brush and

16

brush, well after you thought you'd brushed enough, until you'd collected every strand of hair that was long enough for the ponytail; but he'd always botched the ponytail holder, for Sally's hair was so fine it slipped from the elastic before he could loop it and he'd end up with a sort of herniated ponytail, loose hairs all over the place, spilling down Sally's neck, and Sally angry at him for pinching hairs and he at her for having such fine hair, his hair, instead of her mother's dense curls, which would've made ponytails out of the question. Despite her dense curls, despite her never having made ponytails for herself, despite her anger at Sally for having her father's hair, Joanna had devised them in a flash, her fingers nimble as a weaver's.

"John?" Sayles stood astride the elevator doorsill, the door bumping at his back repeatedly as it tried to close and he prevented it. Rita was already striding down the hall, as if on a solitary errand. "Eight-niner. Ladies' lingerie and lunar orbit. Change here for Mars and Venus."

The virgin stepped aside to let Barnes pass, smiling at Sayles' banter but keeping her eyes downcast.

"Are you free for lunch?" Barnes said.

She looked up at him and saw right through him. "I have a fencing lesson."

And ran five miles before breakfast and played squash after work and backpacked on weekends and on her summer vacation made superalpine climbs in the Himalayas; she was a gourmet cook and a licensed bartender and could—if she wanted to, if she wasn't also a world-class shopper—make her own clothes; she had a black belt in karate, a law degree from Harvard, doctorates in high-energy physics from Princeton (which explained her specific response to a generic question) and Romance philology from the Sorbonne; she wasn't, in fact, a virgin, but she preferred a vibrator, an Orgasmatron. Barnes knew her type; he'd married one.

Nix (aptly named, for he'd gotten to be what he was, the Director's Janus, not on the strength of his own ideas but by finding fault with everyone's else's) spread his tiny pink hands on

17

the table as if about to play some piano favorites. There'd be no telltale dribbles on his blue suit, which had a pin stripe not so much discreet as clandestine. "John, why don't you begin? You all know our area director, I believe."

Barnes put his palms together and thought about saying grace, but just rolled his pencil back and forth between them. "One of our agents, Paul Van Meter, was shot and killed yesterday afternoon while riding in a taxicab on Third Avenue. He was on the job, but it would seriously compromise our activities if that were to be made public. We'd like your cooperation in creating a story that will satisfy the inevitable curiosity of the press—something to the effect that his death was an incident of arbitrary, random violence, perpetrated, perhaps, by someone in a passing car." He closed a manila folder on a sheet of yellow legal paper he'd pretended to consult, though what it was was a list of real estate agents in Hoboken. His sublease on a studio on Ninth Street that reeked of odors from Balducci's was about to expire; Joanna had changed the locks at West End Avenue (and instructed the doormen to call the police, then her, if he came around trying to fast-talk his way in); he couldn't afford Manhattan rents; so he was going to have to go apartment hunting across the river.

"Uh, John?" Chief of Detectives William (Buffalo Bill, after his hometown) Aldrich leaned way forward so that Barnes could see him. "I have a little problem with that, uh, scenario. For one thing, it looks from the ballistics like Agent Van Meter was shot at very close range, one to twelve inches, which makes it unlikely that the perpetrator was in another vehicle. The slug's from a twenty-two-caliber pistol, probably silenced. If the testimony of the cabbie"—Aldrich put on his half-glasses and riffled some papers—"Marvin Needleman, is accurate insofar as he told the squad that Agent Van Meter's posture was approximately the same throughout the trip—what I mean is that he was sitting more or less upright in the back seat—then the angles would seem to indicate that he was shot by someone sitting next to him in the cab, what I mean is by someone holding the twenty-two-caliber pistol approximately like this"—he made a pistol of his right hand and bent his wrist ninety degrees, his arm tucked in to his side—"assuming, based on the statistical probability, that the shooter was right-handed, striking Agent Van Meter approximately here"—he tickled his rib cage just below his heart with the middle finger of his left hand—"the problem with that being the cabbie Needleman's testimony that there was no one else *in* the cab with Agent Van Meter throughout the duration of the journey."

Aldrich looked down at his hand, the forefinger still extended, the other three fingers bent, thumb upright, as if he was wondering if he should enter it into evidence. Barnes thought he should shoot himself in the head with it, for his syntax.

"What else?" Nix said.

"Uh . . . Sorry?" Aldrich took off his glasses and bent an ear with his forefinger.

"You said 'for one thing,' then told us the ballistics militate against a perpetrator in another vehicle, notwithstanding that Van Meter was the solitary passenger of the taxi. Is there a second thing?"

"Well, there's the woman. The cabbie Needleman said there was a woman with Van Meter when he picked him up. When Needleman picked him up. Picked Van Meter up." Aldrich flushed; pronouns were so fickle. "They had lunch together. They were standing outside Trees when he picked Van Meter up. The cabbie Needleman. The headwaiter confirms they had lunch together. Van Meter and the woman. They didn't have a reservation, just walked in. He's never seen either of them before and he's been there two years. The headwaiter. He paid cash. Van Meter. The cabbie Needleman said she leaned into the cab to kiss him. Kiss Van Meter. It could've happened then."

"What trees?" The FBI man, a florid Irish drunk scosh in a pale blue dribble-susceptible polyester suit. The Federal Bureau of Impropriety.

Aldrich, suddenly a sophisticate, smiled. "Trees is the name of the restaurant, Jim."

"An expensive restaurant," Barnes said.

A glance and a smile from Rita, sitting next to Barnes, and a chuckle from Sayles, behind him, and from the mayor's representative, facing him several miles away on the other side of the table, a strawberry blond virgin in a light gray linen suit, horn-rimmed glasses, a floppy burgundy silk bow tie, chugging black coffee, chain-smoking Camel Lights. No dawn runs for her; she stayed trim with nicotine, caffeine and blow.

Barnes played to her. "I think we're getting away from the point here. Our task is to come up with a version of the truth that will be acceptable to the media, not to make it jibe with what only we know to be the facts. The press won't be informed about the forensics, or about the woman."

"What were the, uh, parameters of Van Meter's investigation?" Bailey Rule from Customs, in his formal mode.

"Narcotics trafficking," Barnes said.

Rule laughed his authentic laugh, like jungle drums. "Hey, babe, I don't want a slice outta your action, I just want to scope the layout."

"The layout's irrelevant."

"Mr. Barnes." The scosh from the U.S. attorney's office: rimless glasses, dribble-proof charcoal gray pinstripe suit, repp tie, black wing-tips, a five o'clock shadow at nine-fifteen. "None of us wants to compromise an ongoing investigation, but I respectfully suggest that it's imperative that we know some of the details in order to determine its relevance or lack of it for ourselves."

"Noted."

"Come on, Barnes." The FBI scosh. "Nobody's going to rain on your parade. Look how cooperative we've been about keeping this out of the papers so far—"

"That's a fact, John." Aldrich sprawled forward on the table. "The white-tops that answered the nine-one-one call, the squad, their precinct commander, the guys from Crime Scene, as soon as they found out Van Meter's Colt was government issue, ran it through the computers, came up with you guys, they put a lid on it."

"So we've been giving." Scosh One held his hands in front of his chest and waggled his fingers. "Now we gotta get a little."

"Uh, John?" Aldrich again, flipping through his papers. "Another thing here I got a little problem with. Van Meter gave the cabbie Needleman an address, which turns out to be an apartment building on East End Avenue and Eighty-first Street. It's not his residence. Van Meter's. He lives in Brooklyn. Is it one of your—what do you call them?—safe houses?"

"We don't call them safe houses. And, no, it's not."

"Too expensive," Scosh One said, and laughed a laugh that went with his suit.

"We showed Van Meter's mug shot to the super, to the doormen, but we got a big zilch," Aldrich said. "We tried the cabbie's description of the woman Van Meter was with on them, but the cabbie didn't give us much. Just a looker with a big head of blond hair." Aldrich slumped anecdotally. "You know, one strange thing about this is that Van Meter didn't have any keys on him. Whatever the super and the doormen said, I'd've bet a lot of money that if we'd found keys on him, one of them would've been for an apartment in that building—"

"A *garçonnière,* as the French call it?" The strawberry blonde drummed on the table with the eraser end of her pencil.

"What do *we* call it, Polly?" Scosh One laughed.

Polly. Perfect.

She ignored the scosh, and the poison darts being fired at her by Rita, the senior token woman. "You just said the building personnel didn't recognize Van Meter's photograph, Chief Aldrich."

"Yeah. That's right. Yes. Un hunh." Aldrich was unaccustomed to being interrogated by women—except Mrs. Aldrich.

"Consequently?"

"Look, all I'm saying is we didn't find any keys. If we'd found keys, all I'm saying is we'd've, you know, checked to see if any of them were, you know, for a place on that, uh, premises."

Polly looked at Barnes. "Mr. Barnes?"

He smiled back. "Yes?"

"What do you make of it, if anything—the absence of keys?"

Barnes made nothing of it, since the keys were in his office safe. Sayles, whom the police in the spirit of cooperation had invited to participate in an inventory of Van Meter's possessions, had picked them from the right-hand pocket of Van Meter's suit jacket.

5

Even before he saw the wallet with $1,027 in cash and credit cards, driver's license and Social Security card proclaiming that their owner's name was Charles Fuller Nelson, Sayles knew something smelled. The police assumed Charles Fuller Nelson was Van Meter's fairy tale name and that the cash was buy money; Sayles knew that Van Meter's fairy tale name was Kenneth Meyers and that $1,027 wouldn't buy the right—the approximate—time.

He knew something smelled from the suit, an Oxxford blue, impervious to dribbles, costing two or three times the suit Van Meter would have been authorized to buy for Kenneth Meyers; from Van Meter's hair, which combed straight back instead of parted on the left side; from the contact lenses instead of gold-rimmed aviator glasses; from the gold watch on Van Meter's right wrist. The watch smelled, Sayles, a watch maven, knew, for it was a Cartier Pasha, water-resistant and pressure-proof to 330 feet, never needed winding, a protective crown joined to the case by a fine gold chain, and capped with a cabochon sapphire concealing and safeguarding the winding stem, only 700 of them, each individually numbered, made for the entire world, a powerful new watch for a powerful few men, not a watch for someone who wasn't who he was pretending to be. And what smelled even more was that Van Meter was right-handed and always wore his own watch on his left wrist.

The keys fit apartment 14-D, four rooms, one and a half baths, a terrace, river view, and so on and so forth, in the building at Eighty-first and East End, four rooms out of the Home Design supplement of the *New York Times*. Thomasville, Ralph Lauren,

22

Villeroy & Boch, Yamazaki, Brunschwig & Fils, Einstein Moomjy, Schott, Laura Ashley, Baccarat, Roseline, Bali, Mikasa, ADS, Bang & Olufsen, Waterford, American Standard, Avery Boardman, Erté, Retroneu, Riedel, Thos. Moser, Kagan—all had been enlisted by Charles Fuller Nelson in his spare-no-expense campaign to storm luxury's lap.

"That's Mister Nelson, fourteen-D," the doorman said when Sayles showed him a phony gold shield and a mug shot of Van Meter taken on the slab at the morgue (not a file mug shot like the cops showed, hence their big zilch). "He dead?"

"Hunh? Oh, no. You know how sometimes you take a picture and somebody's eyes'll be closed and so on and so forth? Well, this is one of those pictures."

The doorman shook his head sadly. "You think 'cause I'm a blood I'm a stupid blood? There's plenty of stupid bloods, I just don't happen to be one a them."

"Right. Okay. Sorry. How long was Nelson in fourteen-D?"

"Six, eight months. Since the end a last summer."

"He lives by himself?"

"All by himself."

"Meaning what?"

"Just that."

"You think 'cause I'm a honkie I'm a stupid honkie?" Sayles said. "There's plenty of stupid honkies, I just don't happen to be one of them."

The doorman smiled. "What was the question?"

"The way you said he lived by himself—like there's something strange about living by yourself." Sayles lived with his mother, whose cooking was responsible for his scosh.

The doorman shrugged. "I guess I sometimes wonder, is all."

"Wonder how Nelson gets his kicks and so on and so forth?"

"You might could say that."

"He has men up?"

"Young guys, good-looking. Like, you know, models."

"Any women?"

"Just one."

"Can you describe her?"

"Hard to. Always wears big floppy hats, hair tucked up in them."

"Tall?"

"Five eight, nine."

"Weight?"

"Can't guess weights. Never could. What do you weigh—one seventy?"

One eighty-five and a scosh. "Any identifying marks?"

"Class. She's got the mark a class."

"Nelson ever say what he does?"

"He's an antiques dealer. Ain't he?"

"Anything else? Pets, hobbies and so on and so forth?"

"Mine, or his?"

Sayles laughed. "He ever walk a dog, go out the door with a tennis racket, golf clubs? Does he jog, bicycle?"

"He come out with a spear, one time," the doorman said.

A beat. "A spear."

"You ever been to the Metropolitan Museum a Art?"

"Uh, yeah. When I was a kid."

"You ever been to the room where they got all that ahmah and stuff?"

"What's ahmah?"

"What the knights and them wore, in olden days."

"Armor. You mean he had a, uh, what do they call it, a lance, Nelson?"

"That's it. A lanch. Big, long thing, with a big, fancy handle on it, all gold and stuff. Had to walk it down the stairs, couldn't fit it in the elevator. Reckon he had to walk it up too. Didn't see that part. Must a done it on somebody else's shift."

Sayles took a lap around Barnes's office. "Who's going to tell Susan, is what I want to know. We can't wait any longer; it's going to be in the papers, on TV, and so on and so forth."

Rita, smoking a Marlboro, perched sidesaddle on the window-sill, her narrow skirt tight across her thighs. That was another thing she hadn't liked about Polly, her not knowing not to smoke around the asthmatic Nix—that and that everyone, Nix included, had been too smitten with her to say anything. "I ought to be the one to tell her. We came up together, she and Paul and I."

Barnes wondered: Would three mountaineers who'd scratched and clawed and elbowed and put their feet in one another's faces to be first on a summit say in retrospect that they'd come up together? "I'll tell her. It's my responsibility."

Rita got off the windowsill to grind her cigarette out on the rim of Barnes's wastebasket; her rump invited a caress, a slap. "Perhaps Susan can be of some use to us."

"If you mean put her on the job," Barnes said, "I can't. I've thought about it and I can't."

"I will bet you that she volunteers for it." Rita said it as she said everything, with indignation.

"Even so." Nix's phrase. Upstairs, after all the scoshes had taken their licks, Nix had put an arm around Barnes's shoulders. "That was an admirable performance, John. No one even raised the possibility that Van Meter might have gone rogue. How much, though, are you going to tell Van Meter's wife? Or more to the point, how little do you think she'll accept by way of explanation?"

Barnes had started to say he'd trained her; she was no fool. But he'd trained Paul too. "She's no fool."

"Precisely. Which raises the question of how much she knows already—from him or from her observation of him."

"Susan hasn't gone rogue too," Barnes had said. "Of course you're thinking that that's what I would've said of Paul. But not Susan. I'm sure of it."

"One way to be certain—for all of us to be certain," Nix had said, "would be to put her on the job."

"But if she's straight up, it would just be exploiting her."

Nix had let go of Barnes and shot his cuffs. "Even so."

And Rita was saying now: "I am not saying Susan's gone rogue too, John. I am proposing that we use her to find out who bought Paul."

"We're not in the vendetta business, Rita. I can't send a widow out to avenge her husband's murder."

25

She smiled, for he hadn't grasped her point—the sort of failure she squirreled away in a cache with those contents he expected to one day be buried. "I am not speaking of vengeance. And in any case, if Paul went rogue, then he betrayed Susan as well as the job. It is Paul she will want revenge against, and she will get it by finding out who bought him."

Sayles stopped his pacing. "I like it, J.B. It's got a good beat, you can dance to it. Paul went rogue, whoever got him to was a big hitter, not some ounce man. Be nice to get our mitts on a big hitter. What you're saying—right, Rita?—is Hell hath no fury like a woman scorned. Well, J.B., I'd say Rita's got something, I'd say a woman scorned'd make a pretty fair bloodhound and so on and so forth."

"Susan?"

Barnes might as well have come in in a top hat and tails and a cane, at the head of a line of tap dancers from the word-processing pool. That's how tasteless it was of him to just walk into Susan's office, when he ordinarily summoned her to his, and act as though she couldn't know why he was there.

"Is he dead? When? How?"

He wet his lips preparatory to saying it had been an incident of arbitrary, random violence, perpetrated, perhaps, by someone in a passing car; then wet them again. "I'm terribly sorry, Susan." Terribly sorry, but not unaware that this was an opportunity he'd been alert to from his first sight of Susan Van Meter—Susan Szentmihalyi—smart and svelte and eager, arched over a ballistics microscope as if about to wriggle down the tube to get a better look at the riflings.

Barnes had been doing some scratching and clawing of his own in those days; he'd dragged himself in from the job, and to ensure that he never had to go back out on it again, sank his talons into a rung of the bureaucratic ladder. He taught old tricks to young pups and out of the corner of his eye kept watch on developments on the eighty-ninth floor—and all the way to Georgetown.

Susan's class (he always thought of it as hers—never as Paul's, or Rita's) was a famous class, for equal rights was in the air and half the candidates were women. Barnes taught them—and their male counterparts—a subtle lesson by taking all of them to lunch—all at Sweets—to give credibility to his taking one of them. Susan saw through him—or at any rate looked him up and down for transparency. "Is it a difficult adjustment—having women in the dorms?"

"It hasn't been a sexist policy. It's a dirty work."

"He said, sexistly."

"Is that why you signed on—to make a statement?"

"I don't like drugs. They killed a friend of mine."

A lover, you mean. "A close friend?"

"If I say yes, will you wonder if I've hung around with junkies?"

Do you honestly think we don't know you have? "Have you?"

"He was a vet. He got hooked in Nam. When he got home, well, he couldn't stand peace, either. Now you're going to wonder if I ran around with pinko antiwar types."

From SDS. From the War Resisters League. From Vietnam Veterans Against the War. Her curriculum vitae was in a special drawer in his memory: born on the Fourth of July in a factory town, her father a foreman at Nash (later *American* Motors), a decorated Marine (Guadalcanal), a member of the National Rifle Association, her mother a housewife and president of the PTA, herself a Brownie, Girl Scout and Eagle Scout; a winner of high school letters in cross-country, basketball, swimming and archery; a cheerleader, vice president of her class and queen of her junior and senior proms. At the University of Wisconsin, Susan majored in American History, was a member of the Ski, Rifle, Alpine, Glee and Young Republican clubs and a Tri Delt; she was pinned to a shortstop from Beta, then to a quarterback from Sigma Chi, then took up with a strung-out, shot-up vet. Who turned her head around, radicalized her, knocked her socks off, fucked her brains out, presumably. "Did you?"

Susan tossed her napkin on the table. "Is this official, Mr. Barnes? I haven't lied on the applications about organizations I've belonged to. And yes, I've been in a few marches."

27

And lain down in front of a few bulldozers and liberated a few buildings and lobbed a few balloonfuls of pigs' blood—and never got busted, never got your name on any lists, never got your picture taken. That's what we like about you, Susan—your evanescence. "Tell me about yourself. Is there a man in your life? What do you like to do when you get home?" And how do you like to do it?

Susan leaned way back in her chair. "That sounds like the prelude to a proposition."

Barnes didn't remember any longer what he'd said. *Don't misunderstand me*, probably—with a touch of concern, official concern that she might be the misunderstanding type. It had been his motto—and still was. Just a week ago, taking a lunch hour stroll in Battery Park, he spotted a virgin in blue jeans and a Detroit Pistons jacket sitting on a bench looking out at the harbor, drinking beer from a bag. Didn't he know her? he said, sitting next but not intimidatingly close to her. She said not yet and he laughed and said she shouldn't misunderstand him; he was sure they'd met somewhere. Not unless he'd been to Alaska; she was from Alaska; first time in New York. Why didn't she let him show her around? New York was a great town, but it was tough on tourists. She wasn't a tourist, she was here to pick up two hundred pounds of grass. He laughed and said she shouldn't be so trusting, he could be a narc. She said no, but he was married; she could always tell a narc and she could always tell a married man. She got up and crushed the bag and the can inside it and tossed them in a trash can and wished him a nice life. Wait—this was fascinating. What did married men do? They told you not to misunderstand them.

Susan shut the door and stood with her back to it. "I found ten thousand dollars in Paul's bureau drawer."

"Why didn't you say something?"

"I just did."

"Sooner."

"I found it this morning. I thought he might come home tonight. When was he killed?"

28

"Yesterday."

"Yesterday? And you're on me about not saying something sooner?"

"I'm not *on* you, Susan. We wanted to know as much as we could."

"You've known since yesterday that he was dead. That wasn't going to change. Why the hell didn't you tell me?"

"Georgetown wanted it this way."

Susan snorted. "And when you're bucking for Director, what Georgetown wants Georgetown gets."

Barnes went to the window and watched a cruise ship, all splendid and white, passing Governors Island on its way to the Narrows. He sometimes forgot he was bucking for Director. Perhaps he shouldn't look in Hoboken for an apartment; perhaps he should get a room at the Yale Club until the call from Georgetown came. Or move in with Mia, an Icelandic virgin he'd picked up on a bus. She had albinotic hair, which made her labia, when she was aroused, look an alarming fiery red. The impediment to moving in with Mia was that she was traveling on a tourist visa and didn't have the money for the legal fees for a green card. She was, quite simply, an illegal alien (not to mention a postliterate and a marijuana smoker), hardly a suitable roommate for a Director-bucker. "Was there anything else suspicious? Besides the money."

"He was out all the time," Susan said. "He never called."

"He was on the job."

She waved a hand helplessly. "On the job. You say it as though it explains everything. Paul did too. All of you do. They're just words."

Perhaps he could live with Polly, for whom they were more than just words. She'd cornered him upstairs, after he'd gotten free from Nix, and said she'd been moved by the way he'd talked about his work, about being *on the job;* he made it sound so noble, so dedicated. No, she couldn't have lunch; she had to brief the deputy mayor. Dinner would be fine, but it would have to be next week; she was going to Quogue for the weekend to visit friends—married friends, she took the trouble to say. Why didn't he call her Sunday night or Monday? She wrote her home and office numbers on the folder with the list of Hoboken realtors in it.

"What job was he on, exactly?" Susan said.

Barnes turned away from the window and played with a glass paperweight on Susan's desk.

"You don't know."

"Of course we know."

She shook her head. "No, you don't. That's why you've waited so long to tell me. He went rogue, didn't he?"

An impatient gesture. "Susan, when something's not SOP, it often looks as though someone went rogue. Paul was onto something, but whatever he had, it was't enough for him to ask for an OCD."

She wanted to shake him for turning functionary on her. "He fooled us all. And how easily. We all have such an investment in appearing trustworthy—I was on the job too, don't forget, or nearly—that we can't even see when we're being deluded." Susan put her hand behind her neck and tipped her head back. "I understand you and Joanna aren't together."

Barnes shook his head helplessly. "What does that have to do with anything?"

"Was it because you were seeing someone else?"

He took a deep breath to recover. "It was because of some fundamental differences."

"Good for her, for standing up to you."

Barnes thought about rubbing her neck for her—or offering. "Susan, we don't know enough yet to be talking the way you're talking. But if it turns out to be worst case—"

"Don't talk officialese to me."

"—you mustn't take it personally."

"I can't very well, can I?" Susan said. "I who have no personality, I who have been nothing but a moon of Paul."

Like father, like daughter.

"Why, *no*, Mrs. Van *Me*ter. Carolyn's not *in* school today. But am I mis*take*n, or didn't you call to say she was indis*posed*?"

30

The headmaster was from Virginia and had a drawl that enwrapped you like kudzu.

"Is Jennifer Pohl out too?"

"Yes. Yes, she *is*. But I don't under*stand*. Is there something *wrong?*"

Susan shook free of his solicitude and clumped out of the office and down the steps to the street. Where would *she* go if she were cutting school? She had never cut school. Goody Two-shoes. The Most Likely to Succeed. The Most Likely to Be Deceived.

She found Carrie on the Brooklyn Heights Esplanade, smoking up a storm with Jennifer and three hard-core boys—two with shaved heads, one with orange asterisk hair, all with mental-patient eyes and dead teeth. Their Doc Martens glowered beneath the benches like attack dogs.

"Mom?" Carrie tried her sweetest voice, but it cracked.

"Come home with me, Carolyn."

The boys made gagging noises and giggled. Jennifer rolled her purple-lidded eyes and blew an approximation of a smoke ring.

"Now, Carolyn."

"Muh-ther." Carrie kept her teeth clenched, like a bad ventriloquist.

Susan looked out over the river at Manhattan. She was shocked that she could see her office—well, the building anyway; the floors were indiscrete. All she had to do to see her daughter transgress was look out the window. If she'd looked out the window, or some other, could she have seen her husband?

Carrie was beside her, reeking of tobacco. "It's not what you think, Mom, okay? We're rehearsing a scene from *Julius Caesar,* okay? For English, okay? Honest, okay?"

Which of you is Cassius? "Your father's dead." Not Daddy. Not my husband. Not Paul. *Your* father.

Carrie backed away, bent from the waist. "What?"

"Let's go home. We've got to tell Grandma and Grandpa face to face. We'll take the train to Massapequa. I don't want to drive."

Carrie stood straight, her hands on her hips, not to be trifled with. "Dead?"

"Killed. Murdered."

"Who by?"

A blonde. A blonde he was fucking. "Someone he was investigating."

"Oh, rad. Fucking rad."

"Carolyn."

Carrie turned toward her friends. "You hear that?"

"Carrie."

"My old man got whacked."

Where did she learn to talk like that? From her father—her old man—that's where.

"The narc got whacked by some low-life ounce man."

Susan spun Carrie by the shoulder. She raised her hand to slap her, but lowered it and took Carrie in her arms. They stood like that for so long, crying and crying and crying, that Jennifer and the hard-core boys put out their cigarettes and came to them and touched their shoulders and hands and said that they were sorry for them, was there anything they could do?

They went to Massapequa in the morning. That night they lay together in the guest bedroom, listening to night sounds, watching the patch of light that skated across the ceiling as car headlights passed outside.

"Mom?"

"Yes?"

"Was Daddy..."

"What?"

"Don't get mad, okay? I really want to know the answer. Was he, you know, good in bed?"

"'Good in bed' is just an expression, Carrie, and it's vulgar. Someone who's a good lover—and Daddy was—is good... out on the street, at the dinner table, riding on the subway. I'm not talking about public displays of affection, but then again, I am. I'm talking about someone who's consistently affectionate, not just... once in a while."

"Do you think you'll, you know, marry somebody else?"

"I haven't thought about it at all. It's too soon."

"Would I have something to say about it?"

"If you were living here, of course. If you were out on your own, I'm not sure."

"I miss Dad."

"I do too."

"I feel sick."

"I do too. We must make ourselves eat breakfast in the morning."

"Shredded wheat?"

Susan smiled. "Shredded wheat."

"Remember when I was little and felt sad? You'd say think of something you like to do, or someone you like a lot, or something beautiful."

"Unicorns."

"The trouble with doing that now is I can only think of Dad."

"Umm."

"And that makes me sadder."

"Umm."

"What should I do?"

"Think about unicorns."

"They're not real."

Quite possibly, pumpkin, neither was your father.

6

Cool D saw a shooting star and flinched, remembering incoming.

Wavelets slapped at the houseboat's gunwales. Cars on the West Side Highway thwack-thwacked across a seam in the concrete. A jet out of Newark grumbled overhead, following the river's gash, making the windows tremble. Halyards pinged against metal masts. On a cabin cruiser in the next bay, notional sailors watched a TV sitcom; the laugh track hiccuped at monotonous intervals. A trumpet squalled on the blaster, one of Shiraz's Miles Davis tapes, turned down low. Never quiet, the present, yet like a tomb compared with the past.

New noises: uncertain feet on the dock, and giggling, high-pitched but a man's. It was the giggler who knocked, a crazy tattoo. Cool D stayed in the shadows, drawing his Beretta. Lionel had signaled his okay on the walkie-talkie, but Lionel, lately, was one of D's best customers.

Shiraz uncoiled from the butterfly chair where she'd been reading and went to the door, her body snapping into focus beneath her loose white shift as she crossed in front of a floor lamp: a leopard in a gauzy cage. She stopped with her hand on the knob and tucked her chin into her shoulder, waiting for his leave, hearing it in his silence. She opened the door and stepped back. "Cool D says come in."

A woman came first. She felt the gun, or smelled it, and lifted her hands, high enough to assure Cool D, but not fearfully high. She was dressed for the night's next stop in a little bit of strapless black, over her shoulders a sweater with a woof of magic silver threads, a pocketbook made from some extinct reptile in

34

one hand. After her, like a kid to a carnival, all his senses aquiver, came the giggler, the knocker. His antennae zeroed in on the barker, the main man, and he went toward Cool D, his hand cocked, ready to dap. "What it is, blood?" He was in Rome, and trying out some elementary conversational phrases.

Shiraz headed him off and put a hand on his chest. She flicked his arms up to pat him down, but he drew back and hugged himself, reverting, affronted, to his usual diction:

"Your man, Lionel, has already performed a demeaning and unnecessary search. There's no need to repeat it. I gave my word as a gentleman that I'd come unarmed."

Shiraz hooked a fingernail under his chin and backed toward the center of the room, drawing him after her. "Cool D says chill out. Blood. You come calling you come low and slow, not like you're stepping out in a parade." She went over him expertly, goosing him lightly when she finished, laughing at his shimmy of discomfort.

As if the sweater had suddenly gone out of fashion, the woman twitched it off and hung it from an index finger, offering herself to be searched. Shiraz tossed her head; she didn't do women. "Cool D says sit."

With her arms along the back of the white wicker settee the woman sat, her legs crossed. Her limbs were miles long. She leaned forward to look at the book Shiraz had splayed on the coffee table: *The Mammoth Hunter*. She took a leather-and-gold case from her pocketbook and extracted a cigarillo. She tamped it on the case and looked to her boyfriend, who sat spread-legged in a white wicker morris chair, drumming on his thighs to the music.

Shiraz took her lighter from the leather pouch around her neck and leaned down to strike a light. Their heads close together, their neck muscles taut, the two women might have been boys (beautiful, beautiful boys), for both had sharp jaws and ears made more prominent by their shorn hair, Shiraz's a dense black skullcap, the visitor's blond spikes. Their eyes wrestled momentarily above the flame, which though it shone manfully was overmatched.

"Cool D says smoke," the boyfriend said, and laughed. He was the offspring of movie stars, his late father a specialist in charming

35

scoundrels (Cary Grant manqué, a critic once called him), his mother one of those pouty French blondes who though their films are rarely exported (or perhaps because) have international renown. The handsome features he'd inherited from his father enclosed his mother's empty head; his beautiful body—the sex kitten's legacy—beautifully clothed, *sfoderata* and all in white, was sought after by men and women both (as was his mother's) and (like his mother's) had been attained so often that it had the look of a public garden, ordered and trim but in places worn bare. He took a silver flask from an inside pocket and offered it around. When no one reached for it, he uncorked the top and took hits in both nostrils. The rush made him a star in his own right. "And what does Cool D say to this? We want to cop a K of Cool D's righteous soda. The quality's solid—and how could it not be? He's Cool D—we're looking to cop twenty K's a week, every week."

"Cool D wants to know whom you work for."

Shiraz might have asked if he shopped on Orchard Street; he hadn't worked a day in his life. "What you see is what you get, sister. I'm Kit Bolton, this is—"

"Cool D doesn't want to know names. If you want to be a player you must learn these things. Blood."

Bolton dropped his rap again. "All right. Look. I mean, really. We met your friend, Lionel, all right? It was his considered opinion—"

"Lionel *works* for Cool D."

"—his con*sid*ered opinion that we would have no difficulty obtaining from you twenty keys a week. If that's *not* the case—"

"Cool D knows you've got a big mouth, but he doesn't think your nose is big enough to handle twenty keys a week."

Bolton laughed much too loudly. "And *I* think Cool D hasn't been listening. If Cool D'd been listening, he'd've heard me say—"

"Cool D wants to know what you can pay."

Bolton tossed his hands. "This is absurd. Does Cool D *ever* talk? Wouldn't Cool D like to sit down with us and discuss this in a civilized manner, instead of lurking in the shadows like—"

"Cool D wants to know what you can pay."

"Look, you're the ones who're selling. Don't you...? Isn't it usual...? I mean..."

36

"Cool D wants to know what you can pay."

Bolton's eyes flicked to the woman and back at Shiraz. "Twenty. Twenty dollars. Twenty large. Twenty grand." He made a helpless gesture, for he'd exhausted his argot—and the cocaine had frozen his jaw. "Twenty thousand dollars a key," he added, with great care and effort.

Shiraz smiled. "Cool D says good night."

"Now see here... This is not... You can't just... We came all the way across town... Through the bloody park on foot. We might've been mugged. Really. I mean."

The woman was on her feet. She put the back of her hand to Shiraz's arm to get around her and stood before Cool D, one leg in front of the other, her left arm across her midriff, the wrist supporting her right elbow, her right hand holding her slim cigar a little away from her face, looking like a guest at a gallery opening studying a sculpture.

Which was what Cool D felt like, immutable and fragile at the same time, an approximation of a man, empty but for his armature of bone. He didn't scare easily, Cool D; but this woman scared him as he'd been scared only once before, twelve thousand miles from here and seventeen years ago, in a hut by a river in a jungle. The fear he felt then was the fear he felt now: that his captors, then, that this woman, now, would win him over, would turn him around not with pain but with perfect understanding.

Something pressed down somewhere else on the Hudson and they rose up accordingly. They waited a long giddy moment until they subsided.

The woman finally snorted softly through her nose and stepped away from Cool D, sliding open the window to flick her butt into the river. "The famous Cool D." She spread her hands on the sill and put her face out in the sour breeze. "Frankincense, myrrh—you're like a medieval spice merchant, D, only instead of selling your wares to kings and queens, you're selling to the dregs. Junkies, punks, strung-out Bloomingdale's stock boys, Madison Avenue art directors, blocked writers, lame ballerinas—those're your players. I'm your entrée to a world where players don't have to think at all, forget about twice, about putting money down for something they need and want. All I need is a wholesaler. You could've been it, but I can't do business with someone without vision. And I heard you were good. The day will come when I'll be doing my own wholesaling, D, and when that happens, when I'm looking to make somebody's turf my turf, I'll think of you, D, and think what an easy mark you are."

She pushed herself away from the window, got her sweater and bag from the settee and went out the door.

Kit Bolton stood and wrung his hands and smiled and giggled and shook his head and followed after her.

"Bitch," Shiraz said.

Cool D said nothing. He braced himself against the windowsill and lifted Shiraz up on his hips and did to her what he wanted to do to the blonde.

And out in Riverside Park, her arms over her head and grasping the limb of a tree, the skirt of her dress hiked up to her waist, Rachel Phillips watched the houseboat sway while Kit Bolton thrust at her with the desperation of one who eats when he's commanded to because he never knows where his next meal is coming from. Watched the houseboat sway and imagined Cool D inside her.

Mute and blind witness to this alfresco coupling was the aforementioned Lionel, Cool D's picket, who had indeed searched Kit Bolton but had chivalrously declined to do the same to Rachel. Seeing Kit and Rachel coming up the dock from the boat basin, Lionel had approached them and offered to escort them through the notorious park to Riverside Drive, where their limousine waited. He led the way, and hoped that Rachel was admiring his righteous bones. When she got close to him, he never in his most misogynistic fantasies imagined that it was to shoot him behind the ear with the .22-caliber revolver she carried in her handbag.

It had been an exciting couple of days for Rachel: She'd whacked a narc; she'd faced down a major player and whacked his sideman; in between, she'd had her hair cropped.

38

7

"Tell my colleague here what you told me." Rita Arroyo settled herself on the stretch limousine's jump seat and got her Marlboros out of her bag.

Susan, on the other jump seat, looked the woman all by herself on the back seat up and down. She knew the melody forthcoming, if not the lyrics.

"My name's Grace Lewis. I'm a marine biologist."

Nice name. Nice occupation. Nice voice: husky, Bacallish. Nice body: small but voluptuous. Nice face. Nice clothes. In a word, nice; but deep within her eyes a scary vacancy.

"There's no money in it; you teach or you do research, and I'm not particularly good at either, so I got into designing and building aquariums—for offices, building lobbies, restaurants, like that. I do pretty well. Most of my customers—"

"Get right to the point, I think." Rita blew out a jet of smoke.

So Grace had been busted, and was singing in exchange for the chance to cop a plea. Every minute, Susan knew a little more. She'd begun by knowing nothing, for Rita wouldn't tell her what was so important that she had to have a little of her time, never mind that it was Paul's funeral that was occupying Susan at just that moment.

A hero's send-off it was, though muted, for noisy salutes and ranks of brother law enforcement officers weren't Georgetown's style. The Director was there, and Nix, though they clearly wouldn't be for long, for they bowed their heads as much to consult their watches as out of respect, and their driver never turned off his ignition. Georgetown *had* decided that it wouldn't do to cast one of its agents as the victim of an incident of arbi-

39

trary, random violence, perpetrated, perhaps, by someone in a passing car. The mayor's office and police headquarters had concurred, not wanting to augment the anxiety of citizens for whom incidents of arbitrary, random violence were already pandemic. DRUG AGENT SHOT TO SETTLE SCORE was the headline in the *Daily News* over a story about the press conference at which Barnes and Detective Chief Aldrich hawked this version: Van Meter had most likely been assassinated by a dealer whom he'd put away years ago and who had recently been released from prison; there were several suspects, but their names weren't for publication at this time; nor was the name of the cabdriver, lest he be a victim himself. The press bought it, wore it once, and hung it in a closet; it looked dowdy next to the story in which everyone was making *passeggiatas,* about three young police officers, one of them a woman, who were running an S&M ring in a penthouse apartment on Central Park South.

Grace Lewis took a breath and set out toward the point, if not right to it. "The man I live with, I guess you'd call it, has a boat, a thirty-two-foot sloop. We met the summer before last, in Nassau; I was there buying tropical fish. He berths it at Coecles Harbor, on Shelter Island. His parents have a house out there. It's their boat, really. His name is Kenny. We were in a bar in Hampton Bays last summer and got to talking to a guy who said there was a lot of money to be made using the boat to run drugs. We don't do drugs, Kenny and I—except maybe smoke a little grass now and then. Kenny's done a lot of different things— fished, farmed, driven a cab, taught karate—but nothing that's made him very much money. He saw it as a nice safe way to make some. If he didn't, he figured, somebody else would."

Never, Grace, get involved with anybody named anything like Kenny. It's a kid's name, for guys who never grow up, who fish and farm and drive cabs and teach karate and think they should be doing something better when fish and farm and drive cabs and teach karate is all they can do, who listen to somebody tell them there's money to be made using their boat—their parents' boat, really—to run drugs and act as if they've been given an order. There's money to be made doing just about anything dirty, Grace, but it's only people named Kenny who think the dirt doesn't rub off on you.

"I don't know if you know Shelter Island, but it's real quiet, even in the summer, even on weekends. Not like the Hamptons. In the Hamptons, you can't make a left turn between July Fourth and Labor Day, but you can drive from one end of Shelter Island to the other without seeing another car. It was so simple, the setup. We'd go out in the boat around two or three in the morning; we'd sail out off Gardiners Island and we'd meet a power boat—usually a cigarette, sometimes a cabin cruiser, no names or home ports on any of them. The guys on board wore ski masks. There were usually two of them, sometimes three or four. They might've been Hispanics; they were small, wiry. They never talked; they'd just point directions. But once there was a radio on in the cabin and it was tuned to a Spanish station."

Nobody sings like a first-time felon; they give you detail upon detail as samples of their probity, as if it's going to make a difference, get them a softer fall, or a walk, even, if they tell you absolutely everything. How many heads did they have, Grace? You forgot to say how many heads the two or three or four guys had.

"We'd give them money we'd been given by the guy we met in the bar. We'd stop in Hampton Bays on the way out on Friday night and meet him in the parking lot of a supermarket on Montauk Highway. We didn't talk; we'd go in the store and buy some groceries and when we'd come out the money'd be under the driver's seat. It was always in a sealed envelope, a manila envelope, so we never knew how much money it was, except the envelope was heavy. The guys on the boat'd give us bales of grass, soda, horse, I guess. They were always wrapped and sealed too, so we didn't know what they were, either. Usually ten or fifteen bales, twenty or thirty pounds apiece. We'd sail back in to Coecles—it would still be dark; we never went out that far—and load the bales into my van. I have a van I use for my work. We'd drive in early Monday morning—the first ferry to Greenport's at five-thirty; there're quite a few people who stay over Sunday night and drive in early Monday—and go to a gas station in Queens, a couple of blocks from the Fifty-ninth Street Bridge. I'd drive in the garage like I was there for more than gas and just sit there. Somebody'd come along—I never saw faces or knew exactly how many there were—and unload the van from the back—they had a key—and I'd drive out. They'd leave an envelope with money in it in the back of the van, under the carpeting. That was all there was to it."

Until what went wrong, Grace? Until one day there wasn't enough money in the envelope you gave to the guys in the ski masks or not enough soda or soda that'd been stepped on too hard in the bales you brought back? Until Kenny did something stupid? A guy named Kenny always does, given the opportunity.

"About two months ago, I drove in alone. Kenny stayed out to do some work on the boat. I went to the garage, I was unloaded, I drove off, everything was fine. On the bridge, I noticed a car behind me—a red compact; I don't know makes. When I got onto Second Avenue, he was still behind me. Nothing unusual but when I got downtown—I live—we live—in a loft just east of Chinatown—he was *still* behind me. I panicked. The money was in the back of the van—I'd climbed back at a red light when I was still in Queens to make sure—and I didn't know what to do. I thought about ditching the van, throwing the money out the window, just driving until I lost him—*if* I could lose him. I mean, they only do that in the movies, don't they? Finally I just decided to do what I usually did. I parked in a garage on Elizabeth Street; I put the money in my bag; I went home; I hid the money in a compartment Kenny built under the platform bed. I called Kenny at his parents', but he wasn't there. I called the marina, but he didn't answer their page. I decided to go to a movie. I had to do something to keep from thinking about what might've gone wrong."

Poor Grace. Things always go wrong with a guy named Kenny and he's never around when they do. Not that he'd be any help if he were; a guy named Kenny is a loser and he just drags you down with him when he goes under. But you know that, Grace. *The man I live with I guess you'd call it*—that said it all.

"He was waiting in the hall. The guy who'd been following me. I recognized him from what I'd seen of him in the rearview mirror. I don't know how he got in the front door; there's a dead-bolt lock on it. However he got in, he didn't make any commotion. He had a gun, but he didn't take it out; he just showed it to me, in a shoulder holster. He said, 'Let's go inside, Grace, and have some iced tea with a piece of mint in it.' It scared the shit out of me. Not just that he knew my name; that he knew how I drink iced tea. I think he'd been in the loft when I was away, and maybe saw a glass in the sink or something, but it scared the shit out of me."

Commotion. What a nice word, Grace. But you're a nice kid—not even a kid, a woman. I can see why he was attracted to you. That is the next verse, isn't it, Grace—about how he came on to you?

"He told me everything, the whole setup, more than he could know from watching from shore, or even from another boat, as if he'd been there with us—on the boat, in the marina, in the van, on the LIE, in the garage. He had us cold—but not the guy in Hampton Bays, though. He didn't know his name or the names of the people he worked for or with. He wanted me to work for him until he knew their setup. He wanted me to fuck the guy in Hampton Bays if that was what was necessary. I said I couldn't do that, I couldn't all of a sudden start getting chummy with, let alone fuck, someone I'd hardly spoken to; he'd suspect something. He said I could practice by fucking *him*. He was a good-looking man; I thought seriously about fucking him once, but I knew he meant I had to fuck him until he was through with me, not just once."

It's his intensity you're talking about, isn't it, Grace? His force. There was no way out of it or through it or around it, was there? It surrounded you.

"I told him to fuck himself. He slapped me. I slapped him back. He laughed. He liked it. I told him to get lost, to come back when he had a warrant. He said you want a warrant, here's a warrant, and he took a plastic bag with some white powder in it out of his jacket pocket. Soda, horse—I don't know. Whatever it was, he made me swallow it."

A sharp inhalation from Rita, as though she were hearing this for the first time, instead of conducting a command performance. Rita Meter Maid, they'd called her in the old days, for she'd worn mufti like a uniform and tattered her manuals in the process of getting even the footnotes and the appendixes down

43

by heart. She hadn't smoked in those days, and drank only water; she could run a mile in six minutes and before the sweat dried empty a clip into a bull's-eye. There was gin in the Evian water bottle on Rita's desk these days, or so the slander went, and covetousness in her heart. What she wanted was to be the first woman with her name on the door of an office on Georgetown's ninth floor; murder, sex, factionalism—there were as many theories as there were Rita-watchers as to how she'd pull it off. So what *is* this all about, Rita? And why me?

"I tried to throw up, but he held me and wouldn't let me put my fingers down my throat. I screamed, and he just let me, as though, What the hell? It's New York City. People scream all the time. Screaming's a varsity sport. I told him I'd do anything he wanted, but he had to get me to a doctor. He drove me to Brooklyn. I think it was Brooklyn; I had my eyes closed; I was afraid if I opened them I'd find I was dead. It wasn't an office, just a room in a brownstone. The doctor pumped my stomach out. He was foreign—Indian or Pakistani or something."

Nicely told, Grace. Very nicely told. Once you got going you pared it way down, down to the essentials.

"When Kenny heard about Charles—that's what he said his name was—he freaked, and took off for Florida, or someplace. That made it a little easier to get a job driving for Kit, the guy in Hampton Bays. Kit's short for Christopher, I guess. He's a rich guy who deals to his rich friends. I fucked him. I fucked some of his friends. I fucked Charles.

"I got busted last week. Some bonacker tried to drive his four-by-four up the back of the van on the LIE and ripped the rear doors right off. There was soda all over the road. Half of Yaphank must've been stoned just from the soda in the air. Yaphank. I went through three or four police jurisdictions trying to get them to believe I was working for one of your people. I finally talked to somebody you work with—Sayles, is that his name?—and he said you didn't have any agents named Charles, first or last name. I described Charles and he showed me a picture and I said that was him. Sayles said Charles is dead, so I don't know where that leaves me."

"Susan?"

"I really should get back, Rita."

"There is just one more thing."

Susan leaned against a tree, as if it hid her from the mourners who wondered about her absence.

Rita pawed at the grass like a thoroughbred in spiked heels. "I have not had a chance to say how sorry I am."

Susan pushed herself upright. "Thank you."

"Paul usually wore a diving watch, didn't he?" Rita said.

Susan nearly laughed. "I forgot the brand. He got it from a mail order place."

"He never wore a Cartier?"

"No." Nor anything foreign. He was an American.

"Did he ever wear his watch on his right wrist?"

Susan considered that one for a long time: not the answer, she knew the answer; but the implications of the question. "No."

"Did he ever wear his hair differently? Wear it without a part, for example? On a weekend, say, or when you were going to a party? Or on vacation?"

"No. Never. Not as long as I've known him. He was resistant to styles."

"Did he ever wear contact lenses?"

"No. He thought... No."

"Thought what?"

That they were for women. Vain women. "What, Rita? What're you saying—that Paul was wearing his watch differently, and his hair, and wearing contact lenses? What does that mean?"

Rita sniffed. "What does it mean to you?"

"... He was sending a peril."

Having coaxed the answer out of Susan, Rita tossed her head at it. "Perhaps."

"Addressed to whom? He wasn't on a job; he'd gone rogue. And concerning what?"

"We may never know."

"Barnes didn't say anything about lenses, a watch, hair."

Rita's eyebrows went up. "Ah, well..."

45

*   *   *

Bob Van Meter was an ex-Marine and an ex-cop, Roberta (known as Bob II) Van Meter, an ex-Marine wife, an ex-cop wife; they were also the parents of an undercover narcotics agent (also an ex-Marine), the parents-in-law of a woman who'd been on the job too—or almost. Duty, to them, was no constraint, and they understood from a couple of sentences that Susan was going to have to go on the job, and why, and what they had to do.

"It's nearly summer, Sue," Bob II said. "Carrie'll be out of school and we'll be more than happy to have her stay with us."

"More than happy," said Bob I. "There's the club, the pool, tennis. She'll have a great time. And don't you worry about her missing you, Sue. She'll understand that you've got to find the son-of-a-bitch who killed her dad."

Her dad; not *your* husband; not *my* boy; not *our* Paulie. He'd been a good cop, Bob Van Meter, a beat cop for ten years and a detective for twenty. There were medals and trophies and certificates all over the house attesting to his quality. So how could he be so gullible as to believe that in the middle of a traffic-jammed street in the middle of Manhattan in the middle of a midweek afternoon someone with a score to settle fired one shot with a .22-caliber pistol through the window of a taxicab and killed his son? Her husband. Carrie's dad. Their Paulie. Or did the locution betray the suspicion that it had been some other way? Had some old sidekick called him up and said he hated to be the one to tell him, Bob, but the word on the street is Paulie was dirty, Paulie was into some weird shit, Paulie was wetting his wick with one of the bad guys, she's the one who whacked Paulie, not some ounce man on account of Paulie he did points?

No. Bob Van Meter was in the dark on this one. The NYPD was in the dark. Georgetown had banged down the shutters and was pretending to be bumping into the furniture, and had invited the cops to bark their shins along with them, which they'd done.

Why had they? Where was the good old intermural rivalry on this one? Where was the healthy mistrust of guys who had gotten their asses kicked and were still trying to cover them? Where was the petty, perfectly understandable jealousy of people with more money to spend, more interesting things to spend it on (Jamaica), bigger harvests to reap? Where was the flat suspicion that people who play with dirt get dirty?

Why did he go rogue, the son-of-a-bitch? Paulie. Shit. For the money? For the sex? For the power? The busts he'd made. Beautiful busts. Classics. Like the time...

Fuck it. She was trying to forget him.

Wasn't she?

Then why did she think about him all the time, and affectionately? Like the time...

Montauk. February. Paul had some comp time coming after a job and Susan took some contract holidays and they left five-year-old Carrie at the Bobs' and drove out for three days in the middle of the coldest week of the winter. The wind made them breathless if it hit them just so, but the sky was brilliant and in the lee of dunes they could sunbathe for a while. At night there were so many stars it made them giddy.

They were the only guests in a motel on Dune Road. The place had a dining room and they told the owner they'd eat dinner there the first night. They went to their room and made love and fell asleep and didn't wake until after midnight. "They'll think we lied when we said we were married," Susan said. "Only illicit lovers fuck their brains out."

"Do you want to see if we can get something to eat?" Paul said.

"No."

"Do you want to go back to sleep?"

"No."

"What do you want to do?"

Susan growled and pounced.

They drove to the lighthouse and stared due east and argued about whether it would be England that they would see if they could see that far, or France. They stopped at the library on the way back and looked in an atlas and were dismayed to find that it would be Portugal.

On motel stationery they drew maps of the United States and compared them with the atlas. They had their natal states— Susan's Wisconsin, Paul's New York—in the right place and roughly in the right proportion, and that was about it. Paul's had the Great Lakes bounded by Iowa, Nebraska, Arkansas, Kentucky and West Virginia; Susan's had every state about the same size and rectangular shape except for Florida, Texas and California, which she had bounded by New Mexico, Arizona, Oregon and a nameless state in which she drew tall mountain peaks.

"So do you love me even if I'm geographically illiterate?" Paul said.

"I love you be*cause* you're geographically illiterate," Susan said.

They made love before breakfast on the morning they left and on the way back they listened to WHN and sang along with country songs they didn't know the words to. In the driveway of the Bobs', Susan put her hand on Paul's arm as he started to get out.

"Yes, I had a wonderful time," he said, leaning over to kiss her.

"Here's the thing," Susan said. "The thing is, I've never had a better time and it's entirely possible I may never again and I don't mean that morbidly. So thanks, that's all. Thanks."

"You're welcome. Thank *you*."

"You're welcome."

Carrie, having many times endured the club, the midget pool, the single weedy tennis court, was dubious, and seemed not to understand anything at all. "What if you get killed too?"

"I won't get killed."

"But what if you do, okay?"

"This is something I have to do, Carolyn."

Carrie pushed herself up from her slump and sat forward on her chair, almost formally. "'Revenge, at first though sweet, bitter ere long back on itself recoils.'"

Susan sweated. This was crazy; her deceitful daughter was quoting poetry at her.

"It's from *Paradise Lost,* okay? We're reading it. In school. It means—"

"I know what it means. I'm not acting in hot blood, Care. I'm acting out of a sense of responsibility."

"To who? To Dad? I'd say your responsibility right now is to me. I'd say your responsiblity right now is to not get killed too, okay?"

Her deceitful daughter had a head on her shoulders. "I could get hit by a bus, Care. I could slip in the shower."

"Not if you're careful."

"I'll be careful."

"I think you just want to get rid of me."

"That's absurd."

"We've been fighting a lot lately."

"People fight."

"You're sending me to Grandma and Grandpa 'cause you know they aren't going to let me smoke."

"I should hope not."

"It'll be like prison, okay?"

In prison, dear heart, people smoke and drink and fuck and get high. And watch color television.

"You're sending me to Grandma and Grandpa so I won't be able to see Jennifer."

"She can visit."

"Grandma and Jennifer? That'd be rad."

"You can visit her."

"If I visit her, I'll smoke, okay? Jennifer smokes, I have to smoke. I mean, what else am I supposed to do?"

"You could try obeying me. It's just the two of us now, Care. We have to support each other."

"... I'm scared, Mom."

Susan hugged her. She wasn't scared. *Fear is the loss of your sense of where you are,* John Barnes had told them when they were starting out. Susan knew exactly where she was: She was in orbit around a grave.

8

Susan stood in front of Trees for a while, then walked to the corner, bought two packs of Marlboros, Rita's brand, for she was somehow playing Rita's game, and walked back to the cardboard refrigerator box. She stacked the cigarettes on the sidewalk, the matchbooks on top, and stepped a little away.

It was warmer, and the man was bareheaded and wore only the camel overcoat. From his squat, he studied the cigarettes as if they were passing insects.

"Nam?" Susan said.

He reached a hand out to square up the packs, then drew it back. "Airborne."

Susan nodded. "My husband was a Marine."

As if he'd been meaning to and had been interrupted, he took the top pack between thumb and middle finger, peeled off the cellophane tape, tore the foil and tapped the pack against the palm of his hand. He held it out to Susan. "He KIA-'d?"

"No. And no, thanks; I don't smoke. But yes, he's dead. Would you like a cup of coffee, or something to eat?"

He tore off a match, made a windscreen of his hand and lighted the cigarette. "You a cop?"

"No."

"Bunch of cops around here the other day. Uniforms, detectives."

"Really? It looks like such a quiet street."

He shook the match out, split it, ground the pieces between his fingers until they frayed. "At the restaurant."

"The *Times* gave it two stars. Cops in bunches can't be good for business."

He smoked deliberately for a while. "Looked all up and down the street. Trying to work out where the taxi stopped, what side the guy got in, where the woman was standing, all that."

"Really?"

"All the waiters were out here, acting like they'd seen it all."

"People're funny that way. They don't want to say they didn't see a thing. Of course, sometimes they say they didn't see a thing even when they saw the whole thing."

"Looked all up and down the gutters for slugs, cartridges."

"The waiters? Or the cops?"

"A waste of time. They know he's dead, it means they found his body; they found his body, it means they got a bullet out of him, or out of the taxi; so there was no need to look for slugs, cartridges."

Susan smiled. "Remember 'Alice's Restaurant,' the song? Sometimes cops have to use all their cop equipment."

He smoked some more. "You're something like a cop. I can smell it. He wasn't a cop. He was too..." He lifted his chin at the smoke, as if to say too like it.

Susan studied the smoke, which swirled and was gone. "Did you get a good look at her?"

More smoke. "She's the kind of woman, you see her once, she's one way, the next time you see her, she's different, or you are. A woman like a day. No two days're ever the same. A woman like that's never the same on any two days."

Susan pursed her lips. "Sounds like she'd be hard to handle."

He flicked the cigarette away and was gone, diving into his refrigerator box so swiftly that Susan thought she'd said some magic word. Then he was back, holding a leather eyeglass case. "She dropped these." He held the case out to Susan.

Susan took it carefully, balancing it on her palm. "She did?"

"When she got the piece out of her bag."

Susan opened the case and took out a pair for sunglasses. She held them by the nosepiece and turned them this way and that. "Not prescription. Not much help."

He put the cigarette packs somewhere down inside his clothes. "Only two hundred fifty like them."

51

"Oh?"

He got testy. "In the *world* there're two hundred fifty *pairs* of those glasses."

Susan put up a hand. "My friend, I spotted you for a reliable eyewitness as soon as I saw you, which is why I thought I'd ask you a few questions. You've got a good spot here, you probably don't miss much. But how the *hell* do you know how many pairs of these glasses there are?"

He smiled. "Saw an ad in *The New Yorker*."

Susan laughed.

"There's a dentist's office down the street. His nurse brings me old magazines now and then. I saw an ad for these glasses. Ellesse."

"What's L.S?"

Another sigh. "That's the name of them. Ellesse."

Susan looked at the earpieces. "Right. Ellesse."

He snorted. "Cops."

"If you saw her pull a gun, why didn't you do something, say something?"

Another snort.

Susan put the glasses in the case and the case in her bag. She took out her wallet and counted out three tens. She folded them up and squatted down and took his hand and put the bills in his palm and closed it up. "There it is."

He stashed the bills down with the cigarettes. "There it is."

Which, Barnes wondered, would look worse in a Director-bucker: his affair with Mia the illegal alien postliterate marijuana smoker virgin or with Polly the nicotine-caffeine-cocaine triathlete virgin who was an illegal alien of a sort since she lived in Hoboken, of all places, in contravention of the policy that civil servants live within the city limits? She swore him to secrecy—*him*—about her address, then offered him a toot on a silver spoon and when he declined gave him a long cool look that warned him not to get moralistic with her, forgot about legalistic.

Polly had called him just as he got back to the shop from

52

Paul's funeral, and said she'd decided not to go out to Quogue until Saturday. Was he still free for dinner, at the best restaurant in Hoboken, on her? They'd met in the PATH station in the Trade Center. She'd kissed him on the lips and held his arm against her breast throughout the train ride. The restaurant had bentwood, hanging ferns and canned fifties music for atmosphere, recent college graduates for a clientele and a microwave oven for a chef. The waitress, an Italian-American virgin who had not even been born when Ritchie Valens died, boogied her shoulders to "La Bamba" as she took their orders. Other music: "In the Still of the Night" "Duke of Earl," "Kansas City," "Shimmy Shimmy Ko-Ko-Bop," "Since I Don't Have You." Barnes knew all the words. *How* did he know all the words? He'd gone to Yale, not Syracuse. Or Miami. When Barnes gagged on a red snapper bone, the male recent college graduates (Cornell, he guessed, with a couple of Dartmouths and maybe a Penn) rose up from their chairs as one, ready to execute the Heimlich maneuver. They were alert, they had good peripheral senses; he should recruit them.

He should recruit Polly, who was living a fairy tale. Her apartment was the ground floor of a brownstone across from a Hispanic Seventh-Day Adventist church. She said she sometimes went to the *Miércoles Reunión de Oración*—"to be neighborly." He wondered what she'd do if she lived across from a shooting gallery.

"You brought me off," Polly said when Barnes lifted his head from between her thighs. He nearly denied it, as policy. Sex wasn't what it used to be: women were forever confusing vulgarity with eroticism ("Rub your cock against my clit," was a favorite instruction of Joanna's); there was all that talking beforehand, so they could tell themselves—and their women friends—and their therapists—that they didn't fuck strangers; and *after*wards: word had reached Iceland—*Ice*land—of something called "total orgasm," and if yours were less than total you had a responsibility—to yourself, to your women friends, to your therapist—to articulate their shortcomings (hah!). In college, was it, he'd seen a French film about a beautiful deaf-mute; he'd loved her then and he longed for her now.

53

Or was it worse—worst—that he had fantasies about an affair with an agent who wanted back on the job after years on a desk and who was the widow—the very recent widow—of an agent who went rogue and got whacked? Or worst that she wanted back not exactly in spite of him but definitely not because of him? A Director-bucker ought to be doing his own scheming, not reacting to the scheming—its design all hidden in Marlboro smoke—of his inferiors—his female inferiors. "It's not like riding a bicycle, Susan. You've been away a long time. The SOP's gone through a dozen changes since you were on the job. The markmanship and physical fitness requirements have been tightened way up.... Sit down, please. You're making me nervous."

Which was why Susan stayed standing—that and to keep him from getting behind her, which she knew he'd do if she sat down: get behind her and stand with his hand on the back of the chair—provocatively, paternalistically, arrogantly. "Are you trying to talk me out of it? Aren't you and Rita together on this one? Or was Rita's little performance intended to get me to resign, not volunteer?"

Barnes swiveled toward the window. "Rita and I..." How to find a predicate for a subject whose components were rarely together on anything, and certainly not on this? "Rita and I feel Paul was onto something very major, something that requires special handling. We're dealing with a different kind of player—ones with no records, no MOs, no history. A new ball game. The retail drug business is low-rent, it's dirty, it's sleazy, and that's inhibiting its growth. There're potential customers who aren't comfortable copping on the street and who aren't going to be found copping down in Alphabet City, or at a crack house. There're a hundred apartments on the West Side, in the Village, in SoHo and TriBeCa, in Brooklyn Heights and Park Slope, that cater to them. Therapists, actors, stockbrokers, writers—anybody who wants to can set himself up as a middle-class ounce man, and sell to customers like himself." Barnes faced Susan and tipped back in his chair, feeling nimble again, centered. If she came on the job, he'd run her; she'd be his. "But there's still another kind of customer—one who wouldn't buy a Benz at a dealership that also sold Fords; he just wouldn't. There's a market, and a big one, for someone who sells his soda in crystal decanters instead of glassine envelopes, by appointment only, customized service in the privacy of your own home. It works with everything else; why shouldn't it work with dope? The impediment till now to the development of that kind of market has been that the people who might best exploit it are people like their potential clientele—people who aren't accustomed to working at anything."

"Rich kids," Susan said. "I can't believe a bunch of spoiled brats are going around whacking narcs."

"Somebody's whacking narcs *and* players." Barnes handed her a folder off his desk. "Lionel Leroy James, DOA Riverside Park Friday night or Saturday morning, shot with a twenty-two-caliber handgun, the same gun that killed Paul maybe thirty-six hours earlier. James was a sideman for a big hitter named Dwight Williamson, as you know better known as Cool D. The word on the street is that Cool D's being tested—by whom, no one's sure, but for sure by someone who wants a big piece of his action. Not his ounce men, we don't think; his supplier. This hit would look like a spark-up, if it weren't for the link to Paul."

Susan looked at the mug shots of a handsome black man with an attitude and at his yellow sheet, which was testimony to some fancy counseling; arrested a score of times, he'd gone to trial only three and had incurred one two-year sentence. "So who's Kit? Amazing Grace's Kit?"

Barnes smiled. Susan was so much more fun than Rita. If he bucked his way to Director, he'd promote her to his job and kick Rita somewhere sideways, somewhere out of his hair. To Micronesia. But then he'd be in Georgetown and Susan in New York. Along with Mia. And Polly just across the river. "Suffolk County Narcotics is looking for Grace's nautical friends, and sniffing around in bars and supermarkets in Hampton Bays, but it looks as though that operation's been rolled up. Our only hard lead on any of this at the moment came from a computer search of names and aliases run by your colleagues in Research. A songbird in California, Harry Kellner, told his runner late last winter that some East Coast money was shopping around out there for mules. The man fronting for the money called himself Kit. The L.A. shop had an artist's rendering done from Kellner's description; Grace says it's her Kit." Barnes hoped Georgetown would see integrity in his not having gone and had affairs with felonious virgins like Grace Lewis, attractive as she was; or would they know that he hadn't because she'd slept with Van Meter and he didn't want an agent's sloppy seconds?

Susan put the folder on the desk. "The woman with Paul dropped a pair of sunglasses—expensive sunglasses, a limited edition, if you can imagine such a thing—like that watch Paul was wearing."

Barnes's eyelids flickered. "How do you know about the watch?"

"Rita told me. There're only two hundred fifty pairs of these glasses."

"*What* glasses, Susan?"

"They were picked up by a street person, a man who lives right next to the restaurant, Trees."

"And he turned them over to the cops?"

"He turned them over to me."

"Why?"

"He's a watcher. I asked him if he'd seen anything interesting."

"No, Susan, I mean why were you interrogating him? The cops talked to eyewitnesses in and around the restaurant."

"Not to him—and they won't. He's a sociopath."

A condition Joanna sometimes ascribed to him. Would he end up living on the street? No. He'd end up one of those big-torsoed, bandy-legged ex-cops and ex-firemen and ex-who knew what who hung out around the softball diamonds south of the Sheep Meadow in Central Park, kibbitzing, crisping on the bleachers in the sun, telling war stories, second-guessing anything and everything that moved, going off separately at dusk to their SROs, their rooms at the West Side Y, their memories. "And this . . . sociopath is a connoisseur of limited-edition sunglasses?" Barnes laughed.

Susan now understood Rita's *Ah, well.* "I got a list of the purchasers from the manufacturer."

"Under what pretext?"

"No pretext. I'm a federal agent." Who had never done anything that someone hadn't told her to do—some man. "Polly's running several different cross-checks."

Barnes felt very frightened. "Polly?"

"My assistant."

Less frightened, though still frightened. Barnes scraped at a spot on his yellow paisley tie. "If you *were* to come back on the job, it would have to be with this understanding: We're not in the vendetta business." Who had said that? Oh—he had, to Rita. And what had Rita said? *If Paul went rogue then he betrayed Susan as well as the job. It is Paul she will want revenge against, and she will get it by leading us to the one who bought him.* And what would Susan say?

"Paul went rogue," Susan said. "Unless you're not telling me everything. I want to find out who bought him."

Serious now—Director-bucker serious. "Susan, you're not on the job. I don't have to tell you anything."

Susan sat forward in her chair. "Do you think Paul was sending a peril?"

"How do you mean?"

"The contact lenses. The hair. The watch on his right wrist. The limited-edition watch says he went rogue; wearing it wrong says something else. What? Did you actually go to the trouble of combing his hair the old way so that when I identified him I wouldn't remark on the difference?"

Barnes touched his chest. "*I* didn't, no. . . . So you want to go back on the job."

"Yes."

"With the understanding—"

"That we're not in the vendetta business, yes."

"And one more thing."

"Yes?"

"You voluntarily gave up the chance to go on the job fifteen years ago—the chance to be a pioneer. You may have regretted

57

that decision at some points along the way. It would be perfectly understandable if you had. Paul was—as am I—of a generation that heard the feminists' message and believed much of it to be worthwhile and *still* believed that men should do the heavy lifting. All I'm saying, Susan, is that we can't have any fanatics here; if you have a statement to make, find another forum to make it in; if you want to work hard, then welcome aboard. Welcome back."

Susan just nodded. In a world that had heard the feminists' message and believed much of it to be worthwhile and *still* believed that men should do the heavy lifting *and* equated pioneering with fanaticism, did any woman do anything voluntarily?

Barnes took a folder from his center drawer and opened it. "Your fairy tale—I have been anticipating this visit—is that you're from San Francisco. Old money. Timber, banking, that sort of thing—the kind of money that's just there; no one wonders where it came from. Parents deceased. Your folks are, uh...Aren't they?"

"They're dead, yes."

"Oh. Sorry."

"It'll be three and five years next month. They both died in June."

"Hunh." An opportunity missed to have consoled her. Three years ago next month he'd been sleeping with Debbie the cocktail waitress, five years ago with Chris the aerobics instructor. "You've been away from the scene for a while, traveling, keeping to yourself—"

"In the way only people with the kind of money that's just there can keep to themselves?"

That verged on insubordination. But not Rita's kind; a kind he could live with. "See the storytellers about the details. They'll inculcate West Coast upper crust in you. You'll go see Kellner for a start on your pedigree. He'll put you in touch with the right people. You're looking for some excitement. You've been dealing on a small scale for a while. You have an old boyfriend in pharmaceuticals and can get your hands on an almost unlimited supply of V's and E's—Are you up on your street lingo?"

"Valium. Elavil. To keep from falling off jumbo."

"Jumbo. Good. Crack is jumbo. Good."

"I'm good, John."

"I remember." He'd trained her.

"You trained me, is that what you're thinking?"

He'd trained Paul too. "You were a natural."

"You trained Paul too. He was a natural."

Barnes wrote something, anything, on a scrap of paper and clipped it to the folder. "You'll need a fairy tale name. Something, well, patrician."

"Saint Michael," Susan said.

Barnes pursed his lips. "Not bad. Where'd you get it?"

"It's my name. My maiden name."

"Right. What is it again? Szyz—"

"Szentmihalyi."

Barnes rubbed his hands together. "Well, Saint Michael it is, then."

9

Bob Seger sang "American Storm" in the Toshiba's headphones.

Ted Scally sauntered to the beat, then sidled up to the barricade that kept the unticketed from the wing where the planes came and went, checking out the limo drivers, who held up signs with the names of their prospective passengers on them, looking like panelists on a TV game show. He ignored those whose signs were professionally printed, or bore the names of organizations or corporations, and picked out one with a sign that was hand lettered—but neatly—MISTER DELL, and walked straight up to him. "That's me. I'm your man."

The driver had goofy curly hair that his cap sat in like a bird in a nest. He looked at Scally's sweat-stained Stetson, his buckskin jacket, his abused jeans and boots, and looked as if he would weep. *"You're* Mister Dell?"

Still engulfed in the music, Scally lip-spread it. "Yep. Where you parked?"

The driver said something Scally couldn't interpret. He hung the earphones around his neck. "Problem, dude?"

"I'm sorry, sir. I expected a much older man. A wheelchair. The boss said there'd be a wheelchair."

"My old man. He couldn't make it."

The driver brightened. "Your *father.*"

"Right."

"He couldn't *make* it. You're here in*stead.* He couldn't *come.*"

"He died."

The driver whipped his cap off. "Oh."

"Yeah."

60

"I'm sorry."

"You got a name, dude?"

"Lawrence. Lawrence Peel."

"*Law*rence?"

"Well, Larry. But you should call me Peel. The boss thinks it sounds more, well, you know. . . . *He* thinks anyway."

"Lead the way, Lar."

Peel tried to, and to put his cap on and stand deferentially aside all at once. He rocked on his heels until he had his balance. "Your luggage, Mister Dell. I need your luggage checks."

"Just the pack." Scally tossed it at him, caught the sign that Peel dropped in catching it, and threw the sign in a trash basket.

Peel held the pack out in front of him as they hustled along, to keep the trail dust off his uniform. "I'm sorry I wasn't able to meet you at the gate, Mister Dell. This is a sterile airport."

"Name one that ain't."

"I mean, that's what they call it, sir—an airport where you can't meet arrivals or departures unless you have a ticket."

"Why would you want to meet a departure, Lar?"

"Hunh? Oh, yeah. Well, see someone *off*, then."

They were on the sidewalk in front of the terminal. On the horizon, Manhattan looked like a scale model of itself. "You know the way to Southampton, I guess, Lar."

"South*ampton*? The boss said the Waldorf."

"Yo, Larry. Take a good look at this face. *I'm* the boss. Scally got in the gray Mercedes Pullman 600—six doors, bar, TV, VCR, radio and cassette deck, compact disk player, phone. Who needed a car with six doors? Oh, yeah—the wheelchair. He put the earphones back on and played air guitar to the rave-up in "Like a Rock," the mix coming together deep inside his head. He turned the TV on and found a ball game—Mets-Cubs—and watched it without the sound. That was the wonderful thing about baseball—it was an accompaniment to life where every other sport was an interruption. As they pulled away from the curb, he looked out the smoked window in time to see a mean-looking nurse pushing an octogenarian in a wheelchair out the door. The nurse looked left, then right, then left, and so did the old man, much more slowly, his head bobbing at the end of his frail neck. Scally hoped it wouldn't bob right off; there had been enough innocent victims.

Rachel Phillips took a long hit on the glass pipe and held it out to Scally—but not so far out that he wouldn't have had to get up to get it if he'd wanted some.

"Nope. Thanks."

"An abstainer? Or you're already high?"

"High on life." He flashed his all-American hot-dog smile, the smile that turned snow bunnies into drooling succubi, made waitresses allow him substitutions, generally got him out of jams, though sometimes in them. This rich bitch wouldn't fall for the smile, though; she could see from the dental school bridgework that it had no pedigree.

"You come highly recommended." Rachel put the pipe aside and rose up out of her nest of soft pillows like a cobra and was suddenly all business. "If your services aren't too costly, you sound like just the sort of man we can use."

"'If.' 'Sound.' 'Sort.' You're not too sure."

Her eyes got hard. "When it comes to taking in outsiders, I can never be too sure."

Scally thought: He should close down his skiing school and open one for rich bitches who wanted to be drug dealers; he would teach them to rap and moonwalk and, above all, that caution was bullshit and that all that mattered was that those you were cautious of were scareder of you than you of them. "I get five points of the retail price of everything I move. You can raise your eyebrows as high as you want to, sweetheart, but you'd be surprised how close that comes to not even covering my expenses. Anyway, if you want to bargain, you shouldn't do business in a place like this."

There was no place quite like this, a replica of Monticello erected by Rachel's grandfather (an alumnus of the University of Virginia though hardly a Jeffersonian Democrat). When the house became Rachel's (her grandparents and parents were all dead by the time she was twenty-five—of, Rachel liked to think, obsolescence), she made some changes, tossing out the Chippendale, the Louis XVI and Charles X, the Regency, Victorian, Georgian, Queen Anne and Directoire, the chintz and the faux tortoise, the Wedgwood and the majolica, the Persian Sultanabads, the van Ruisdaels, the dog portraits, the botanical prints, and putting in a little high tech, a little Judy Rifka, Rosemarie Castoro, Jean Dunand, Daum, Ulrica Hydman-Valliem, Gallé, Marcel Coard, Ruhlmann, Kurt Ziehmer, Frank Nadell, Robert Zakanitch, Martine Bedin, Carmen Spera, Roger Mitchell, a sauna, a squash court, a Nautilus room, a solarium.

Scally went on: "Fact that I'm sitting here, instead of doing twenty mandatory, means I'm good, highly recommended or not, so you can take it or leave it, 'cause if you leave it someone else'll take it. Oh, yeah, and I get six O's off of every load to keep my nose in trim, and my friends'. Six O's before the load gets stepped on." He put his boots up on her limited-edition coffee table, not knowing that's what it was but nonetheless achieving the desired effect.

Rachel Phillips was silent for a time. She was not one of those patrician women who daydream of coming upon the chauffeur in his undershirt, a cigarette in his lips, a lock of hair down on his forehead, grease on his hands and sweat on his brow, and of giving herself up to him espaliered on the bonnet of the Daimler. Decidedly not. She didn't even care much to rub elbows or anything else with her own kind, a coolness that had led her to inscribe a circle within her circle (or, she liked to think, outside it and above it), passage across whose circumference was restricted to those to whom Rachel gave her cachet. The New Four Hundred got their antics written up in *New York* and their pictures in the papers; the Fortymost, as Rachel's set was known, were always a step ahead of the gossip columnists' legmen, out of range of the *paparazzi*. They went to clubs, restaurants, islands, ski resorts no one had ever heard of, and by the time someone had, and went there, the Fortymost were gone. Their parties echoed all over town, but no outsider ever witnessed the source of the noise. "Shadowy," the newspapers

63

called them, an adjective they also often imputed to terrorist organizations, with which the Fortymost did share one characteristic: an unswerving conviction that it was all right for them to play God.

But. Rachel liked to get high; and the more she did the harder she found it to get there again in the same old ways. Soda, rock, dust—they were no different from tobacco or food or mere alcohol; you did them until you'd, well, done them, and then you did a little more, until you ran out or you slept. The sun adamantly set on beaches and ski slopes and came up again to extinguish parties; yachts put into port, cars ran out of gas (and there were all those signs ordering you about), airplanes were a kick on take-offs and landings but otherwise flew themselves; clothes got quaint, sex irksome. For a time, she'd tried to make do by having more, more of everything, more at once. It worked—for a time, until it occurred to her (under a circumstance worth recording: She was in Rio, having flown in the Learjet from Lyford Cay, because it had been raining there, sitting on the railing of a twelfth-floor terrace of the Sheraton, wearing only an Elsa Peretti necklace, a baroque pearl set in eighteen-karat gold and hanging from a silk cord, smoking a Ritmeester Senior, washing down a Dilaudid with 1979 Roederer Cristal champagne, half a gram of soda up her nose, listening to Sting on her Aiwa's phones, mooning Ipanema and the Avenida Niemeyer, watching through the scrim of nervous curtains as Kit Bolton fucked a transvestite prostitute who'd just fucked Rachel, tied to the bed, or pretending to be, by her Oscar de la Renta beaded purple silk shirt and white silk pants), it occurred to her—and occurred again to her now—that should she give the slip to her caparisoned entourage and take a look at how the other ninety-nine point ninety-nine percent lived, maybe take up with a man who called her sweetheart, the result might be some altitude, some uplift, a jolt. "My partner's in Mexico right now making arrangements for regular shipments. You're to meet him in El Paso tomorrow. I have plans for you for tonight."

Scally sighed at the amateurishness of it all. "If you're going to tell me the setup every time we talk, you may as well rent a billboard. I wouldn't go to El Paso to meet Tina Turner. I steer clear, on principle, of former members of the Confederacy. I pick my own routes, and if you think they're roundabout, you're welcome to think so. I have my own plans for tonight and I don't fuck women I work with; it confuses things."

Rachel smiled. She was already feeling it—the altitude, the uplift, the jolt.

Scally knew not to look at that smile too long; it could blind you—like the sun, like polished snow. And he knew not to play games with this woman, lest playfulness dilute his rage and deflect him from his errand.

Rachel was on her feet and on her way to the French window, trailing a hand after her. "Let's go outside."

She had changed the grounds too, uprooting the boxwood parterre garden, the bowling green, the holly maze, the dwarf box flower beds, the azaleas, iris, delphinium and Oriental poppies, making way for a tennis court and a swimming pool. For privacy, she'd kept the hedgerows of red maples, apples, Washington hawthorn, holly, rugosa rose and fire thorn, edged with day lilies, periwinkle and Virginia creeper.

There was an acre of lawn in front of the house and an acre behind, the latter with stables, corral and exercise ring on its far side and bisected by a low rail fence. Something about the light said that somewhere around here was the ocean, but Scally couldn't see or hear or smell it.

"Do you ride?" Rachel said. "No, you're a skier. An Olympic prospect. Until something happened, something went wrong."

So she had something on him. Well, there was plenty to be had; and it was all in the public record—DWIs, barroom brawls, a couple of GTAs, a million curfew violations, AWOLs and insubordinations. Missed gates, illegal skis, poles and waxes: *Ted Scally is to international competitive skiing,* someone once wrote, *as Bonnie Parker and Clyde Barrow were to banking.* "Friend of yours?" He lifted his chin toward the stables, where someone had driven up in a white sports car, what make he couldn't tell from this distance.

"That's Nick. Nick Ivory."

"Ivory Tower?" She'd sneaked him a look when she'd said the name, as if she thought he'd be impressed, so he'd tried to sound it.

"Were you a fan? He has some tapes of unreleased material that're just marvelous. You'll hear them."

Scally'd hated Ivory Tower. Ivory Tower, Led Zeppelin, the Doors: it wasn't music; it was bombast. Give him the Stones. Give him the Dead. Give him Bruce. This rich bitch wouldn't understand Bruce. She'd never felt the darkness on the edge of town, hidden on the backstreets, been trapped. "That fence for jumping?" He shaded his eyes to look at it.

Her smile again. "Watch." She sat on a stone bench, leaving room for Scally.

It wasn't much room, and he stayed standing behind her.

A stable door was opened from the inside, making a maw he couldn't penetrate. A horse whinnied; it came stepping sideways out the door, it's rider—"Jesus Christ"—dressed all in armor, blue armor, and carrying a shield and a lance from which a pennant stood straight in the breeze from the unseen ocean.

Rachel laughed. "It's a bit of a shock the first time, isn't it?"

Scally watched the horseman walk his mount to the middle of the fence, where he leaned down and pulled into place a device holding a row of target rings. He walked the horse to the end of the fence and turned to face the rings. He lowered the lance and adjusted his hold on it. He shut the visor of his helmet. He kicked the horse lightly into a trot, then a canter. He picked off the first ring in the row with the tip of the lance and raised it so that it slid down toward the handle. He rode the course ten times and all but one time collected a ring. He moved the lance in what might have been a salute to them and rode back into the barn.

Scally watched and in his mind he heard the phone ringing and him answering it, just enough this side of dead drunk to tell the mouthpiece from the earpiece and mumble something into it:

Mister Scally?

Fug is zis?

Mister Scally, I'm with the Suffolk County, New York, Police Department.

I'm innashent, offacher. Haven't been in New York in yearsh.

There's been an accident here, Mister Scally, involving a friend of yours.

Dough dough anybody on Law Island.

Ornella Vitti? I'm not sure if that's how you pronounce it. O-r-n—

Just like that, cold sober. *What happened? What the fuck happened?*

You do know Miss Vitti, then?

What the fuck happened?

We found your name on an envelope in her things.

What the fuck happened?

She's, uh, dead, sir.... I'm sorry.

Now the hangover, just like that. *You don't mean dead. You don't mean it. You don't.*

I'm afraid I do, Mister Scally. Mister Scally, are you next of kin to Miss Vitti, or if not, do you know some way I can reach her next of kin?

How did she die?

Well, if you're not the next of kin—

How did she die?

It's just that I really should be speaking to her next of kin.

We were lovers. How did she die?

...Right. Okay. Well. She washed up on a beach out here in Sagaponack. A fellow who'd had a couple too many the night before feel asleep on the beach, took a walk when he woke up to try and get sober, he found her.

She's an expert swimmer. The holiday they'd spent in Baja. She would swim so far out in the Gulf that he'd lose sight of her and when she came back to him she wouldn't be even a little breathless.

Well, that may be, Ted, but I said she washed up on the beach, I didn't say she drowned, and even with expert swimmers there'd come a point when they'd have so much horse in them

67

it'd kind of override the expertise, if you know what I'm saying. Not to mention the stab wound.

Horse?

Heroin.

No.

Yes.

Stabbed?

After the horse'd killed her, the coroner thinks. There was an accumulation of blood in the lungs and chest cavity that he says is consistent with a drug overdose. She had a seizure, he reckons, went into a coma and never regained consciousness.

Then why was she stabbed?

And with what's an even better question, Ted. Made a hell of a hole in her, whatever it was. Fellow who found her, he took one look at that hole, he passed out right there on the beach next to her. Tide coming in woke him up. Coroner thinks it was some kind of spearlike implement. She had burn marks on her wrists too, like maybe she'd been tied up. And one more strange thing is she wasn't wearing a bathing suit or anything, and all her clothes were in a duffel bag sitting right out there on the beach. That's where we found the envelope with your name on it.

What do you mean, spearlike?

Like a spear, Ted. Like a spear. There's an Indian reservation over at Shinnecock, we're going to go over and have a powwow with some of the braves, though I've never seen a bow and arrow around that reservation, let alone a spear.... Ted ... Mister Scally? ... Ted?

Scally had gone away, leaving the phone dangling, to find another bottle, and another and another.

10

Cool D raised a finger and the towel-head dropped out. Only the slope was left.

Henry Aaronson leaned forward on his folding chair, putting his head between Cool D's and Shiraz's. "You going to drive this car, D, or just look at it? Or sit in it and pretend like you're driving? My grandson does that. Hours, he sits in the car in my daughter's driveway, moving the wheel back and forth and making little rum-rum noises. The *mazik.*"

"Cool D says it is not a car; it is a Duesenberg Model J."

"Yeah, and what kind of mileage does it get is what I want to know. For two hundred large you should get at least twenty highway."

"Cool D says please wait outside, Henry. He want to concentrate on the bidding."

"Yeah, and Henry Aaronson says a guy who's in the trouble Cool D's in shouldn't be throwing two hundred large away on wheels, especially when they're not even new wheels, they're nineteen twenty-nine wheels. Kraut wheels. Nineteen twenty-nine was not a good year, D, and the Krauts may make good wheels, but they're still Krauts. You should be sensitive to that, you know. Your people and my people, we got a lot in common. We're *mishpocheh.*"

Shiraz patted Aaronson's hand. "It'll just be a minute, Henry. Wait outside."

"There's a coffee shop on Madison," Aaronson said. "I'll be there."

"The bid is on the aisle to my left," the auctioneer said.

The slope touched his temple.

69

"It's two hundred twenty thousand dollars against you, Mr. Williamson."

"D, maybe you shouldn't."

Cool D raised a finger.

The slope touched his temple.

"Two hundred fifty thousand against you, sir."

"D."

Cool D hesitated, but raised his finger.

"The bid on the aisle is two hundred fifty thousand. Fair warning at two hundred fifty thousand."

The slope folded his arms.

The auctioneer knocked it down. "Thank you, gentlemen. The next lot, number twenty-six, is a nineteen thirty-nine Bugatti. I'd like to start the bidding at one hundred thousand dollars."

"You got the wheels. I can see by your face you got them. You want a bagel? You want coffee? Just water? Here, take mine. She brings you water, this waitress, she'll want a bigger tip. Listen, D. Here's the thing. The narc that got whacked in a taxi? Someone he collared did his nickel, got out, whacked him, is what the cops're saying, but that ain't what went down, D. What went down is *she* whacked him, the *shikseh,* the *shikseh* that whacked Lionel. It was the same piece, a twenty-two Smith."

"Cool D wants to know how you know this."

"Shiraz, all these years we've been doing business together, I tell you something I know, don't ask how I know it. Is that too much to ask?"

"Are they going to arrest her for the narc's murder?"

"No. Or for Lionel's. 'Cause the cops don't know she whacked the narc, the *shikseh,* or that she whacked Lionel. The feds know, but they're not telling the cops. Why? I'll tell you why. They want to use her. They're getting *bubkes* these days, the feds, the cops—especially the feds. Not even *bubkes—makkes.* Everything used to be nice and neat and tidy. There were—what?—twelve, fifteen, twenty major importers; a hundred or so major wholesalers; two or three hundred ounce men, at the

70

most. Now everybody and his mother's an importer, everybody with a boat, a plane, a suitcase, even. There must be a hundred crack factories, two hundred, which means—what?—an apartment is all, with a couple of coffeepots, a stove, a hot plate, even, some scales, some spoons, a carton of baking soda, Arm and fucking Hammer. Not like the old days having to find someplace to put fifty-five-gallon drums of ether, acetone and HCL. The factories supply three, four, five houses each, a day's supply at a time so if there's a bust a day's supply is all the cops bag or all that goes down the toilet, out the window.

"The cops put heat on the houses, they go out in the street. Out in the street they got steerers, they got cashiers, they got *shleppers*. You try and make a stop-and-cop bust, who you going to bust? You bust the steerer, he's got no scratch on him, he's got no soda, no J, no rock, all he did was say something like 'Jumbo, jumbo. Crack it up.' You can't bust a guy for that. He could be selling tickets to the circus. You bust the cashier, all he's got is scratch, he could've made it pushing a rack on Seventh Avenue, he could've found it, a pony could've come in, his rich uncle could've died, he could've won the Lotto. You can't bust a guy for having some scratch on him. You bust the *shlepper*, he's got —what?—a *pekl* on him, two *pekls*—no works, nothing like that. You can bust him, but how long're you going to put him away for *shlepping* a couple of *pekls*? You get real lucky, you tail the steerer to the cashier, the cashier to the *shlepper*, the *shlepper* to the ounce man, you bust the ounce man, even if he doesn't beat the rap, which I can't think of any reason why he shouldn't, he's got a good bondsman, a good lawyer, a judge that's been greased, there's another ounce man—there're a dozen other ounce men—waiting to take over his action. *Bubkes. Makkes.*

"And that's just the cops I'm talking about. The feds don't bust ounce men. They fly around in helicopters, they ride around in boats, they see a fishing boat with no fish in the hold riding low in the water, they get on the bullhorn, tell the poor bastard to heave to. They bag a few bales, they hold a press conference, they brag how it's worth a million, two million, ten million, big

71

fucking deal, who've they got to go with it? Six Colombians and a couple of *shmucks* from Patchogue. They need a big *macher*, the feds, and they need him so airtight he'll do twenty mandatory. They think the *shikseh*'s connected to a big *macher*, and you know what, D? She is. She made a deal with Lorca. She told you she was going to go after your turf, and she's done it. She whacked your *nuchshlepper*, Lionel, and bought your importer right out from under your fucking nose. And you're throwing your money at fifty-year-old Kraut wheels."

"Cool D wants to know if the feds know about her deal with Lorca."

"No, they don't—for two reasons, the first being that *I* just found out about the deal this morning when I called Lorca to make sure everything was on between us as per usual and said, '¡*Hola, Enrique! ¿Qué tal, amigo?*' and he said, 'Fock off, jou Yew bastard. I don't need your focking beesness.' Nice way to start the day, hunh? And the second being that the feds don't know who the *shikseh* is. They don't know her name, her rank, her serial number, they don't know shit about her, except that they know she came out of nowhere and all of a sudden she's a big hitter."

"Cool D wants her eliminated," Shiraz said.

"For doing what, eliminated? For whacking your *nuchshlepper* Lionel? Hey, Lionel was supposed to tap people down, D, make sure they weren't packing heat. She could've whacked you, the *shikseh:* you ought to give her a fucking medal for only whacking Lionel. For making Lorca a better offer, eliminated? Lorca's a *gonif*. The fuck is he going to do—say, 'No, *gracias,* I will stay with my *hermano,* Cool D, who is a cheap motherfocker but I love heem'? D, D, D. Wake up, baby. Will you wake him up, Shiraz? Will you slap some sense into him...

"I got to go. I got an appointment. You ever play handball, D, anything like that? Sometimes you play a guy who is nowhere as good as you, he's all over the court, in the way, underfoot, he mishits the ball, his game's got no rhythm to it, he makes you fucking crazy, he *beats* you because you never get a chance to

72

play your own game. My advice is do not fuck with the *shikseh*, she is one crazy broad, she will burn you up if you get too close to her, she will burn herself out in a very short time, may even burn Lorca up with her, or the feds will be down on both of them, things won't be so crowded, the status will be quo. Good afternoon, D. No, I will get the check, I insist. Enjoy your new wheels. What do you got to do now—have somebody haul them out to your place on a truck or something? Doesn't make any sense to me, buying wheels too expensive to drive. Shiraz, a pleasure as always."

Cool D tore a strip off a paper napkin.

"Henry's right, D," Shiraz said. "Lionel fucked up."

Cool D tore off another strip.

"And he's right that the situation on the street has changed so much that this might be an opportune time to reassess our position."

Another strip.

"You've got to get off it, D—this misguided loyalty you feel to your people. You got it in Nam and you oughtn't to have felt it then. You were taken prisoner because your buddies let you down."

D rolled the strip into a ball.

"And you've got to get off this infantile macho feeling that you've lost your balls just because you've been outsmarted by a woman. Act your age, D, not your shoe size."

D tossed the ball into the water glass and rolled up another strip.

"Let's chill out for a while, D. Go someplace. We could go to Georgia and see your momma and go to New Orleans and see my dad. Take a ride on a riverboat. Have some fun. We don't have much fun, D. Henry can look after things,, or we can just let them slide altogether. Start over when we get back or start over somewhere else. New York's lost its glitter, D; it's just a flat ugly town with a lot of miserable people. We should check out San Diego. You liked it when you were in the hospital there. You said it was pretty. Pretty is something New York ain't."

Cool D tossed another ball and hit the rim of the glass.

"You know, Henry told me once—he was flirting in his innocuous way—that his one regret in life is that he never balled a *shvartzeh*. He didn't say that; Henry's always a gentleman around me. He said 'made love to a black woman.' I know you feel the same way; you want white pussy. And when you can't have it—and you can't have it, D; this isn't the sixties; the streets aren't full of white chicks trying to make amends for four hundred years of oppression—you want to kill it, so you don't have to think about not having it. That's not very professional, D. Not to mention not very humane. I'm going to go now—down to the marina. I want you to go uptown or upstate, whichever. Tomorrow or the next day or the day after, I'm going to decide whether I'd like to go down south for the rest of the summer. Or somewhere else. And you decide too, and you let me know. But don't come around until you've decided, hear?"

Shiraz left.

Cool D wiped off Aaronson's knife with what was left of the napkin and bent it into a question mark.

11

The bum crawled back as far as he could into the cardboard refrigerator box. Too many people were looking for him these days; he might as well be back in Cupertino, California, his name on the mailbox and in the phone book, wife, kids—four, were there, or were there three?—pool, tennis court, Mazda (his), Volvo (wife's), BMX dirt bikes (kids'), PTA, Little League, Jaycees, Cub Scouts, never too busy to, always had time for, Employee of the Year at... at... Where had he worked?

He had nearly, the day the woman came around, the woman who looked not quite like a cop but almost, he had nearly... nearly... Nearly what?

Nearly forgotten his name. He'd been sure she would ask him his name, especially after he gave her the...

The sunglasses.

But she hadn't asked.

Had she?

He smoked the last of the...

Marlboros.

He'd smoked the last of the Marlboros she'd given him, even though it hadn't been that long ago, it had been...

He'd saved a couple of the butts and had found a whole, intact, entire Winston on the street, not too far from where he'd found the...

Sunglasses.

Winston tastes good, like a... Like a...

He had a crust of pizza too, and an apple he'd lifted from a Korean market. And he had the thirty dollars the woman who looked not quite like a cop but almost had given him and that he was making sure he didn't touch until winter. He was rich. He didn't need anybody. Why was everyone looking for him?

Well, not everyone. Just the alligator man.

His kids—there were three of them: Amy, Kevin, David—his kids, when each was two or three or so, had sung a song about an alligator man.

No. Alligator *pie*.

> *Alligator pie, alligator pie.*
> *If I don't get some.*
> *I think that I shall die.*
> *Give away the green grass,*
> *Give away the sky.*
> *But don't give away*
> *My alligator pie.*

He was dressed like a hippie, the alligator man.

No, no, no. Like a yuppie, I mean. A navy blue alligator shirt, tan slacks, a madras belt, navy socks, brown loafers. Bass...

Injuns? Nobody dressed like that anymore. Well, a few people at... at... A few people at wherever he'd worked dressed like that. The ones who'd gone to prep schools and Ivy League colleges and had wives named Pidge and Muffy and kids named Carter and Maitland and... and...

He'd carried a sport coat over his arm. Cocksucker. No, no, no. *Seer*sucker.

*Wee*juns.

Someone. Is knocking. At my door.

"You?"

A man. Is knocking. At my door.

"You there, You?"

You there you. You there you. You there you.

Hugh. He's saying Hugh. You there, *Hugh?*

Who's Hugh?

You.

Me?

"Hugh? It's Mike."

76

Mike the kike. Mike the kike the CPA. Mike the kike the CPA from Erie, P.A.

"Hugh, it's Mike, I just got back, I just got back from Philadelphia, I was squeegeeing on Houston Street, a guy in a Coupe de Ville gave me an Andy Jackson, I decided to go to Philadelphia to look for work, I got myself a Nedick's hot dog and a Nedick's orange drink, I took the Amtrak train, I was sitting there with my little tray with my Nedick's hot dog and my Nedick's orange drink on the Amtrak train, I went to Philadelphia, there's no work there, either, I came back, I'm back, there was a guy, Hugh, asking about you, you were out squeegeeing, I didn't tell him anything, I figured he was from, you know, your wife, he looked like, maybe, I don't know, an insurance investigator or something."

How about a cop? Did he look like a cop, or maybe like somebody who's not quite a cop but almost, the way the woman he gave the sunglasses to looked not quite like a cop but almost?

"Hugh?"

He was left-handed, the alligator man. He wore his watch on his right wrist and carried his sport coat over his right arm and used his left hand to take off his sunglasses and put them on top of his head.

How do you know he had his watch on his right wrist, Hugh, if he carried his sport coat over his right arm?

Because he moved the coat aside a little with his left hand to look at the time.

How'd you happen to notice that, Hugh?

I notice things. In Nam, I was in . . .

Intelligence?

Yeah.

"Hugh? Hugh, it's Mike. I know you're in there, Hugh. I can smell you. Ha ha. Just kidding, Hugh. Ha ha. Just kidding. But I know you're in there. . . . Hugh, is there something you want me to tell the guy if he comes around again looking for you?"

Tell him I know he carries his gun in an ankle holster on his left leg. Tell him I know he wears contact lenses. Tell him I know he's left-handed.

Ankle holster? What, did you see it or what?

It was windy. His pants were pressed against his leg, like. I could see the holster.

Jesus, you do notice things, don't you Hugh? Contact lenses? How the hell could you tell he was wearing contact lenses?

Like I said, it was windy. He got something in his eye, under the lens. He got over against the building, out of the wind, and took the lens out and got out whatever was in his eye and put the lens back in.

I thought you said he was wearing glasses, Hugh.

Sunglasses. He had them up on his head when the wind blew something in his eye.

"Hugh, I'm gonna go now. I'm gonna go down to Houston Street and squeegee. You wanna come? . . . No? Well, I'll be back tonight, I guess."

He'll be back too, the alligator man. At night. Maybe not this night, but some night. He knows I saw him. And he knows I saw him the other time too, the time he went to the restaurant with the woman, the blonde, only she had her hair up and was wearing a hat, the kind bullfighters wear. No. Not bull-fighters . . .

Gauchos.

Her hair up and a gaucho hat and she looked altogether different, for she was the kind of woman, you saw her once, she was one way, the next time you saw her, she was different, or you were. A woman like a day, he'd told the woman who looked not quite like a cop but almost. No two days were ever the same. A woman like that was never the same on any two days.

What're you, some kind of poet, Hugh?

Sounds like she'd be hard to handle, the woman who looked not quite like a cop but almost had said. Very hard to handle, he knew; his wife had been that kind of woman.

Back at night because he knows I saw him and he knows I saw him the other time, the time he went to the restaurant with the woman, the blonde, with her hair up and a gaucho hat, the woman who shot the guy the woman who looked not quite like a cop but almost was asking about, the guy who looked almost like a cop too, except he was too...

Too what, Hugh?

> *Alligator pie, alligator pie.*
> *If I don't get some,*
> *I think that I shall die.*
> *Give away the green grass,*
> *Give away the sky.*
> *But don't give away*
> *My alligator pie.*

12

"Miss Saint Michael?"

"Yes?"

"I'm sorry to wake you. We're starting our approach to LAX. Could you please bring your seat forward?"

"Certainly. I wasn't asleep. It's all right."

"Can I take your coffee cup?"

"Please."

"I hope you've enjoyed your flight."

"Very much."

First class, VIP, Moët & Chandon, Chateauneuf-du-Pape, filet mignon, fresh-ground French roast, Jack Nicholson movie, feather pillow, Viyella lap rug. Out the window, twilighted Los Angeles spread out like a sequined cape, hemmed by the burgundy Pacific. What wasn't to enjoy? And hadn't she earned it? Eight exhaustive weeks of training, retraining and re-retraining, at the end of which she was a certified dissembler—though not so skillful that she hadn't blurted her first destination to her daughter, who'd done nothing but ask.

"Cali*for*nia?" Carrie had said.

"Forget I said that. I'll call when I can, but I can't be sure when that'll be."

"Like Dad."

"Like Dad."

"Dad got killed."

Not *whacked*, at least. "I'll be careful."

"Are you going to keep on doing this? I mean, after you find the man who killed Dad?"

Not so skillful that she hadn't almost said it was a woman, not a man, hadn't almost forgotten the disinformation that had been vended to the media. Maybe she wasn't going to be good at this, except that she heard herself say things like *disinformation vended to the media* more often these days, except that she hadn't said it was a woman. "I have to pay the rent."

"And you couldn't pay the rent just working in Research?"

Touché. "There's something else, Carrie: Just working in Research is just that—just working in Research. There's a war going on in this country and the bad guys're winning. If it were a real war—a war that threatened our lives and our freedom— you'd understand that I had to fight in it."

"Quiet desperation," Carrie said. "Dad used to say that people live lives of quiet desperation—"

Dad didn't say it; Thoreau said it.

"—and they've always found ways to turn on or tune out and they always will. So what difference does it make, really?"

"Did Dad say it didn't make a difference?"

"No, but..."

"He made a difference. He couldn't do anything about the people who want to turn on or tune out, but he did what he could about the people who tried to exploit them or take advantage of them." Christ, what drivel. And yet, it was true. How could what was true have come so startlingly undone?

"You're not going to be able to talk about your work—just like Dad. You hated that he could never talk about his work."

"Did you?"

"I don't know. I guess."

"Dad's work embarrassed you—around your friends."

"A little. I mean, it's not like they're junkies or anything, but..."

"But they're suspicious of authority."

"Yeah."

"Are you?"

"I don't know. Yeah. I guess."

"There's nothing wrong with healthy skepticism, Care, as long as it's well-informed."

"What does that mean?"

81

"It means it's not enough to know how much something costs; you have to know what it's worth." Someone—Oscar Wilde?—said *that*, more or less.

"Grandpa said you went through your training a lot faster than anybody expected."

"I'd been trained before. This was a refresher."

"He's proud of you."

"I guess he is, yes."

"He said he hopes you kill the son-of-a-bitch. He didn't say it to me—don't go yelling at him; he said it to one of his friends on the phone."

"I hope I don't have to kill anyone."

"You've got a gun, though."

"Yes, I've got a gun."

"Dad always said the trouble with guns is the people who have them think it's not enough to just have them, they have to use them."

"He was talking about people with no training."

"If you find the man who killed Dad, will you kill him?"

"You've watched enough television, Care. I'll read him his rights." After I've scratched her eyes out.

"You could say you had to kill him because he tried to kill you. Who would know?"

"Is that what you'd do?"

"I don't know. I guess. Maybe."

"Don't judge me if I don't, Care."

"Have you ever been to California?"

"Forget I said that."

"I've forgotten. Have you?"

And just like that she was back there, skinny and pale and callow and stunned by the bright and the warm, which coaxed her to loose the grip she'd had on herself for a score of Wisconsin winters. "Yes."

"Why'd you have to think about it?"

Because it was in a part of her memory that didn't willingly give things up. "It was a long time ago."

"Was it a vacation?"

A pilgrimage, sort of. "No."

"Muh-ther."

"What?"

"You went there with a boyfriend, didn't you?"

"A friend, yes."

"A *boy*friend. Someone you knew before you met Dad, right?"

"Yes."

"Was he cute?"

Cute? She'd never thought of him as cute; it was a word that wouldn't stay pinned to a man in a wheelchair. Or in a coffin. "Yes."

"What was his name?"

"Joe."

"Joe what?"

"Joe Cook. He was someone I knew in college. He wasn't *in* college, but he hung around the campus and I sort of went out with him—"

"What do you mean, sort of?" Carrie giggled.

"He was in a wheelchair."

"Oh."

"He was wounded in Vietnam and I really don't want to talk about him anymore."

"I hear that," Carrie said.

"Good."

After a while Carrie said, "How did you meet him?"

He had swept her off her feet. Literally. Whipping around a corner from one of the classes he wasn't registered for to another, he'd cut her legs out from under her and wound up with her in his lap.

It hadn't hurt a bit. "Home, James," she'd said.

"Joe. Where's home?"

"It was a joke, Joe. Put me down."

"I've got a car, if you live off-campus."

"Put me down."

"Can't. We're going too fast."

"Then stop."

"Never stop when you're just getting started. That's my motto."

"'I'm an asshole' should be your motto."

He laughed. "What's your major?"

"American History. Put me down."

"No kidding? Ever hear of the A Shau Valley?"

"Ever hear of the Lindbergh kidnapping?"

He laughed. "Go figure. You've heard of Valley Forge and Gettysburg and San Juan Hill and Belleau Wood—"

"And Guadalcanal—my father was there—and Normandy and Inchon."

He'd stopped by now, but she hadn't gotten off his lap. "You see? You know those places just off the top of your head, and you'd come up with more if you put your mind to it. But the A Shau Valley was just a couple of seconds ago, historically, and you've never heard of it."

"I didn't say I hadn't heard of it. I just . . ."

"Don't know what it stood for."

"Yes. I mean no. I don't."

"Susan Szentmihalyi." He read the name off the cover of a notebook. "Is that how you pronounce it?"

"Close enough. Joe what?"

"Cook."

"What did it stand for—the A Shau Valley?"

For a moment, he was back there, as she, twenty years later, would be back in California. Then he returned to Madison, Wisconsin, on October 4, 1968. "Will you have dinner with me? Tonight, tomorrow, whenever. My place is best for me, not to be seductive but because it's easier to do my own cooking than to get to a restaurant, up steps, into booths, under tables, all that. I make a great pot roast. If you don't eat meat, I make a great chicken. I make great fish, great spaghetti, great salad. Everything below my waist is dead. Everything. But like deaf people you've read about who can see better and blind people who can hear better, I've got some new places that turn me on. My ears,

84

if you can believe that. And I can touch you and ... so on. ... I'm just trying to answer the questions you're surely asking in your mind."

She was wet, whatever he was trying to do. "There's something you should know."

"You're not a lesbian. And you're not a seminary student."

"Worse. My parents voted for Goldwater in sixty-four, and I would've if I'd been old enough. I'm treasurer of Students for Nixon."

He smiled. "We should have some interesting conversations." He lifted her off his lap as if she were an infant. "There. I put you down. Let's not put each other down, all right? And maybe something nice'll come of it. Susan Szentmihalyi."

"You said he got sick," Carrie said.

"He was in a lot of pain and took a lot of drugs for it. He was always looking for a more powerful painkiller and heroin was it for a while until he needed so much of it that it didn't just kill the pain, it killed him."

"So why'd you go to California with him?"

"I didn't go with him, exactly. I went to his funeral."

"His parents lived there?"

"His parents were dead. He had a brother and two or three sisters. They wanted him buried along with his folks."

"What town?"

"Carolyn, why're you asking so many questions?"

"I want to know, okay?"

"Barstow. It's nowhere. It's in the desert."

"Is he the reason you became a narc?"

"He's the reason."

After a while, Carrie said, "I sometimes wonder—if you and Dad hadn't met, if you'd both married other people, and both had kids, would they be anything like me, the kids, or not at all like me, or—What's the matter?"

"Nothing."

"You're crying."

"I'm going to miss you, that's all."

"I'm going to miss you, Mom."

Redondo Beach: a house with a view of a taco franchise; posters on the walls of Heather Locklear, Samantha Fox, Vanna White; Sade on the stereo, She-Ra: Princess of Power on the television, with no sound; on the Goodwill couch, his head on one arm, his feet on the other, Harry Kellner, white sport coat, blue T-shirt, white pants, white espadrilles, gold watch, hair finger-combed back, whiskers, Wayfarers: Don Johnson manqué—the old Don Johnson, before he got new threads and a new do. Except for the snowy miniature poodle asleep on his stomach.

"Know why I turned songbird?" Kellner said. "The H never asks."

The H, Susan had figured out, was for Hemingway, Barnes's work name—Barnes as in Jake.

"He thinks it's 'cause I was looking at a double sawbuck at Q, but it's 'cause I've got it—the big A. A year, two, three—who knows?—I'll be the late great Harry the K. Unless they find a cure, in which case I'll still be the late great Harry the K, 'cause everybody I sang about's going to come looking for me."

If Harry was gay, then why the posters? Unless he didn't want his junkies to suspect. Junkies were funny that way; they didn't want the shit that was going to kill them one way or another stepped on by an ounce man who might have AIDS. "Tell me about Kit."

"I already told the H."

"Tell me."

"I helped a guy draw a picture of him. Look at the picture."

Susan waited.

Eventually, Kellner flipped a hand. "Like I told the H, a month, six weeks ago, I got a call. A dude was in town from New York, he wanted the names of mules who make runs out of

Meh-hee-co, could I be of assistance? He had good references, he was willing to pay for the referral, I just happened to know someone who was looking for a gig that'd take him east every so often, we smoked a J, we did a little business. Like I told the H, he was six one or two, skinny, nice threads, dirty-blond hair, brown eyes, I think. Like I told the H, said his name was Kit, but who the fuck uses their right name? Like I told the H, that's all I know. He blew into town and blew out. I don't even know where he stayed. He's the type who'd stay at the Marmont, if he stayed in a hotel, or maybe the Riot House, if he's into slumming."

"Who's the mule?"

Kellner wagged a finger. "That song I don't know the words to. The guy's a friend, we did points together, I got him the mule work as a favor, I don't want to fuck him over."

"Kit's people whacked a narc, Harry. It's them I want, not your mule. But he's the way to them."

Kellner played with the dog's toes for a while. "He'll know it came from me."

"Of course he'll know, Harry. I'm going out to play; I need some credibility. I'm going to be dropping your name all over town."

Kellner nodded. "That why you parked your wheels right in front of the house?"

Her wheels were a royal blue Testarossa loaned her by the L.A. shop, which had seized it in a raid on a yacht in a Palos Verdes marina. Its owner used the boat to smuggle horse and kept the car on davits on the deck for trips into town wherever he docked. "That's why. It's also why you're going to get me invited to some parties while I'm out here. Who's the mule?"

More toe business. "I don't like telling you."

Susan took a black leather-bound notebook from her bag and tossed it at Kellner, startling the dog awake. "Don't tell me. Write it down."

Kellner sighed, and wrote it down.

"And an address."

"He moves around a lot."

"Harry, whatever deal you made with Barnes can be unmade. Who knows? Maybe Q's got just the climate for someone with the big A. Maybe you'll live there a long time."

Kellner wrote again, clipped the pen back in its holder and tossed the notebook back.

Ted Scally. Spruce Colorado.

"What's back east that wants a gig that takes him there every so often?"

"Hunh?" Kellner said.

Susan stood. "Get me invited to some parties, Harry. I'm at the Beverly Hills."

Malibu: a house like a spaceship, all curves, no angles; two bars in the living room, one by the pool; a tray of cocaine on the coffee table, an ivory-handled straight razor to cut it, a crystal snifter of hundred-dollar bills for snorting; on another table some glass pipes and gold butane lighters and a cut-glass bowl of crack. More Don Johnson clones. Women so thin they were painful to look at. Everyone suntanned. Everyone screaming to be heard over Duran Duran on the stereo. No one making any sense and no one minding.

"'Ello, luv."

"Hello."

He laughed. "No, no, no. You're supposed to say. 'Aren't you. Nick Ivory? 'Ave all your records. Been in mourning. Ever since. The band broke up. Please, Nick, please. Get back together. Go on the road. Cut an album.'"

Susan handed him her highball glass. "Would you get me a drink? Club soda with a piece of lime. Not a twist, a piece."

He laughed and got it and brought it back but didn't hand it to her. "'Ave you seen what Georgia's. Done to the loo? A great flaming red tub. Quadriphonic speakers in the 'eadrest. 'Ydrotherapy water jets. Moisturizing mister. A blood telephone. No sensory-deprivation tank. For Georgia. For Georgia. A sensory-satiation tank. Known Georgia long?"

Susan took her glass from him. "You look like Keith Richards."

"The bloody 'ell. Seen Keith lately? Aged, he is. Grizzled, gnarled. Care to see. My etchings? My digs. Are right up. Solstice Canyon."

There'll be men after you, Susan, Barnes had said. *Lots of men. Sometimes it'll seem every man. The only way to keep them at bay is to establish from the outset that you're there on business—that even your small talk at parties has business behind it. Don't ever let them see you relaxed, because if they see you relaxed they'll have all the edge they'll need.* "Would you introduce me to Georgia, Nick? I want to ask her who does her catering."

Ivory looked over at the coffee table, where two girls in chic punk were on their knees giggling at their combined inability to roll a hundred into a tube. He looked back at Susan, looked closely at her eyes. "Sober. Clear of eye. The earmarks of a, uh, player."

"I have an acquaintance who sells wholesale to . . . chemists, you'd call them."

"Condoms? Toothpaste? That sort of thing?"

"Prescription items."

"Ah."

"He has an overstock problem."

" 'Appened with the first record. Me and the lads did. Everywhere you looked. Overstock. Sold four of them, finally. One to each of our mums."

"He'd like to trade it for something."

"Sort of a barter arrangement."

"Yes."

"You're an extremely lucky. Young lady. Out of this entire multitude. I'm the bloke. You should be talking to."

"I wanted to talk to you at Leah's the other night, but you were taken."

"You were at Leah's? Didn't see you. I'd remember. I'll never forget you. As long as I live."

"You were with twins. How is it with twins?"

Ivory laughed. "Bet you've done it. With twins. Bet you've done. Everything."

89

"Nick?"

"Yes, luv? Didn't get your name."

"I can't talk to you when your nose is down my dress."

"But it's so. Lovely there. Like the promised land."

For Susan too. Well, like a rumored one, one dreamt about over a sink of dirty dishes, perhaps, or on the Gowanus with a flat tire in the rain, or in August on the subway or February in the slush, or any time at all when the realization came that the way things were was the way they were going to be for, as Nick Ivory might put it, ever. Oh, Susan would people the land differently, and change the decor and the stimulants, and turn down the music, but she'd keep the ocean and the stars and the sense induced by the wind in her face that she was riding on the continent's prow.

There'll be other seductions, Barnes had said. *Money, power, freedom to do what you want, when and where you want. As long as you can be yourself, you can withstand the temptations. Don't playact, don't bullshit, don't pretend, and you won't be vulnerable. It sounds contradictory, I know, because the essence of what you're doing is acting, bullshit and pretense; but if you can hold on to your self, your sense of who you are and where you are, you won't break.*

How about waver a little? Susan was used to having a big effect on younger men—mailroom boys, delivery boys, the butcher's son and the greengrocer's, even friends of Carrie's, the less anarchic ones: they could see beyond her maturity to her femininity and admire it without being threatened by it. And she could flirt with them with impunity, knowing they weren't clever enough to besiege the pedestal they'd put her on.

But rock-and-roll stars. Never mind that he'd wasted to look twice his age, that he was enslaved by his appetites, that he'd probably never read a book in his life—or read only books by Aleister Crowley. He worked on her, the way she'd been worked on first by Elvis, by Jimmy Dean, by Brando, who had known— *how* had they known?—that there was a thing like a clitoris in a girl's mind and had touched it just... so.

"Nick?"

90

"Won't do it. Again, luv. I promise. Cross me 'eart."

"I have to go now"—had to get some air, get her bearings, listen to Bach on the Testarossa's tape deck and remind herself that *that* was music. "Can you come around to my hotel tomorrow for lunch? The Beverly Hills. We can talk... barter."

"I'm absolutely. Devastated. That you're leaving, luv. But the prospect. Of dining with you. Elevates me spirits. Just a little. 'Ow do you call yourself?"

"Susan Saint Michael."

"Lovely name. Suits you. Shall we say oneish?"

"Twelve sharp, Nick."

13

"What do I do?"

The stoner handed Carrie a Super Cub. "Just hold this under the pipe, okay?"

She juggled the lighter as if it were aflame, and handed it back. "I don't want to, okay?"

"Hey, it's way rad. You'll love it."

She put the pipe down.

Jennifer snorted. "Narc genes."

"Fuck you, Jen."

The skinhead picked up the pipe. "My turn."

The stoner punched the skinhead in the arm. "You had a turn, asshole. It's Carrie's turn."

"That's okay, okay?" Carrie said.

Jennifer leaned down to see Carrie's eyes. "Narc genes."

Carrie hugged herself. "I just don't want to do it, okay? All the stuff I've read about it..."

The skinhead laughed. "Oh. Right. Sure. What do you expect? You expect to read in the *news*paper that it's rad? You expect the dweebs who put out *news*papers to tell the world it's out*standing*? Think of what that would do to the dweeb tobacco companies that advertise in them, the liquor companies."

"The *air*line companies," the stoner said.

The skinhead laughed. "Right. Oh, rad. I mean, why fly to Hawaii or something when you can crack it up?"

"Narc genes," Jennifer said.

"Fuck you, Jennifer, okay?"

"Then do it."

"I don't *want* to."

"'Cause you have *narc* genes."

Carrie got off the mattress that was the stoner's bed and went to the window. The apartment was on 103rd Street and had a view of a brick wall that some sunlight shone on through an unfathomable process of incidence and reflection; the rooms smelled of boy-ripe clothes, junk food remains, semen spilled willy-nilly for want of a human receptacle. Copies of *Hustler, inCider* and *Kerrang!* One book: *The Two Mrs. Grenvilles.* Albums and tapes by Murphy's Law, 7 Seconds, Agnostic Front, the Cramps, Slayer, Hellhammer, Nasty Savage and Future Tense—but nothing to play them on. A videocassette of *National Lampoon's Vacation,* ditto.

"Now I want you to write Jennifer's address and phone number," Bob II had said, "and also her mother's office number."

"Okay, Grandma." Carrie wrote Jennifer's address and phone number, which was better than saying she wasn't going to Jennifer's, she was taking the Long Island Rail Road to Atlantic Avenue and meeting Jennifer at the subway and going to Manhattan, and a number she made up, which was better than saying she didn't know Jennifer's mother's office number, Jennifer's mother didn't work, she lived on alimony and hung out at a bar in Carroll Gardens with her boyfriend, the president of the Brooklyn chapter of the Hell's Angels.

"Now, you be sure to call us when you get to Jennifer's."

"Okay, Grandma."

"Do you have enough money for a movie?"

"Yes, Grandma."

"Now, make sure you don't see anything that's rated PG-thirteen."

"*Grand*ma. I'm *fif*teen."

"Carolyn."

"*Okay,* Grandma, okay?"

"Give me a kiss, dear."

A careful kiss, lest Bob II's parchment skin crack.

"Go give Grandpa a kiss too."

93

"He fell asleep watching the ball game."

"I'll tell him you said goodbye, then."

"Okay. Goodbye."

"Have fun, Carrie."

"Okay."

"Do you want to take a sweater? Sometimes those movie theaters're so cold."

"I'll be okay, okay?"

"Do you want to take some fruit to eat on the train?"

Oh, right, Grandma. Crucial. How about a baloney sandwich on white bread with mayo? "No, thanks."

"Now, don't eat too much junk, Carrie."

"I won't."

"Call us before you leave and we'll pick you up at the station."

"I'll walk, okay? Thanks, okay?"

"You're sure?"

"Good*bye,* Grandma, okay?"

"Goodbye, Carrie."

"Bye."

"Bye."

"So what's it gonna be?" the stoner said. His name was Rob or Ron or Rick or something. That was the skinhead's name too. The stoner was standing too close to her. Even if he had taken a bath recently, he would've been standing too close. "You gonna crack it up or what?"

"Uh..."

"'Cause if you're not, then maybe you should, you know, split, 'cause we wanna have a good time and if you don't, well..."

"I do, okay? I do want to have a good time."

He stood closer. "Well, then?"

"I just don't..."

"Don't what?"

"...I don't know, okay?"

He put his hands on her shoulders, then turned her toward the mattress. "Look at Jennifer. She's having a good time."

Carrie looked and looked away, but the image persisted of Jennifer on her back, the slip she wore for a dress up around her waist, her fishnet panty hose down around her ankles, still with her one Doc Marten's and her one high-top black sneaker on, still with her panties on, the skinhead lying between her legs, nuzzling at her neck.

"See?"

"What?"

"She's having a good *time*. We could have a good time too."

"Is...?"

"Is what?"

"Is there another room?"

"No."

"Well, then..."

"Well, then what?"

"Well..."

"Hey. Are you shy or something?"

"No. Yes. No. It's just..."

"What?"

Caroline sneaked a look to see just how far Jennifer was going. Nothing had changed. She still had her Doc Marten's and her sneaker on. She still had her panties on.

"Looks like fun, doesn't it?"

"I don't know. I guess."

The boy let her go and took the pipe from his pocket and lighted the Super Cub. "Here. Try this."

"I don't... I don't..."

"Just *try* it. You don't like it, hey, fuck it."

"Doesn't it...?"

"What?"

"Don't you, you know, have to have more?"

He laughed. "You don't *have* to have more. You wanna have more, you have more, but you don't *have* to have more."

"Honest?"

He laughed. "Honest? Whattaya mean, honest? Do I look like a dweeb?"

He looked like an alien. "No."

"So don't ask me honest, okay? I mean, if I tell you something, I tell you straight. Don't ask me honest."

"Okay."

"Okay?"

"I said okay, okay?"

He heated the bowl.

"But..."

He turned the stem toward her.

"I just... I don't..."

He put his hand at the base of her skull and pulled her head toward him, toward the pipestem.

Carrie put a knee in his groin and ran—out the door, down the stairs, through the lobby, out the door, down the steps, into the street. Which was no better place to be, for all along it, propped in doorways, sitting on stoops, up against walls as if splattered there and stuck and unable to move, were people like him, men, boys, a girl or two, hissing at her, jeering, leering.

Narc genes. Narc bones. Narc brains.

14

In Aspen and Vail and Squaw Valley, and even in Zürs and Courcheval, they made Spruce jokes:

Why was the town council petitioned to replace the clock on the Spruce town hall? Because it wasn't a gold Rolex Oyster.

What has a fur coat, a straw up its nose and goes down a mountain on its knees? A Spruce skier.

How many Sprucers does it take to make a martini? One to mix the gin and vermouth and one to fly the olives in from the south of France.

Ted Scally hated Spruce. He hated the Main Street boutiques and the restaurants with no prices on the menus; the gourmet food shops and the funiculars with heated cars and hostesses in skating skirts serving mulled cider; the cops who wore rabbit fur trooper hats and white turtlenecks and bright blue ski jackets and designer jeans and looked like the assholes who covered skiing on *Wide World of Sports*—except in summer, when they went bareheaded and traded their turtlenecks and ski jackets for blue shirts and red ties and royal blue blazers and looked like the assholes who covered tennis or golf or baseball.

The only thing Scally liked about Spruce was the airport, a vestige of the days when he'd loved Spruce, then a place a couple of hundred skiers in the world had heard of and a couple of dozen had skied; when Main Street was the only street, with a bar, a coffee shop (with prices on the menus *and*, the only Spruce joke of the time went, samples of the food on the menus too), a general store and a gas station; when there was one cop, who wore a watch cap and Levi's and a flannel shirt and an army-surplus parka, and in the summer traded the parka for a sheepskin vest and the watch cap for a Cat hat; when the only way up the mountain was on a T-bar that broke down two or three times a day; when après-ski meant you were too tired to move, and condos and fondue were movie stars, weren't they, and princes and vicomtesses and sheiks and senators were people you read about, if you could read, not tripped over every time you turned around.

Scally sat on the split-rail fence outside the so-called terminal, peeled dead skin off his left arm and watched the Spruce Airways de Havilland Otter coming down the valley, looking lost and scared, the way it always looked. The sunburn on his forearm and a pain in his butt were souvenirs of his drive from Mexico in a Dodge van with three salamis, a pound of provolone, two loaves of Italian bread, a bag of trail mix, six quarts of Gatorade, a box of NoDoz, tapes by Tom Petty, Juice Newton, Sandy Rogers, Bruce, Tina, Dwight Yoakam, the Swan Silvertones, and nine hundred pounds of cocaine.

A piece of cake, even getting across the border. Especially getting across the border, since his escort had been the police chief of a town in Jalisco state whose name he never got but where he'd been treated like a native son.

The Otter touched, bounced, touched, bounced, touched and stayed down, its tail coming up and up as the pilot did everything but drag his feet to stop before he ran out of runway, airport, clearing. It was always exciting to see a landing at Spruce, always a kick to see the faces of the passengers as they disembarked. Another joke: Who invented Valium? The first person to fly an Otter into Spruce.

Four passengers. Heavy for an almost-summer Wednesday afternoon, though Spruce was the beneficiary of a climatological quirk that left snow on the slopes through June. No problem picking out the one he was there to meet: tall, anorexic, wearing a mink vest and jeans that had probably been washed in Perrier —or—champagne—to fade them. She looked like she had her head on straight, though, hadn't flown in higher than the plane and was still somewhere up overhead, juiced and frantic and sending off signals, *Bust me. Bust me.*

Scally hopped off the fence and walked around to the front of the tar-paper shack—SPRUCE INTERNATIONAL AIRPORT, said the hyperbolic sign over the screen door—and went inside. The big dumb fuck behind the counter looked up from *Nugget,* then looked again.

"You're Scally, aren't you?"

"Nope." He went through the other screen door.

The woman came right at him, which was good for his self-esteem since each of the three taxi drivers waiting along the chain-link fence looked as though he might any minute decide he'd had enough of hacking, and drive over to the Frontier Mall and kill some shoppers with a deer rifle.

"Scally?"

"Ted." He smiled; he thought it was funny.

No name in return. No handshake. No smile.

"Welcome to Spruce."

A little tired sigh that said that either she'd been here a thousand times or she couldn't wait to get out. "I'd like something to eat. Let's go to Maude's."

Been here before. Of all the places with no prices on the menu, Maude's (which had no name on the door and an unlisted phone number) was the one with the prices most likely to kill. "Sure." He took her bag—a Vuitton, natch— and held the screen door for her. She smelled good—of herself, not some scent.

The big dumb fuck had come out from behind the counter. "Yeah, you're Scally. I saw you one time at Sun Valley. You lost to some Eye-tie. You had the last run and you choked. Missed two gates."

"Oh, *that* Scally. I'm his brother."

The big dumb fuck screwed up his face. "Didn't know he had a brother."

"Well, I used to be his sister, but I had one of those operations."

He was a smart dumb fuck; he didn't even have to think about that. "You did some time, didn't you?"

"That's right. Killed the manager of a jerkwater airport."

The big dumb fuck retreated a step.

"Then sodomized him."

The big dumb fuck went back behind the counter.

She was at the other screen door, propping it open with a lizard boot. "Was that for my benefit?"

Scally got behind her and took the weight of the door and let her go down the steps ahead of him. "The blue van."

She stood a ways off from the van, her hands on her hips, while he opened the rear door and put her bag inside. Then she kicked at a rear tire and watched the dust shimmer up. "I don't mind a little local color, Ted, but this is fucking ridiculous."

He laughed.

"Where've you been in this? Hell?"

He laughed again. She was funny. "Oh, here and there."

She said, "Fuck it," and walked around to the passenger's side.

He got in and reached under the dash and fiddled with the ignition wires and got it started. He smiled at her. "Had a key once, but I lost it."

She had an elbow on the windowsill and her head propped on a hand, watching him. "Around the time you lost everything?"

Another smartass rich broad who knew his life story. "That piece of rope there's a seat belt. Hitch it around this bar and it'll hold you well enough. You'll want it on; the road's for shit. But you know that; you've been to Maude's."

She ignored the rope and put a boot up on the dash. "I told Kellner I didn't want to deal with someone with an attitude problem. He assured me you were a professional."

He was chastened, having worked so hard in the first place to convince Kellner that he was serious about wanting to be a full-time bad guy, that the six months since he'd gotten out of the fire camp for his last GTA had been enough of the straight and narrow for him, thanks. He didn't say a word until off the shit road and onto the paved. "Kellner said you're looking for a wholesaler back east."

100

"Then Kellner got it wrong."

"Okay, he didn't say back east. He said—"

"Listen. Scally. I want some food and I want a drink. After that we'll talk. You don't have to bullshit with me. You don't have to reminisce. Just do what I tell you and keep your—What the fuck?"

He had pulled onto the verge and braked hard and jolted her and her chin struck her knee. She pressed her hand to her mouth and he wrenched it away and pulled her to him and kissed her hard, with teeth and tongue, then thrust her away and popped into gear and burned rubber getting back on the road.

She hit him behind the ear with the heel of her hand. His head rang but he kept driving. He sensed that it was a punch that could've killed him if she hadn't pulled it. "Cunt."

"Asshole."

"Ball breaker."

"Motherfucker."

He laughed.

She laughed.

Scally did a power slide into a U-turn. "Fuck Maude's. We'll go to Maggie Reno's." Which was not in Spruce but in Spruce Junction—junction of what, no one remembered (if anyone ever knew), and, the only Spruce Junction joke went, where you'd make the insertion if you wanted to give the planet an enema. Maggie Reno's. It sounded strange to hear himself say it, for he hadn't been to Maggie's, hadn't spoken of it, had tried not to think about it, since the time when he had gone there nearly every day with Ornella.

The storytellers hadn't taught Susan about a place called Maggie Reno's, but a place called Maggie Reno's sounded good to her, as Scally's mouth had felt good even while it's being on hers had revolted her, as his face had looked good after a week of meeting men with faces made from the same cookie cutter of rage and despair. His face not only looked good, it looked too goddamn much like Joe Cook's.

"So when you say you want a drink, you mean a club soda."

Susan sipped it.

"Kellner says you're from San Francisco. Pacific Heights?"

"Hillsborough."

"I lived there in seventy-two. Noe Valley."

She gave him the look that Hillsborough gave to Noe Valley.

"Kellner said you'd been in Europe for a while."

"Five years."

"Whereabouts?"

"Everywhere."

"Business or pleasure?"

She laughed.

"What line's your old man in?"

"You mean my father? He's been dead for years. I have no idea what he did."

"You just cash the inheritance checks," Scally said. "Do any skiing in Europe?"

"In the winter?"

"And in the summer?"

"I lay very still."

"Were you with one guy, or a lot of different guys?"

"I don't remember."

"You just lay very still."

"Be careful, Scally."

"Ted. . . . You're going to like Rachel."

"I have no intention of liking her. I just want to do business with her."

"You're birds of a feather. She'd done it all too—looking for that something they leave out when they stick a silver spoon in your mouth."

"God, what a tiresome cliché."

"I'm a tiresome guy."

"That you are."

"But you like me. Rachel does too. It's fear, really. You're afraid of me, both of you, because you know that I've seen the future and it isn't you."

Susan laughed. That was pure Joe Cook—apocalyptic Pogo.

"Go ahead. Tell me about him," Scally said. "Someone you used to know who was just like me. That's what you're thinking."

Joe Cook had done that too—burgled her mind even when she was home with all the lights on.

"You remember that song, a couple of years ago? 'Bad Boy'? Miami Sound Machine?" He sang a bit, more than passably, about how he made her feel so good.

Be careful, Susan. Be very, very careful. "Here's the address in Oakland." She wrote it on a napkin, turned it for him to read, then took it back and balled it up and dropped it in her water glass. "You pick your route and your timetable. There'll be somebody there every night between ten P.M. and two A.M. I'll be here until Saturday, at the Boyd. In New York, I'll be at the Pierre. Call me when you get there and've arranged a meeting with your people. Any questions?"

"Don't you want to look at my goods?"

"Then have you step all over the load anywhere between here and Oakland? There'll be a chemist there to look at your goods."

He smiled. She was good. Very good. Nice and simple. In and out. No energy wasted on details that didn't matter. No horning in on his end of things. Plenty of room to improvise. And careful about what she had to be and not about what she didn't. She wasn't going to like Rachel at all, or Rachel her; Rachel couldn't keep her hands off what was no concern of hers and was careful when she could be careless and when she should be careful didn't give a fuck.

15

"Susan's gone out to play," Barnes said. "We won't be hearing from her for a while."

Rita smoked.

"This fellow Scally's a puzzle."

And smoked.

"On track to an Olympic skiing medal until he derailed himself; he broke training rules, defied coaches, insulted the national Olympic hierarchy, alienated his teammates and finally broke the law." Barnes flicked pages of the yellow Research Department file that Polly had brought him. Susan's Polly. He and *his* Polly had had their first fight, a minor classic: she'd wanted to tape a WNCN stereo simulcast of a Channel 13 telecast of the Kirov Ballet's *Swan Lake*; he'd asked her to wait—just a few goddamn minutes—so he could listen all the way through to George Thorogood and the Destroyers' "One Bourbon, One Scotch, One Beer," which she'd stumbled over on NEW-FM on the way to NCN. She'd called him an aging hipster; he'd called her a snob—and a record pirate.

"He's had several felony arrests—assault, D and D, robbery armed, GTA—and one conviction, on one of the car thefts. Nothing to do with drugs and no indication that he used them; he's a beer drinker; he used to brag about it in newspaper interviews." When it came to drinking, *Barnes* was a snob. If you were going to drink, drink something that was at least eighty proof.

Rita drew an ugly Rorschach on the pad on her lap.

"There is a connection to narcotics by way of an old girlfriend —an Italian Olympic skier named Ornella Vitti. She died two

104

years ago—interestingly, just before the GTA that landed Scally in jail, which might mean that his infraction was a reaction to the tragedy, although they apparently were no longer involved. He was living in Los Angeles at the time, whereas she died, also interestingly, in Suffolk County—Sagaponack, to be precise, which is part of Bridgehampton. She was found washed up on the beach, but the cause of death was an overdose of heroin, administered by injection. The needle mark was the only one on her arm, and from published interviews with her coach and teammates it appears she had had no previous involvement with any controlled substance.

"She also had a stab wound and burn marks on her wrists, as if she'd been trussed up. The stab wound was from a 'spearlike implement,' which the police eventually despaired of identifying more precisely, settling on the speculation that whoever was with her when she OD'd decided to dispose of her body by dumping it in the ocean, tied a rope around her wrists to facilitate moving her, and in jettisoning her body caused it to strike some 'submerged object.' An implement like a spear fits rather nicely—or is it rather too nicely?—with the anecdote about Van Meter's lance."

Rita lighted a new cigarette from the old and ground the old one out in the ashtray on Barnes's desk.

Barnes closed the folder and sat back in his chair. "What's Scally up to? He approached Harry Kellner, with whom he'd done points, about the possibility of getting into the transportation end of the business, especially making runs back east. Back east. Why should the location be important to him, especially since he was to the west born and bred? *Had* this Vitti woman's death had an impact on him? Is he committed to some kind of vigilante revenge? Against whom? Against narcotics traffickers in general, or...? If the people Van Meter went rogue with collect swords and lances, do they occasionally use them? And does Scally know that?"

Rita smoked.

Barnes sighed. Another woman unhappy with the status quo. After Polly'd kicked him out, he'd called Mia and asked if he could come over. She'd hung up on him, making him for a moment, just a moment, think about calling a friend over at Immigration and Naturalization. "Say it, Rita."

She put out the new cigarette. "Why are you running Susan, John?"

"As opposed to?"

"As opposed to me."

"For auld lang syne? You came up together—you and Susan and Paul. And it is because of you that Susan's back on the job—because of your going behind my back and telling her things that were none of her business."

Rita contracted her nostrils. "You are too involved with policy and planning—"

"Don't forget politics."

"—to run an agent day to day. You are an administrator."

"I'll manage. Running Susan's an incentive to keep the paperwork from backing up."

"And when you are away from the shop and she sends a peril?"

"That's why we have duty officers, Rita. I can be reached anywhere, anytime."

"I could not reach you last night."

You cunt, Rita. You chocha.

"A little after midnight. You did not answer your beeper and you left no number with the duty officer."

Because a Director-bucker couldn't very well leave the Jersey number of a woman who ought not to be living in Jersey—and who sometimes carried her cocaine in a pair of hollowed earrings, for a quick toot at the office or at the movies or a party or in an empty elevator or anywhere at all. The old wooden escalators in the middle of Macy's were a fun place; for some reason, not very many people rode them.

And a Director-bucker couldn't very well call the duty officer after that woman kicked him out and leave the number of an illegal alien postliterate marijuana smoker. And couldn't very well call after *she* turned him down and leave the number of a bar in the Village he'd gone to with the intention of closing it

106

down. "The beeper must be broken. I didn't leave a number because I had the beeper."

"It is SOP to always leave a number, beeper or no."

He'd met a virgin in the bar, a virgin from Hickory (*Hick*-reh, she pronounced it), North Carolina, who was waitressing by night and taking acting classes at the HB Studio by day. "What did you want to tell me, Rita? Or were you just testing?"

Rita stretched her neck. "Aaronson made contact."

"And?"

"Lorca has broken with Cool D. He has a new arrangment, Lorca has, with a new player—the woman who whacked Cool D's sideman. And whacked Paul."

The virgin from Hickory—the hick from *Hick*-reh—had gone back with him to the studio on Ninth Street that reeked of odors from Balducci's, but had left in tears after she saw his look of dismayed disappointment that her breasts tumbled nearly to her waist when she took off her bra. He couldn't very well have called the duty officer to tell him *that*. "That was to be expected."

"Aaronson expects Cool D to retaliate."

"If he whacks Lorca he'll be whacked right back. A spark-up between them would be a favor to us."

"Retaliate against the woman."

"Ah."

Rita got out another cigarette and struck a match and from behind the flame said, "Why are you playing dumb, John?"

He smiled. "Because I am dumb. Does Cool D have a better idea than we do who this woman is? Does Aaronson? She's smart, she's quick, she doesn't leave a dirty trail. We're all dumb, compared with her."

"It is difficult for Aaronson to get a description out of Cool D and his people without arousing suspicion. She has short blond hair, however, almost like a man's, and is apparently extremely attractive."

Barnes leaned forward. "*Short* blond hair? The woman with Paul had a big loose mane." He tried not to sound as though she sounded interesting.

"Perhaps she had it cut."

"And you propose to do what—canvass every hairdresser in New York?"

"Not every. The kind of woman who would buy limited-edition Ellesse sunglasses would go to only a certain kind of hairdresser." Rita hurried on, before he could remind her of the limits of their resources. "I have been going over the list that Polly prepared—regarding the sunglasses."

Susan's Polly.

"Some of the purchasers can be eliminated geographically or because of their ages or genders. We have to proceed on the assumption that the glasses were not bought as a gift, though they might well have been. Of the two hundred fifty pairs, only twenty were sold to women between the ages of twenty and forty whose primary residence is in the forty-eight contiguous states."

"Any with short blond hair, almost like a man's, and apparently extremely attractive?"

"Polly is still collecting photographs."

His Polly collected photographs too, she'd revealed just before *their* spark-up—self-portraits in assorted lingerie, taken with her Pentax's timer as foreplay to masturbation; it was the only way she could turn herself on. Why did she get them developed and printed? Why not? No, it hadn't occurred to her that the lab technicians might vet them, might even make copies. *He* could have as many prints as he wanted, to stimulate himself when they weren't together. He imagined them circulating around Georgetown and wished she'd taken more care with the framing and focus; if discredited he was going to be, let the evidence be high-quality. And he wished he *had* taken some prints, since she was just the kind of principled cunt who wouldn't kiss and make up. Would Mia? Would the hick from *Hick*-reh? "There's also the question of the reliability of this witness of Susan's—this street person. Those sunglasses could've fallen from the sky, for all we know. I've sent Sayles uptown to have a talk with the fellow—if that's even possible."

Rita carefully rolled the ash off her cigarette and studied it for a moment before speaking. "Aaronson had to tell Cool D that the

108

newspaper stories about Paul's death were disinformation we vended them."

"Had to?"

"He felt it was something they would expect him to know."

Barnes rubbed his eyes. Conditioned air always dried them—and Rita's contractionless staccato made them heavy. "The next time Aaronson makes contact, arrange a get-together between him and me."

Rita blew out a jet of smoke. "For what purpose?"

"I want to hear from him—not from you—how his operation's going. A case officer and his field man—or hers—are like a pair of lovers; they can't always see the bigger picture. It's not a criticism, Rita, it's a fact. I want to make sure the operation's not going stale. We've invested too much in Aaronson's fairy tale not to have it producing optimally."

His secure phone rang. "Would you excuse me, please? That'll be Nix." He'd already talked to Nix this morning, but he'd had enough of Rita.

She left behind a contrail of Marlboro smoke.

"Barnes."

"It's Red, John," Sayles said. "Our homeless eyewitness isn't homeless anymore."

Barnes waited.

"He's gone to the big flophouse in the sky."

Barnes exhaled through his nose. "When?"

"Last night or early this morning."

"How?"

"I've had to kind of pussyfoot around this and so on and so forth 'cause the Homicide scoshes want to know why I'm so interested in a wino, but what it looks like is he got so polluted he passed out and strangled on his own vomit. There were four empty Scotch bottles in his, uh, house. Cutty, if you can figure that. You don't happen to know if Susan gave him any money, do you? He had thirty dollars on him, which is kind of a lot for a wino, even one that drinks Cutty and so on and so forth. You think it's our money?"

"She didn't mention payment, but even if she made one, the police won't trace it."

"So I should keep hush-hush and so on and so forth that this was a guy we wanted to talk to?"

"I don't see any point in telling the police, no. It would just confuse things."

"There were some winos hanging around who knew the guy. One of them ID'd him as Hugh Morgan, said he's from California and used to invent computers. The company he worked for decided not to build some computer he invented and Morgan took a long walk. Left behind a wife and a couple of kids and so on and so forth. It's a hell of a world, isn't it, J.B.?"

"Yes," Barnes said. "Yes, it is."

"The thing is, John, Morgan's buddy tells me Morgan hated Scotch. He only drank wine and when he could afford something better he drank vodka. Or am I just fishing here for something that's not going to bite and so on and so forth?"

"I think it's a dead end, yes."

"Okay, but just one more thing, though. Morgan's buddy says Morgan was afraid somebody was going to kill him."

"I think it's a dead end, Red."

"He called him the alligator man."

"Come back to the shop," Barnes said.

16

Shiraz dreamed that Howlin' Wolf invited her backstage, then beat her with his guitar because she had been talking and giggling during his set. The guitar was made of glassine and burst. Snow spilled out and filled the green room, floating upward, as in a child's glass paperweight.

The snow was cold and she was cold and she felt for the sheet, which she'd kicked off in the dream.

She couldn't move.

She wanted to wake enough that she wouldn't fall back into the dream, and she turned onto her back until it had dissipated.

Tried to turn, but she couldn't move.

A woman laughed. Not in the dream, or another dream. There. In the bedroom of the houseboat.

A laugh of delight—delight that something hoped for but not to be counted on had come to pass.

A curtain billowed in the breeze from the open window, then luffed, then was sucked against the screen by an outgoing current.

The moving air chilled Shiraz, for she was naked. Yet she never slept naked; she liked the feel of an oversized cotton undershirt, even on the sultriest nights.

She had been undressed, as well as bound, for it was because she was bound that she couldn't move, bound hand and hand and foot and foot, each end tied to a bedpost with a rope that cut at her wrists and ankles. "Who's there?"

The sound of pots and pans rattling.

No. Something more substantial. Something like . . .

Like what?

"For the love of God, untie me."

A lugubrious voice, artificially deep. "Cool D say chill out. Bitch." And the laugh again, contemptuous this time. Still a woman's laugh. The laugh of a woman at a woman, which was not the laugh a woman ever laughed at a man.

"It's you, isn't it?" Shiraz said.

The pots and pans again. The...whatever.

"Let me see you....Turn on the light, bitch."

A shape, a rush of air, a slap Shiraz had sense enough of to turn away from but that she couldn't altogether evade.

A noise like cymbals in her ears.

"Jesus. God. Damn. Christ. Oh shit, oh shit, oh don't, oh don't."

Pincers, metal pincers, gripped her chin and turned her head up. The grip was almost gentle—not comforting, but competent. Shiraz opened her eyes. They were more accustomed to the dark now and she could see...She could see...Could see...

"For the love of God, don't hit me again."

The creature patted Shiraz's cheek with its metal fingers. Its metal beak came close to Shiraz's face. Its hollow breath was short and urgent. "Shhhhiraaaaaz."

"It's you, isn't it?"

"Shiraz, Shiraz, Shiraz."

No. It couldn't. No. It wasn't.

It was.

The creature's metal hands were on her thighs in an ungainly, scraping caress.

"No. Please, don't."

"Shiraz."

"Please."

"Shhh."

"Oh God."

"It's out of God's hands."

"Please."

"It's out of Cool D's hands."

"Please, please, please."

"It's in *my* hands."

And Shiraz screamed as first one, then two metal fingers thrust inside her.

"Yes."

Screamed.

"Yes, yes."

Screamed.

"Yes."

Moaned.

"Yes, yes, yes."

Fainted.

"Yes, oh yes. Oh Shiraz, yes. Oh God, yes. Oh Shiraz."

The light went from red to green. Marvin Needleman put his cab in drive and his mind in third: "Pete Rose. Everybody says he's too old, I read in the papers how old he is, he's ten years younger than me. The funny thing is, when I was thirty-two, thirty-three, and Pete Rose was just coming up, I'd look at him and I'd think, 'This is a grown man, and I am just a kid.' Not just Pete Rose—all ballplayers. It's on account of when you're a kid, you think of athletes as men, so even when you get to be a man yourself, you still think that way, even though, by the time you're thirty-two, thirty-three, the ones who're playing're younger than you. It's only when you get to be fifty-five, sixty, probably, you can finally put their age and your age in, you know, perspective.

"Eva Marie Saint. She's another example. *On the Waterfront* came out—when?—in the fifties. She plays a girl—nineteen, twenty years old; Karl Malden plays a priest. I had a crush on her—she was about my age—and I had, you know, respect for him, for the character he plays, 'cause he was older. Couple of months ago, on television, they reran this TV movie about the Green Beret doctor who supposedly killed his wife and kids back in the sixties, right after the Manson thing. I saw it when it was on the first time, a couple of years ago, but I didn't notice something I noticed the second time, which is Karl Malden's in the movie playing the wife's father, the Green Beret's father-in-law,

113

and guess who's playing his wife, Karl Malden's. Eva Marie Saint.

"So it's like if you drew two curves—you know, like we used to do in math—and this curve is my life and this curve is Eva Marie Saint's life. And then you draw two more curves—and this one's Eva Marie Saint's life and this one is me looking at Eva Marie Saint over the years and thinking that she's a certain age in relation to me—"

"Could you make a turn at the light, please?"

"Uh, yeah, sure, but this isn't your street. You wanted the Port Authority Bus Terminal."

"The middle of the block'll be fine."

"Yeah, sure, but there's nothing here. I wouldn't walk around this neighborhood if I were you, buddy. This is not a good—"

"Turn the engine off."

"What're you talking about? Hey, is that a gun?"

"That thing you've always wondered, Marvin—does it hurt? Well, it's not going to."

"Hey, buddy, look. I'll give you everything I got, but don't—"

114

17

Nick Ivory, on his back on the bed, sighted through an empty Jim Beam bottle. "Young Christopher Bolton. Two points. Off the starboard bow."

One knee on the bench of her vanity, Rachel did a line off the glass top through a rolled-up bill.

"Scally's here," Kit Bolton said. "With this Saint Michael woman." He leaned against the doorframe, miming insouciance, but his heart ached that he had to knock these days.

"Come in, Kit. Come in. Don't be bashful. It's just us. Naked savages."

Bolton took a small step into the room. "Scally's trouble, I think. I think—"

"Fuck-ups relinquish the privilege of second-guessing, Kit." Rachel did another line. "I need Scally; until I can train my own mules, I'm stuck with him." She unrolled the bill, saw it was a one, crumpled it and threw it away. She stood straight and closed her eyes for a moment, to feel the rush.

Ivory curled up with the bottle. "There's a lyric there. If I still. Wrote lyrics. I don't still. Write lyrics. Do I, luv?"

Bolton sniffled, wanting a toot, knowing Rachel might offer him one or she might not. "You can't still be pissed off about the thing with Grace. The thing with Grace is history. The thing with Grace was an accident. How could I know someone was going to total her van?"

Rachel dipped her right shoulder, than her left, and her silk dressing gown fell off her like ruby liquid onto the parquet floor. She considered herself in the full-length mirror, touching her pale nipples with the tips of her middle fingers. "Accidents happen to the accident-prone."

"Another lyric," Ivory said. "You're fairly bursting. With them, Rach."

"But we got what we wanted, right?" Bolton was sweating. He sweated often these days, especially when Rachel said *I* when once she'd said *we,* meaning just the two of them. "I mean, we're major players, aren't we? That's what we wanted, isn't it? So it's worked out for the better, hasn't it?"

Rachel yanked open the doors to her closet and stood with her hands on her hips, as if saying to her clothing, *Well?*

"Scally could be a narc, that's all," Bolton said. "Nick thinks he could be a narc too." He was sorry he'd said that: In the old days, he and Rachel shared lovers, men and women; but she'd kept Ivory to herself. If Kit couldn't have him too, he wanted him gone, not seconding his motions.

Rachel was going through her garments like someone punishing a band of unruly children, giving one after another the back of her hand. She stopped and stepped back, hands on hips again. "Nick doesn't think, Kit. Nick short-circuited years ago. He's just going through the motions."

Ivory rolled over and raised the bottle in a salute. "She's right, mate." He tapped his forehead. "Fuck all's 'appening. Up 'ere."

Without looking, as if she were taking potluck, Rachel put a hand in the closet and plucked a pair of black silk pants off a hanger; she shook them out and stepped into them. "Let me tell you something about narcs, Kit. It's something I've told you before, but I'll tell you again in the hope that this time it'll sink in. What color are narcs?"

Ivory, looking at his reflection in the mirror above the bed: "Narcs are . . . magenta. With blue, polka dots."

Bolton shook his head. "You mean. . . . What do you mean?"

Rachel got an ivory silk camisole from a drawer of a dresser built into the closet and slipped it on. "They're white—the color that rules this country. What color are dealers and pushers and junkies?"

"That's an easy one, Kit," Ivory said. "Come on, Kit. You know. The answer, lad. Buh, buh, buhllll—"

"Black," Bolton said.

"Bravo, Kit. Bloody good show. We'll 'ave you back. Next week. To try for the jackpot."

Rachel stood before the mirror and jabbed at her blond spikes. "So doesn't it make sense to you that if black dealers and black pushers are making junkies out of as many black people as they can, black people who might otherwise be making de*mands*— doesn't it make sense to you that it would be in the best interests of white men—and white narcs—not to interfere? Drugs're the new slavery, Kit—updated genocide."

"Sounds spot on to me," Ivory said. "If kaffir dealers. And kaffir pushers. Are... What was it you said again, Rach?"

Bolton looked sideways at the residue of cocaine on the vanity. Sometimes when he imagined he'd done some blow he could get his courage up as much as if he had. He tried it now. "But the narc you whacked... You said he... The whole operation was ... Then why did you whack him?"

Rachel found a pair of black low-heeled sandals and dropped them to the floor and kept her balance with a hand against the closet door as she worked her feet into them. "I forbid you to talk like that—like some... thug."

"'Orrible, Kit. The way you talk. Bloody 'orrible."

Bolton hung his head. "I just don't like all this killing."

Ivory stretched and scratched his testicles. "Put a sock on it, Kit. Jesus bloody Christ."

Rachel came to Bolton and lifted his chin with a knuckle. "We're playing for keeps, Kit. The killing's necessary to establish our credibility. If more's necessary, it'll be done. You don't have to like it. Now go see to the guests. We'll be out in a moment."

He wanted to say that she should see to her own fucking guests. He wanted to say that if she was going to fuck other people she shouldn't expect him to greet her guests while she did. He wanted to say.... But he went.

Ivory sat up and swung his feet off the bed. "Do you think maybe. Young Christopher's. Outlived his usefulness, Rach?"

Rachel wet a fingertip and dabbed up the cocaine. "I still need him for his show business contacts." She scrubbed at her nostrils and gums. "Get dressed. Let's go talk to Scally. And this Saint Michael woman. We'll see if she's everything you say."

"Everything. And more."

Scally put his elbows on the terrace parapet and looked straight down at Beekman Place. "You don't drink. You don't do blow. You don't smoke grass or cigarettes. You could be a narc. Unless you're a nun. Except nuns don't wear dresses like that."

Susan, her back to the parapet, held her glass of club soda against her bare chest and enjoyed the chill. The dress was from the wardrobe of the mistress of a Corsican drug smuggler who'd been busted in his Central Park South penthouse after handing a narc ten keys of scag in a Gucci shopping bag. The smuggler was doing points; the mistress had been deported, *sans* her designer clothes. Not just a narc: Paul. She had him to thank for the Ungaro.

"Be careful of these people," Scally said. "Very careful."

Scally was an awkward ingredient in Susan's juggling act. She hadn't expected him to be around so much, and she felt inhibited by him and by knowing his curriculum vitae. She wasn't yet sure how much he knew and how much he supposed, and how much of what he supposed was the offspring of his distaste for the people he supposed it of. And she didn't like that he had less distaste for her than for them; was it that she had too much class, or not enough? Or was it because he'd mauled a kiss on her and all she'd done in retort was hit him, which had been to play by his rules? She moved his beer bottle away from the brink. "You be careful."

He took a swig from the bottle and put it back where it had been. "See those lights? Shea Stadium. You a baseball fan? No, of course not."

Susan surveyed the guests, dancing to Cars on the stereo in the living room, snorting soda out of silver flasks that were passed from couple to couple, moving their mouths, their eyes everywhere but on their partners.

118

"Polo, right? Tennis. Not golf; nothing you have to walk around in the hot sun to watch. Horse racing, certain prizefights, certain college football games, sports car racing, bullfights—after a morning on the beach, lying very still. . . . I've been reading a book about a baseball player, a minor-league player, a true story. He was talking about a knuckleball, which you don't know, since rich people don't follow baseball, unless they own a team and even then they don't know shit about the game, is a pitch a pitcher has no control over, he just grips it—with his fingertips, actually, not his knuckles—and throws it and it doesn't have any spin on it, it just floats, and wind currents push it around, and it might go up and it might go down, nobody knows—not the pitcher, not the batter, not the catcher. To be a good knuckleballer, he says, a pitcher has to surrender to the pitch and just throw it; he says it takes a completely uncomplicated man to do that."

Susan turned to look at the lights. She was interested. This was Joe Cook talk: baseball as a metaphor for life.

"I'm looking to become that kind of man."

"What kind of man is that, Ted?" Rachel stood in the terrace doorway, undressed from the waist up by the light behind her.

Susan heard a hum of appreciation from Scally and felt a little awed herself.

Rachel didn't move from the doorway, milking the effect. "I'm Rachel Phillips. You're Susan Saint Michael, from San Francisco. Do you know Patsy Fallon and Steven Littlejohns?"

Don't playact, don't bullshit, don't pretend. "No."

"Really? How strange."

"Is this a test?" Susan said.

Rachel smiled. The test would come later. She descended the three steps to the terrace and offered a hand.

Susan ignored it.

Rachel laughed. "I'm sorry. Of course that wasn't a test. You passed the test with flying colors with the quality of your merchandise. I trust you found ours satisfactory."

"I've heard no complaints from my customers."

"Who *are* your customers, exactly?"

119

"Who're yours?"

Rachel laughed. "What're you drinking?"

"I'm fine, thanks."

Rachel took Susan's glass and took a sip. "Club soda."

"I think she's a narc," Scally said. "She doesn't drink, she doesn't do blow, she doesn't smoke."

Rachel put the glass down. "She's here to do business. There's a time for all that." She took Susan's arm. "Come on. Let's go where we can talk. Excuse us, Ted."

At the door to the living room, Kit Bolton oozed out from among the dancers to block their way. "Remember me?"

Susan had been barely through the door when he'd hurled himself at her like a desperate puppy. He hadn't had to say his name for her to know he was Amazing Grace's rich Hamptons type who dealt to his rich friends, that he was Harry Kellner's dude from New York, six one or two, skinny, nice threads, dirty-blond hair, brown eyes, the type who in L.A. would stay at the Marmont, if he stayed in a hotel, or maybe the Riot House, if he was into slumming; he hadn't had to say anything at all for her to know that he was supernumerary.

"*Is* there something, Kit?" Rachel said, and when all Bolton did was stammer, got a better grip on Susan and led her through the crowd.

Susan went with some dread. It had been easy, till now, to pretend to be something she wasn't, someone she wasn't, because she'd been pretending to men. Had it been easy because she'd spent a lifetime pretending to men that she was who they believed her to be? Barnes had raised the possibility, on the eve of what he'd called her graduation, though there was to be no ceremony:

"This isn't intended to be a therapy session, Susan," Barnes had said, "but I want to ask you to look at your personality and try and understand something about it. All the sports you did as a teenager, and in college—the outdoor stuff, the riflery: Were you being the son your father never had?"

"There's probably something to that."

"Why didn't your parents have other children?"

"They didn't have much money. I never asked, but I think that was the reason. I liked being an only child. You are too, aren't you?"

"This fellow you were involved with—the Vietnam vet—"

"His name was Joe Cook."

"He radicalized you, as the saying went. He changed your outlook from a rather conservative one to one that if not radical was at least liberal."

"When I met him I believed that America knew what it was doing in the world. He suggested that, in fact, it hadn't faced up to some contemporary realities—guerrilla warfare, for example. I'd say I was enlightened, not radicalized. And I was hardly the only one. Nor was he the only one to make the suggestion."

"If it hadn't been for him, would you have had the same epiphany?"

"Was I the child he never had?"

"His Eliza Doolittle, his Galatea, his Trilby. Take your pick."

"He was a friend," Susan said.

"... You and Paul began as peers, you became lovers, you ended with him—I don't think you can dispute this, objectively—as your superior: superior in rank, superior in responsibility, superior in salary, superior in prestige—"

"He did the heavy lifting, yes. I was the son he never had."

"More to the point, you didn't protest the arrangement—as you hadn't protested the arrangement with your father, as you hadn't—"

"Where is this leading, John? If it's not a therapy session, what is it? Can I use it on the job?"

"You're used to playing a role with men. My observation of your relationships with women—both professionally and personally—is that you're much more your own person. I've heard you tell Rita off, when she deserved it, and I've heard you praise her when she deserved that. This could present a problem on the job in that I can't imagine you suffering the fools you will certainly encounter. The very rich *are* different from you and me, and the difference isn't just that they have more money; they have a different outlook. It literally *is* an *out*look, because they spend much of their time in enclaves and compounds, in seclusion, sequestered. Cut off. You can take on their coloration—put on their clothes and their accents and their manners and

121

their style; learn their lingo and their pedigrees—but it's going to be difficult, dangerously difficult, to take on their thought processes. You know the old ditty about proper Bostonians, about the Cabots and the Lowells and God. Whichever of them it was who talked only to God, well, the implication is that He sat up and took notice. These aren't people who are accustomed to not getting their way, who can even comprehend not getting it. And what's true about the men goes double for the women."

Susan and Rachel had gone through the apartment to the south side of the terrace. From this altitude, Manhattan looked comfy, like a toy city.

Rachel studied not the view but Susan. "I want more E's and V's. Can you get them?"

Susan moved out from under Rachel's scrutiny and sat on the steps. "Not in the same quantity—and not right away. But these transcontinental transactions aren't efficient for either of us. I can connect you with someone here in the East who has access to prescription drugs. That was, for me, simply a starting point. I want to do in California what you're doing here. California has the reputation of being on the leading edge, but the fact is, California's three hours behind New York in more ways than one."

"How do you come by your connections?" Rachel said.

Susan said, "Who does your hair?" And did you just have it cut? And are you the woman who whacked my husband? You are, aren't you? This was too easy. Or was it that life wasn't all that complicated? Good guys, bad guys—there were finite numbers of each; once you'd narrowed it down by gender, race, age, class—and geographically—you weren't left with all that many to choose among. What was difficult was knowing what to do now. In the Wild West, she'd whack Rachel and back out the door and be gone and that would be that; but these were litigious times, and the streets were full of bad guys who had no more fear of justice than they had of the sky's falling.

Rachel laughed. "We're all flying out to Southampton tomorrow. Can you join us? Nick'll be out there; his place is just down the beach. He was quite taken with you. It's a better place to do business, I find. There's less tension; one doesn't rush into things."

As if to demonstrate just how tense it was, the sky over Rachel's head exploded in a puff of golden fire. Then again, in blue and bright red.

"What on earth...?"

Rachel glanced over her shoulder, then put out a hand. "Come look."

Not fire, but fireworks. Susan could hear the crumps now, as the rockets went up from barges in the East River, then burst in balls and umbrellas and pinwheels. The fire was reflected in the river, and smoke began to veil it and it looked like the Styx. "But why?"

Rachel put an arm around Susan's shoulders. "It's the Fourth of July."

Susan was doubly startled—by the embrace and by the realization that it was her birthday.

"Oh, Sue," Bob II said. "How terrible. Carrie's out."

"Out where? It's after midnight."

"She's at Jennifer's, Sue. They went to see the fireworks and she's sleeping over. There were fireworks tonight on the East River. Where are you, Sue? You sound close by."

"Is Carrie okay?"

"She's just fine."

"...How's Bob?"

"He's fine."

"And you?"

"Just fine. How're you, Sue?"

"I'm fine." Except that I'm breaking every rule in every book by calling you.

"Carrie remembered your birthday, Sue. She was wishing she had some way to reach you."

"Tell her I love her."

"Can't you call again, Sue? She'll be home around two or three in the afternoon."

"... No."

"Oh."

"Good night, Bob."

"Good night, Sue. Happy birthday."

Susan hung up the phone in Rachel's den.

In the hallway, Ted Scally, who had watched Susan slip in the den and heard her dial and listened on another phone, hung it up.

18

Some scosh was pounding on Red Sayles's door.

He pulled the blanket over his head.

"Martin!"

Some scosh yelling about Martians.

He put the pillow over his ears. Wrong number. We don't handle invasions. Martians've invaded, call Customs. Call INS. Maybe they handle invasions. Call the marines. For sure, they handle invasions. Invasions, revolutions, civil strife and so on and so forth.

"Martin, wake up."

Mar*tin,* not Mar*tians.* That was his name, Martin, though only his mother, who'd given him the name (and his scosh), called him that—his mother and the computers that issued his checks and his bills and so on and so forth.

Sayles lifted a corner of the pillow. "What, Ma?"

"Telephone."

"I'm asleep."

"It's the police."

"I'm innocent."

"Come to the phone, Martin."

Sayles got up and put on his pajama top and went out the door to the phone on the landing. His mother was halfway down the stairs, groaning and wheezing. "Go back to bed, Ma. It's three o'clock in the morning."

"I'll make you something to eat."

"Ma."

"It's three o'clock in the morning."

"That's a good reason not to make something to eat." That and his scosh.

"You have to eat, Martin. Everybody has to eat."

Sayles sighed and picked up the receiver. "Yeah?"

"Sayles?"

"Yeah."

"This is Chief Aldrich."

"Yeah."

"I'm trying to reach Barnes."

"He's not here."

"You know where he is?"

"Home, probably. It's three o'clock in the morning."

"Can you give me his number?"

"I can't do that, Chief. You'd have to call the duty officer."

"I called the duty officer. He wouldn't give me his number."

"You should've asked him to beep Barnes."

"He said he'd beep him and give him a message to call me. That was an hour ago. I called the duty officer back and he said he'd beeped Barnes every three minutes but he hadn't called in. He said if Barnes didn't want to respond to the beep he couldn't make him."

"I guess he's out of pocket."

"What does that mean?"

"It means I don't know where he is. You want to give me the message, I'll tell him when I see him in the morning and so on and so forth."

"It's about the cabbie Needleman. The cabbie who drove Van Meter. He got whacked. On West Two-eight, between Nine and Ten, kind of behind the Post Office garage there. There's a playground and some projects. It's real quiet at night. A holdup, looks like. The shooter got away with his fare box, his wallet was empty."

"We don't handle holdups, Chief. You guys handle holdups."

"It wasn't just a holdup, Sayles. It was a homicide."

"You guys handle homicides too."

"Yeah, well, who handles the coincidence of him being the guy—the cabbie Needleman—who was driving Van Meter when Van Meter got whacked?"

"Was he whacked with a twenty-two, Chief?"

126

"A thirty-eight. It was a professional-type hit, though. One shot in the back of the head."

"Times're tough. I guess hit men're having to whack cabbies to make ends meet."

A pause.

"Why don't you smartass fed fucks tell me what's going on?" Aldrich said.

"Sorry, Chief?"

"Van Meter was dirty, wasn't he? He had something going on the side, didn't he? The broad he was with was fucking him for nose candy and he held out on her and she whacked him, didn't she?"

"Hey, Chief, we never said she didn't whack him. We just didn't tell the press she whacked him."

"She whacked Van Meter, and now she's whacked the cabbie Needleman, or somebody whacked him for her, so he wouldn't finger her."

"I don't think so, Chief. I mean—"

"He's got a wife and a kid, the cabbie Needleman, and you just hung him out to dry like a fucking sitting duck. You smart-ass fed fucks."

"Thanks for calling, Chief. I'll tell Barnes about the—"

Aldrich hung up.

"—coincidence."

Sayles hung up and went to the bathroom and back to the door to his room.

"Martin?"

"I'm off the phone, Ma. I'm going to bed."

"I made a ham sandwich."

"No, thanks, Ma."

"You have to eat, Martin."

Sayles went downstairs and ate the ham sandwich and a pickle and a chocolate chip cookie and drank two glasses of milk. Everybody had to eat. Everybody had to die. Just because they started dying in droves didn't mean there was a connection, did it? Connection with what? What was a drove anyway? Was it anything like a scosh?

"Where're you going, Martin?"

"To make a phone call."

"There's a phone right here. I'll make you another sandwich."

"It's business, Ma. I'll use the upstairs phone."

Sayles didn't know Aldrich's number, so he called police head-quarters and asked for Aldrich's extension. The operator said Aldrich wasn't there, it was three-thirty in the morning, and Sayles said he was, he'd just talked to him, though he didn't know that Aldrich hadn't called from home, and the operator said it was his nickel and put him through and Aldrich answered.

"It's Sayles."

"What do you want, you smartass fed fuck?"

"You said we hung him out to dry, the cabbie Needleman. But we didn't hang him out to dry, because the disinformation we vended to the media didn't mention the cabbie's name, so the only people who know Needleman was the cabbie and therefore a witness are your guys and my guys and the guys who were at the meeting the other day and Needleman himself, and if he shot his mouth off around his garage or whatever, then it's his problem, but if he didn't, then it's our problem because there's been a leak, unless it *was* a holdup, in which case it's just a coincidence."

"Needleman was an owner-operator," Aldrich said.

"You mean he didn't work out of a garage?"

"Correct."

"Then it's our problem. Unless he shot his mouth off in some bar, to his buddies, his kid, his brother-in-law, his wife."

"His wife says he told her what happened and no one else. He doesn't go to bars. He works and he comes home. We've been over this, you smartass fed fuck."

"Then it's our problem."

"Correct."

"Unless it *was* a holdup."

"It was a holdup, all right. Whether that's *really* what it was, I couldn't say, I wasn't there, I didn't whack him."

"Chief?"

"What?"

"I know you're ticked off. You're right to be ticked off. You're going to be more ticked off when I tell you what I'm going to tell you. I'm going to tell you three things: The first thing is there's a big hitter named Cool D, a sideman of whose got whacked in Riverside Park a couple of days after Van Meter got whacked. This you may know because there's paperwork on it somewhere, a parkie found him, there were homicide D's and so on and so forth. We got called in because the DOA was the sideman of a big hitter and we did what we maybe shouldn't do but we sometimes do it anyway, which is we said we would do the ballistics ourselves, as, you know, a friendly gesture with a copy to you guys, and we ran what we got through our computers to see if it rang any bells with anything we're working on and so on and so forth and it did. It rang bells with Van Meter's shooting because it was the same gun, and we kind of, you know, forgot about sending you guys a copy.

"The second thing is there was a homeless guy who lived on the street where Van Meter and the broad had lunch. He lived right next door to the restaurant, in a cardboard box. He found a pair of shades he said the broad dropped when she leaned into the cab to whack Van Meter. He gave them to one of our agents. We've got a list of people who own such shades because they were expensive shades and only two hundred fifty pairs exist in the whole world. About forty-eight hours ago, the homeless guy died. There were white-tops there, there's paperwork on it somewhere, but it's not paperwork you would've seen because the uniforms in the white-tops didn't know there was a connection with Van Meter's getting whacked and it looked like natural causes, aspiration of vomitus induced by excessive consumption of alcoholic beverages, Cutty Sark, and so on and so forth.

"The third thing is, yes, Van Meter was dirty, yes, he had something going on the side, yes, the broad he was with was probably fucking him for nose candy and, yes, he probably held out on her and, yes, she definitely whacked him, or something like that.

"The reason I'm telling you all this is it looks like we're looking

129

at a situation where somebody else might be dirty too, one of your guys or one of my guys or one of the guys who were at the meeting the other day and so on and so forth, and we've got to put an industrial-strength housecleaning operation in effect ASAP. You tell whoever you have to tell and I'll tell Barnes because I have to tell him what you told me and what I told you. And then we'll talk—and you'll tell us who you told and then we'll know just exactly how many people know and we'll put an industrial-strength housecleaning operation in effect ASAP and so on and so forth."

"You smartass fed fucks," Aldrich said.

"Yeah."

"Sayles?"

"Yeah?"

"Thanks."

"Yeah."

"Sayles?"

"Yeah?"

"Happy Fourth of July."

19

"What's free-range chicken?" Aaronson said. "Is that like home on the range?"

"It's been a long time, Henry," Barnes said.

"When you said meet you at Trees I thought you were saying 't'ree's,' like, you know, 'Two's company, t'ree's a crowd.' This is where Van Meter, *alav ha-sholom*, ate before he got whacked, isn't it? *Haimish*, Van Meter was."

"Speak English, Henry."

"I liked him. I'm torn up. A hell of a way to die. How's Susan?"

"Well enough."

"She take some leave, or what?"

Barnes looked up at the waiter. "I'll have the cold pasta, with a salad. And a glass of white wine."

Aaronson looked once more at the menu for something like a pastrami sandwich, but nothing about it had changed. He closed it with a flourish. "Me, too."

When the waiter had taken the menus away, Barnes said, "Rita tells me there's been yet another accident involving one of Mister Williamson's associates."

Aaronson flicked his hands. "I loved her, Shiraz, in a way, never mind who she was, what she did. You know what it's like, John. You get close to these people, you can't help it. The feelings, they got to be genuine or they'll cop to your being a *momzer*. Out of the blue, Shiraz getting whacked. I expected Cool D to whack the *shikseh* for whacking his *nuchshlepper*, Lionel. I also expected D to whack one of Lorca's people on account of the *shikseh* made an arrangement with Lorca. When Shiraz, *aleha ha-shalom*, got whacked, I figured Lorca'd

131

whacked her, just to, you know, get a jump on D. But Lorca says he didn't whack her. He's a *gonif,* Lorca, but I think I believe him. He went out of his way to tell me he didn't whack Shiraz, he asked me to give his condolences to Cool D and say he didn't want a spark-up. 'I don't keel weemin,' Lorca said, and I don't think he does. I think he *shtups* dogs, but I don't think he keels weemin. Which leaves the *shikseh* as the number one candidate for who whacked Shiraz, *aleha ha-shalom,* to make it perfectly clear to Cool D that not only does she have the stones to whack his *nuchshlepper* and make a deal with his wholesaler, she's got the stones to whack his old lady." Aaronson leaned forward and whispered. "You heard what they did to Shiraz? Rita told you?"

Barnes nodded. He'd never seen Rita so close to losing it. She'd braced herself in his doorway and ignored his invitation to come in and have a seat; she hadn't looked at him, or at anything; she hadn't had a cigarette in her hand; she'd started speaking Spanish until he'd reminded her that he spoke only a few obscenities; she'd waited so long that he'd wondered if she'd come to tell him she was in love with him. "Shiraz is dead," she'd finally said. "She was stabbed with a sword, or some long, sharp instrument. Stabbed . . . in the vagina."

"A hell of a way to die," Aaronson said.

The waiter brought a virgin to the next table—a virgin with brown hair cut punk short, wearing a black silk blouse with padded shoulders, gray linen slacks, black leather shoes like a bicycle racer's. She had gold-rimmed glasses and a stainless-steel watch and a thin gold chain around her neck. She carried nothing in her hands, which was what he'd liked about the virgin in the elevator, but he liked this one even more, for she'd gone empty-handed out into the world—no pocketbook, no wallet or change or keys (her slacks had no pockets), no wherewithal but complete confidence that she'd make her way. She reminded him of the virgins on Fire Island, where the Barnes family, when there had been a Barnes family, spent its Augusts, accoutred only with bikinis, something to hold up their hair, a bracelet or two, a necklace, striding along the strand with the uttermost certainty that they would encounter someone who would look after their needs.

Barnes couldn't will the virgin to look at him, and he looked back at Aaronson. "Rita says that Mister Williamson discovered the, uh, remains, and has taken care of their disposition himself. There's been no official complaint."

Aaronson made a face at the euphemisms. "Who's he going to complain to? He can't holler cop."

"More to the point, how does he plan to respond?"

"That's the thing, John. We'll never know till he does it. He doesn't talk, D. I don't mean he's—what do you call it?—mute; he just doesn't talk. Shiraz, *aleha ha-shalom,* she did his talking for him. You'd sit there and ask him a question and she'd answer and you'd ask another question that the answer to the first question made you think of and she'd answer that too, like she knew everything he was thinking. You could go on like that for hours. I guess they talked to each other, when they were alone. Who knows?"

The waiter brought their salads and Barnes waited until he'd gone. "How does Lorca know about Shiraz?"

"It's a tight little world, the world of the big hitters."

"And how much does Lorca know about the... *shikseh?*"

"*Bubkes.* Not a lot. Or maybe he knows everything. I can't *nudzh* him. He'd make me."

"Perhaps Lorca would be more forthcoming to a woman."

"Who? Not Rita. He'd make Rita in a New York minute."

The virgin hadn't ordered a drink; she was sipping a glass of water and thinking about something that made her lips curl with amusement. "A witness to Van Meter's accident has been eliminated. The driver of his taxi. It was in the papers as robbery, but it was clearly an execution. Tell Lorca that, and tell Cool D. I want them to know that this woman and her people aren't pushovers."

"I think they've figured that out, John."

"Tell them. If Lorca, in particular, is more vigilant, he might find out something that so far we haven't been able to." The virgin's date had arrived, another virgin, with the same haircut and the same glasses. She was older and her hair was gray; she wore a yellow oxford-cloth button-down shirt, white Dee Cee

133

painter's pants and blue espadrilles. She'd brought the money—in a Kreeger wallet on her belt—and whatever else they needed in a Dolt backpack. They kissed discreetly but passionately. They touched hands, elbows, knees. They smiled and laughed. They ordered margaritas, straight up with salt.

Their waiter brought the cold pasta and a second waiter hovered after he'd gone away. "Mister Barnes? There's a telephone call for you. Would you please follow me?"

Barnes followed him to the end of the bar, which had but one customer, a man with a military mustache, in a tan suit. Barnes turned his back to him and picked up the phone. "This is Barnes."

"Red, John. Are you ready for this?"

That was what Polly—his Polly—had said to him on the phone that morning. *Are you ready for this? I don't want to continue our relationship.* Before she could tell him why not, he'd said they hadn't had a relationship. No? She'd thought they'd had the beginnings of one. Maybe so, but he wasn't going to count it as one. They'd never danced together and he'd never come in her mouth, so it hadn't been a relationship. He'd hung up on her before she could on him.

"Aldrich just called," Sayles said. "The homeless eyewitness, Morgan, usually bought his booze at a liquor store on Park Avenue South. The owner feels sorry for winos, he gives them a discount, which you could argue is not what you should be doing if you feel sorry for winos and so on and so forth. The owner says Morgan never bought any Cutty from him, he drank vodka, like Morgan's buddy told me, or wine. Never any Cutty. But get this, John: the night Morgan bought it, a guy came in the store and bought four fifths of Cutty, a guy the owner never saw before, never saw again. The cops have an artist with the owner now, trying to come up with a composite, because what it could be is that it wasn't natural causes, aspiration of vomitus induced by excessive consumption of Cutty, what it could be is somebody forced Morgan to excessively consume enough Cutty to make him vomit, held his mouth shut so he'd aspirate it, whacked him to keep him from telling anyone what he saw the day Van Meter got whacked and so on and so forth."

134

Barnes waited.

"You there, John?"

"Is that it?"

"That's it."

"I'll see you at the shop." Barnes hung up.

"You don't remember me, do you?" the man with the military mustache said.

Barnes smiled and shook his head. "Sorry." He went back to the table.

"This isn't bad," Aaronson said of the pasta.

"Something's come up, Henry. I'm going to have to leave. If you have any questions about how to proceed, now's the time, otherwise you'll communicate with Rita by the usual channels."

Aaronson shook his head. "No questions."

Barnes put a fifty under the ashtray. "Enjoy your lunch. No need to account for the change. I hope it won't be as long before our next meeting."

"*Alevai*," Aaronson said.

Barnes smiled at the virgin in black. She gave him a cool look, but long enough that her friend looked from her to Barnes and back at her with puzzlement.

Barnes touched the arm of a passing waiter. "Is there a back way out? I'm a federal agent, on business."

The waiter laughed. "Sure. This way."

20

The woman's name was Lillian, which she pronounced with the accent on the last syllable, as if she were French, though she said she'd been born and raised in Brooklyn too, just like the girls. She was tiny and had a dancer's turned-out walk and pulled-back hair. She wore baggy shorts and a tube top and had the radio turned to K-Rock. She wasn't as young as she felt, and Carrie was uncomfortable in the way she was uncomfortable whenever she ran into one of her teachers outside school, wearing casual clothes and trying to look like a normal human being.

Lillian led Carrie and Jennifer down the longest hallway they'd ever seen and sat them in the living room, which had the highest ceiling and the biggest television, and said she'd be with them in a minute. Carrie leaned back in her chair and watched Lillian go down the hallway to a bedroom, probably. Lillian went through the door like a thief, but nonetheless Carrie saw the face of a girl her age, looking as frightened as Carrie felt.

Jennifer rolled her eyes and made a gagging sound at the music: "Kiss," by Prince. Carrie knew it wasn't cool to like Prince, but he always made her want to dance, and you couldn't ask anything more of music than that. Her mother liked Prince, especially "Purple Rain," which could make her cry if she was in a certain mood. She missed her mother, even though Jennifer said it was stupid to miss her, that Carrie had an opportunity most kids would kill for.

"You're on your *own*. You're *free*. No 'rents. God, that's so rad."

"My father's dead, Jen, okay? He was murdered, okay?"

"I know, okay?"

"My mother's off doing something that I don't know what it is, but it's dangerous, okay?"

"I *know,* okay?"

"Kids would kill for that?"

"Ooh, Carrie, you're such a *dweeb.* It's just an ex*pression.*"

The door down the hallway opened and Carrie leaned back and saw the girl come out, then Lillian. Lillian walked behind the girl to the front door and helped her with the locks and patted her on the shoulder and closed the door behind her and locked it. She walked back down the hall, her hands in the pockets of her baggy shorts, almost skating on the parquet floor on the balls of her bare feet. There was an exercise bicycle with all kinds of dials on the handlebars in front of the television and Lillian swung it around and sat on the seat and started to pedal. "Well, what can I do for you young ladies?"

Jennifer looked at Carrie, who looked at the floor. "Well, like, you know what we want, right?" Jennifer said.

Lillian smiled and pedaled a little faster. "There're so many things you could want. Why don't you tell me?"

Carrie stood up. "Let's go, Jen, okay?"

Jennifer stared.

"We have to say what we want, okay? If she says anything it's illegal, okay? She could be arrested, okay?"

Jennifer laughed. "We're not *narcs.*"

Lillian craned her neck, but kept pedaling.

"Her father's a narc," Jennifer said. "That's how she knows this stuff."

Lillian stopped pedaling.

"My father's dead," Carrie said.

Lillian got off the bicycle and bounded to Carrie and put her hands on her shoulders. "You poor thing."

"He got whacked."

"Come with me, both of you," Lillian said. She held Carrie's arm and led her down the hall. Jennifer followed, her Doc Marten clumping and her sneaker squeaking.

21

Scally was a fucking armorologist, practically: He knew about Viking hide shirts, German shirts of mail, full Gothic steel armor, jousting armor with tournament helmets and staghorn saddles, Renaissance associated armor for man and horse; he knew a Frankish helmet from a sallet, a visored basinet from an armet à rondelle, a barbute from a parade helmet; he knew about lances, gonfalons, vamplates and coronals; he'd hefted falcions, dress rapiers, two-handed swords, poleaxes and hammers, maces (flanged and studded), flails, daggers, awls and halberds; he knew how to wind a crossbow and had fired a bolt at a tree.

He heard poetry in the anatomy of a suit of armor: heaume, bowl, sight, visor, breaths, pauldron, rerebrace, couter, vambrace, tasse, gauntlet, cuisse, poleyn, greave, sabbaton; he heard it in the shoptalk of heraldry; gules, azure, vert, purpure, sable, or and argent; ermine, vair and potent; engrailed, indented, undé; bend, pale, fess and chevron, pile, cross, saltier and chief; per pale and barry, label of three points, cross botonée, lozenge, dolphin, unicorn, gryphon and rose.

He had been a quick study and Nick Ivory an enthusiastic teacher, giving Scally the run of the temperature- and humidity-controlled storage vault he'd had built for his armor collection in the basement of his house on the beach in East Hampton; encouraging him to look at and even take over to Rachel's, where Scally was staying, some of the books from his library; letting him try on one of the copies he'd had made of full suits of armor, copies that were wittily displayed around the house: at a piano in the living room; by a sink in the kitchen; reading *Le Morte d'Arthur* in a rocker by the window in one of the guest bedrooms; on the toilet in the bathroom off the den; peering, a gauntlet shading its eyes, out over the ocean from the lawn; by the net on the tennis court, a stainless-steel racket raised in triumph, a gauntlet extended to shake the hand of an imaginary defeated opponent. Ivory had even instructed Scally in the use of the crossbow and stood alongside him as he fired it, never showing any fear that he might suddenly become the target.

None of which made any sense at all. Unless Ivory'd just forgotten about Ornella. Unless he'd had nothing to do with Ornella. Unless he never imagined that someone who'd loved Ornella would come looking for her killer. Unless she hadn't been killed and the cops had been right, that she'd killed herself with an overdose and whoever was with her, frightened of having to account for a dead body, had dumped her in the ocean, where she'd struck some "submerged object."

Whoever was with her. It should be easy enough to find out who that was. *Say, Nick, you probably know I used to do some competitive skiing, and there was this girl I knew on the Italian World Cup team. A couple of years ago, right around here, as a matter of fact, she died. At first they said she drowned and then they said she OD'd and fell in the water or something. And I was just wondering if you knew anything about it, if maybe you knew if she had friends around here or something, I could stop by and say....What? I don't know. That I was sorry to hear about it. She was a hell of a skier. Ornella Vitti was her name. Ring any bells?*

Right. And then when he says, *Never. Heard of her, mate,* then what do you say? Do you say, *She also had marks on her wrists like somebody'd tied her up and she was stabbed in the stomach and her guts were all over the place and I was just wondering, Nick, if maybe you and the other rock stars and playboys and former tennis greats and baby moguls and heirs and scions and wimps you hang out with were playing one of your stupid-ass knights in armor games and after she OD'd, or maybe even before, you tied her up and hung her from that fucking target practice thing at Rachel's place and took a poke at her with one of your fucking lances and then you dumped*

139

her, or had some of your ex-roadies dump her, in the fucking
ocean? How 'bout it, Nick, hunh, hunh, hunh?

Right.

So if these people are right out in the open about the armor
and all that shit, what's in the storeroom in Rachel's stable?

Let's go see, shall we?

An armorologist but not and never was and never will be a
horsologist. He hated the spindly-legged things; you could never
tell what they were thinking. Or if.

Scally tightroped his way down the stable's aisle and hoped
the regular tenants weren't thinking what to do about a horse-
hater among them—a predawn horse-hater.

There were six of them—big mothers—wide awake at four in
the morning and curried to a sheen. By whom? Rachel's spread
had no quarters for grooms—and, in fact, none for any servants
at all. Gardeners and poolmen and handymen and maids and
cooks came and went all day long and there were often five or
six pickups parked in the drive and gaggles of blacks down at
the gate waiting for spouses or taxis to pick them up, but he
never saw anyone around the stables except Rachel and Ivory.
He couldn't imagine Rachel doing her own grooming, but then
again he could; he could imagine her getting off on it and maybe
even getting the horses off too, like some Tijuana whore.

The stable's double doors were never locked; a hasp, a staple
and a wooden peg on a piece of string tied to a nail in the door
were all that kept them closed. The storeroom lock, a combination lock with four settings, was a serious lock, impervious to
picking, breaking or cutting. But not to common sense. Scally
had seen a million locks like it—or a dozen anyway; his mother
had one on the gate to the road to her house on a mountaintop in
Big Sur (or had the last time he'd visited, back when California
still belonged to Mexico)—and the combinations had all been
selected according to the same principle: they had to be easily
remembered by a lot of people—hands, neighbors, utility
workers, local cops and firemen and tradesmen, prodigal sons.

140

The easiest combination to remember was the current year, or, if you felt you had to be a little clever, the year backward.

He tried the year and the lock didn't open. He tried the year backward and it did.

A horse nickered and Scally said, "Yeah, people're weird, aren't they?" He propped the door open with a rake and waited a moment for the light from the stable's single pale bulb to seep into the storeroom.

Another nicker.

A bolt of light through the chinks in the siding.

A car, its engine cut, rolling on its momentum, its tires crunching the gravel drive.

Scally shut the door and set the rake aside and put the hasp over the staple and the lock through it and spun the numbers and climbed the ladder to the hayloft. A stupid thing to do, since he'd taken out the wooden peg to open the double doors and had had to leave it hanging when he went inside. Better, if someone were to challenge him, to say he'd had a hankering to look at some horseflesh than to be found lurking among the bales.

Too late, for just then the double doors were pushed wide open and after a moment Rachel backed through them in a Jeep. It was a foggy morning, and chill, yet she wore only a short-sleeved white cotton shift and her feet were bare. With her cropped hair, she looked like a latter-day Joan of Arc, speaking of armorology, since there was a picture of Joanie in one of the books he'd read on the subject.

Rachel backed right up to the storeroom door, clucking to calm the horses all the while. She got out and worked the combination—was there a fraction's hesitation there? did she glance his way out of the corner of an eye?—and opened the door and propped it with the rake. She threw back an old blanket on the bed of the Jeep. Under it was a long, narrow wooden box that Scally knew from movies and television if not from life contained guns—rifles, Uzis, M-16s, grease guns, whatever. A gunologist he wasn't: guns made him nervous and gunologists more so; they were always pointing the damned things one way and then looking another, like up at the ceiling while they chugged a Stroh's.

Rachel got one end of the box down to the ground, then got hold of the rope handle at the other end and worked it off the bed and down, then dragged it little by little into the storeroom.

The stupid rich bitch. He should hop down and lock her in there and let her shoot her way out and then explain to her that guns were for grownups and that if she was going to play with grownups she'd better get some grownups on her team because the amateurs on her team now were sure to cave in when the going got tough.

Where did she get the fucking guns and why hadn't she asked him to haul them and what had she traded for them and why hadn't she asked him to haul *it*? And why didn't he just take her now? He'd seen the armor; he knew as much as he'd ever know it that Ornella had been impaled on one of those lances, after she'd overdosed, probably, as her punishment in one of the sick games Rachel and Nick were so good at thinking up.

The first night out they'd had a cockfight: some blacks from Sag Harbor brought the birds and handled them and the rock stars and playboys and former tennis greats and baby moguls and heirs and scions and wimps and their respective fuckers sat around a portable pit set up alongside the tennis court and threw money at one another and screamed and carried on. The next afternoon they'd had what everyone called a joust (pronouncing it, every one of them, *jowst*), but which Scally, because he was a fucking armorologist, practically, knew wasn't a *just,* which was a charge with lances, but a mounted tourney, in which there was close-order fighting on horseback with sword, ax, mace or flail. Some of the rock stars and playboys and former tennis greats and baby moguls and heirs and scions and wimps brought their personal horses in vans and trailers and some of them had their own armor, which this guy, a onetime Broadway musical prop man or something, who made Nick's copies, also made for his friends, and they also had weapons that were blunted but otherwise looked like the real thing, and they tore around Rachel's backyard, beating one another over the head while their respective fuckers sat in the shade and drank gin and tonics and did delicate ladylike daytime quantities of blow and screamed and carried on.

There was some big game coming up in a couple of nights. Rachel had told Ivory to tell Scally to be sure and be there. "Susan will. Be there," Ivory had said, smirking the way girls in high school used to smirk when they told him some girl who had a crush on him would be at some party.

What was the question? Oh, yeah—why not take her now? Because it wasn't time to take her. Why not? Because it just wasn't time, that's all.

Rachel was out of the storeroom now and spun the numbers —oh, shit; she didn't spin all four, just the last; people're weird that way too, they leave combination locks set except for the last number so they don't have to bother with all the numbers, and that must've been the way the lock was set when he opened it, but he hadn't noticed because he'd tried the year first, then the year backward, and he'd spun all the settings when he closed the storeroom door and for sure she'd noticed that and she *had* glanced up his way—and got in the Jeep and drove out of the stable, clucking at the horses, and stopped outside and hopped down and shut the double doors. He could hear that she latched them and put the peg through the staple and for sure she'd remarked that they weren't latched and pegged when she came through, so why hadn't she challenged him, why hadn't she greased him with one of the grease guns?

Who the fuck knew why Rachel did anything? Or didn't?

Now what, asshole?

Now climb down and find a window that'll open and climb out. Asshole.

Hello. Who's this?

Scally took his foot off the top rung of the ladder and moved back in the hayloft.

The double doors opened and Susan Saint Michael came through and shut them and stood with her back to them, getting her bearings. She wore blue jeans and a black turtleneck sweater and black exercise shoes. Her hair was up and tied in a blue bandanna. Commando Woman.

What the fuck was with her? She didn't smoke, she didn't drink, she didn't do blow or grass or pop pills; she didn't tumble

143

when the rock stars and playboys and former tennis greats and baby moguls and heirs and scions and wimps hit on her, which most of them had done, as had a few of their respective fuckers. And what about that phone call to a woman named Bob, and her concern about someone named Carrie who was sleeping over at someone named Jennifer's but who hadn't forgotten Susan's birthday? *Was* she a narc? If she was, then she'd entrapped him. Or had she? He wasn't paying enough attention to things these days. He was trying so hard to be a convincing bad guy that he wasn't thinking about the consequences of being so convincing that he'd get himself busted. That was the way he'd used to ski—all speed, no control. It was nice to know that he'd matured.

Susan walked the length of the stable to the storeroom, shushing at the horses, who must've been ready to kick somebody between the eyes by this time, and held the lock in her hand and studied it. She moved the last setting and the lock opened. Smart woman. Or was she well trained? Or both?

She stayed five minutes by his watch, locked the lock and moved only the last setting, shushed at the horses, and went to the double doors.

The doors opened and there was Rachel, carrying something that Scally, not being a gunologist, didn't know the name of but that was fierce and black and ugly. Nick Ivory, at Rachel's shoulder, had one too.

No one said a word. Susan untied the bandanna and shook out her hair. Rachel came close and tapped Susan down for a weapon, then took her by the elbow and jerked her toward the door. Nick stood aside to let the women out, then went out and shut the double doors and latched them and set the peg.

One of the horses sighed a long, weary sigh.

22

Barnes, shirtless, in a pair of old khakis, sat with his bare feet up on the dining table of the studio on Ninth Street that reeked of odors from Balducci's, a finger marking his place in a biography of Diane Arbus he'd been skimming by the light that spilled over from the kitchen, thinking about one witness's recollection that what had mattered for the Beat generation was not how good an Abstract Expressionist you were, but how well you played the bongos and whether you could dance all night.

That was what everything came down to, finally, wasn't it? What mattered wasn't how good you were at your job, your art, your craft; what mattered was your style. Joanna had never understood that that was what his promiscuity, his philandering, his unfaithfulness (her words), was all about. He fucked around because he was good at it, and because being good at it—or something like it—was all that mattered.

Barnes thought about waking the cowgirl slut virgin, calling Joanna, and having the cowgirl slut virgin tell her just how good. That the cowgirl slut virgin slept on the convertible sofa that when opened nearly overwhelmed the tiny studio was the reason Barnes was sitting at the dining table to read. That the cowgirl slut virgin slept was because he'd fucked her so well, fucked her brains out, fucked her to a fare-thee-well, fucked her unconscious. *What matters, Joanna, isn't how good a husband or a father or a provider or an agent I am; what matters is how well I fuck. Tell her that, whatever your name is.*

Margaret. The cowgirl slut virgin's name was Margaret, which didn't go at all with her salmon pink buckskin dress with fringes on the short sleeves and thigh-length hem, with her white

145

tooled-leather boots, with her fat silver-and-turquoise bracelet, with her five necklaces of beads, with her teased and sprayed bleached blond hair, with her scarlet push-up bra and G-string panties.

Barnes met her in Balducci's, where he'd gone to get some tortellini for dinner. (When in a studio that reeks of odors from Balducci's, eat Balducci's food.) She was ahead of him on the express checkout line, with a container of yogurt and an apple. She dropped the apple and he picked it up and handed it back and said here you are... Eve. She said he had her bollixed up with someone else; her name was Margaret. He said he'd just read in a novel set in San Antonio that Sam Houston's last words were "Texas... Texas... Margaret." Margaret said she didn't know he was dead. Barnes believed he was, yes. Sam Houston? The fellow who directed *Prizzi's Honor*? Anjelica's father?

Margaret was from Eustis, Florida, and was staying at a cousin's on Charles Street until she found a job as a photographer's assistant (the Arbus biography was hers) and her own place. Her cousin, a lesbian ("My Aunt Charlotte would *die* if she knew that, but it makes no never-mind to me"), spent most nights at her lover's, leaving Margaret by her lonesome. Barnes suggested they go to Charles Street, in the hope the cousin and her friend would stop by (he imagined—no, he was certain— that they were the virgins he'd seen in Trees), but Margaret wanted to see his place, for it was her dream to one day live in a luxury high-rise too. She was a ways from fulfilling it, for the photographers to whom she'd shown her portfolio (mostly pictures of cats, her specialty) had seen a future for her, if they saw one at all, in front of the lens, not behind it, and had wondered if she'd thought about doing some nudes: *Not porno, babe; we're talking strictly adult high-concept here.*

The phone rang and Barnes got to it before the first ring died, though he wondered why, for he wanted Margaret gone. He'd seduced her, while they ate their respective dinners, by echoing her contempt for the men who weren't able to see beyond her breasts to her soul, and now felt only contempt for her for not having heard that it was double-talk. "Hello."

146

"Red, John," Sayles said. "You're not going to believe this."

Barnes waited.

"Remember the doorman in the building where Van Meter had his little pad on the side?"

Barnes waited.

"Anyway, the doorman, his name's George Foster, like the ballplayer, you remember he told me Van Meter had these young guys coming up to his apartment, and we thought Van Meter was maybe, uh, you know? Well, he saw one of them, Foster, walking down the street right past the building and there happened to be a cop out front giving parking tickets and Foster told him he thought the guy was wanted for questioning in connection with something or other and the cop stopped the guy and told him to hang on for a minute while he checked into it. Who says there's never a cop around when you need one? Foster still had the number I gave him in case he remembered something he forgot to tell me and so on and so forth and the cop called me and guess what."

Barnes waited.

"It's Jack Collins. Our Jack Collins. You recruited him, didn't you, John? I mean, him being from Yale and so on and so forth."

"Is he with you now?"

"Oh yeah."

"You're at the shop?"

"Yup."

"I'll be right there." Barnes hung up and rubbed his eyes and stretched and nearly had a heart attack when Margaret put her arms around his hips and cupped her hands over his genitals. He broke out of her grasp and turned and slapped her.

"Hey!"

"Don't ever do that to me."

"Do what, you bastard? You liked it well enough a little while ago."

Barnes got a clean Lacoste shirt from the hall closet and a pair of socks from the dresser and put them on, leaning his back against the wall to pull the socks up.

"Fuck 'em and forget 'em, hey?" Margaret had turned to face him and lay propped on one elbow, a cowgirl slut odalisque.

147

Barnes remembered another thing he'd read: Raymond Chandler on a woman so beautiful you'd have to wear brass knuckles every time you took her out. Margaret wasn't beautiful, but walking with her just the few yards from Balducci's exit to the building entrance he'd felt like Moses strolling through the Red Sea as men fell left and right at the sight of her body; her escort would need an Uzi. "I'll call you."

She was up and dressed and out the door and down the stairs before Barnes could get the rest of his clothes on, or he would've gone after her to give her back her book. It took class he hadn't imagined she had to leave wordlessly like that and he wished he'd gotten her last name—or her cousin's—so he could call and make up and see her again.

"There were five of us," Collins said. "John Broughton, Carlos Pérez, Dick Freund, Charlie Peck and me. Van Meter interviewed each of us separately four or five times and then met with us as a group twice before he told us what the job was. He said someone conveniently located had gone rogue, that he'd been assigned to find out who and had handpicked us to assist him. We were all new—Charlie's been on the job eighteen months, the rest of us all under a year—but that was the point, Van Meter said. We weren't part of any cliques, any factions; we weren't politicized. Not to put too fine a point on it, we didn't have any friends on the eighty-ninth floor or in Georgetown.

"Van Meter said our primary role at the outset was to give credibility to his fairy tale, which was that he was a well-to-do antiques dealer, a homosexual. Our job mainly was to visit him at his fairy tale address, on East End Avenue; he wanted a string of young men coming and going in the evenings. I went up maybe eight or ten times; I'd go on a Tuesday and then again the following Thursday, then might not go for a week, then go on a Monday. The point was to make it look as though there were more of us than there were; I'd dress differently each time —sometimes in a suit, sometimes in jeans and a T-shirt—and I guess the others did too. I wasn't in contact with them after the last collective briefing."

"But you'd see them around the shop," Barnes said.

"Yes. But we never talked about the job—Van Meter's job. We were all on other jobs; Van Meter's was on the side—although in my mind at least and I'm sure in the minds of all the others it had top priority."

"Did he ever discuss compensation?"

"He'd give me expenses each time I went up. More than just cab fare—fifty or a hundred bucks. I understood that everything had to be off the books and that once we'd completed the assignment there'd be compensation, time off, promotions."

"He promised you those things?"

"He didn't have to. When a senior agent asks you to help him flush out someone conveniently located who's gone rogue, he doesn't have to promise you anything."

"Go on."

"It was makework, mostly. Van Meter usually stayed in the study, working at his desk, occasionally talking on the phone, and I'd sit around and read or watch television. Sometimes I'd help him go through catalogues, looking for antique ordnance, mainly: pistols, rifles, arms and armor; most of it was American, from the First World War, the Civil War, some from the Revolutionary War, but there were some European items from the sixteenth and seventeenth centuries. I'd read to him out of the catalogue and he'd check the data against other catalogues or reference books. The most outgoing he ever was about what he was doing was that he had a client who collected the stuff."

"Client, or clients?"

"Extrapolating from things he said just in passing, a man in his thirties or forties, possibly English, who'd made a lot of money in the music business—or maybe movies or the theater."

"Were Van Meter's phone calls overhearable? Did he have visitors while you were there?"

"He kept the study door closed when he made calls. There was one visitor, a woman: she came by quite late—twelve-thirty or one; I was usually gone by that time, but he asked me to hang around without saying why. Why, it was clear when she got there, was so she could see me. Van Meter took her into the

149

study by way of the living room, which wasn't the shortest way; he ignored me, but she couldn't.

"She was tall, five seven or eight; slim, one twenty or so; early to mid thirties; blond hair worn up under a black flat-brimmed, flat-crowned hat, a gaucho hat; blue-green eyes, very pale eyebrows and lashes; some discreet eye makeup and skin blush, but no lipstick; a black linen suit, cut like a man's business suit, worn without a blouse; no bra, perhaps a camisole or a teddy, off-white panty hose or stockings—panty hose, I'm almost sure; black low-heeled shoes with gold bits across the instep—not Guccis, but handmade; a Cartier tank watch on her left wrist, nothing on her right, no jewelry around her neck or on her fingers; a small black alligator bag with a shoulder strap; she smoked a cigarillo while she was with him in the study—a Ritmeester Senior."

Sayles laughed. "Jesus, John. This guy is *good*. What kind of perfume was she wearing?"

"Jovan," Collins said. "Island Gardenia."

Sayles laughed.

"Go on," Barnes said.

"Van Meter got whacked. That was the end of it."

"Didn't you think someone might pick up the ball?"

"Yes, but who was *I* to ask? And ask whom? There was the risk I'd ask the someone conveniently located who'd gone rogue."

Barnes went to the window and looked out over the Hudson at the flames of some major industrial fire in New Jersey. Nowhere near Hoboken, unfortunately. "Was that always the way Van Meter put it? 'Someone conveniently located . . . '?"

"You mean did he ever use something other than an indefinite pronoun?"

Barnes turned to face Collins. He was good—and good-looking: Fresh-faced and determined to see freshly what the fogies above him saw through stale eyes, he reminded Barnes of himself, twenty years earlier. "That's what I mean, yes."

Collins shook his head. "Van Meter never said 'he,' not even generically."

"And that told you what?"

"Well, it's been my observation, in professional conversations and in personal ones, that when someone"—Collins laughed, and looked relieved when Barnes smiled—"when *people* use indefinite pronouns, or vague nouns, they're concerned that the definite pronoun, or the accurate noun, will be too...vivid for the particular situation."

"I wish I was sure what you guys were talking about and so on and so forth," Sayles said.

Collins crossed his legs and for the first time looked comfortable. "My girlfriend always says 'person' when what she means is 'old lover.' We were talking recently about going to Mexico and she said, 'I went to Mexico just after grad school and the person I was with got dysentery and I never want to go back.' If it'd been just a girlfriend, she'd've said that."

"Oh," Sayles said.

Barnes turned back to the window. "So you felt the someone conveniently located who'd gone rogue was a woman?"

"Yes. If Van Meter had said 'he or she,' as if taking cognizance of the language's innate sexism, it would've been too pointed. The indefinite pronoun raised the possibility without hitting us over the head with it."

"After Van Meter's death, you didn't talk to the others?" Barnes said. "Broughton, Pérez, Freund or Peck?"

"Pérez and I had lunch in Battery Park one day and talked about going over the eighty-ninth floor, going right to Georgetown. We decided we shouldn't. Van Meter never said that the someone who'd gone rogue wasn't conveniently located in Georgetown."

"What were you doing walking past that apartment building?"

"My mother lives on Gracie Square. I'd had lunch with her and decided to walk down East End to Seventy-ninth to get a crosstown bus. I live on West Eighty-first. Call it natural curiosity."

"I call it an egregious breach of procedure," Barnes said. "Never invade a fairy tale from any entry other than the one that's been established."

151

"Yes, sir."

"And if a fairy tale address is ever so proximate to your mother's—or that of anybody else with whom you're intimate—mention it to your job runner."

"Yes, sir."

"This is as far as this goes, Collins. Consider the ball picked up and consider yourself to be back on this job and refrain from discussing it with Pérez or any of the others, at lunch or any other meal, in Battery Park or any other venue."

"Yes, sir."

"Uh, Collins," Sayles said. "Or maybe you know the answer, John. Why the, uh, homosexual thing? Why did Van Meter want it to look like he was, you know, gay and so on and so forth?"

Barnes watched the fire.

"Sir?" Collins said. "I've thought about that, sir, and I think it might've been because of the woman. She was inordinately attractive, sir. Breathtaking. The kind of woman you're afraid to look at and yet can't not. I thought about myself, sir; I thought that if I were on a job that brought me into contact with that kind of woman, I'd appreciate having a fairy tale that, well, that precluded intimacy. I think the only explanation that a woman like that would accept for a man's not being attracted to her would be that he was homosexual."

"That's good," Sayles said. "That's real good. The only trouble with it is the cabbie Needleman, the waiters at the restaurant, the people who remember seeing Van Meter with the woman, they all said they were very lovey-dovey and so on and so forth."

"I've heard that speculation, sir," Collins said, "and what I've hypothesized is that perhaps their display of affection was misinterpreted. Perhaps their kisses were merely platonic."

"That'll be all, Collins," Barnes said. "Thank you very much."

"Yes, sir."

"We have your phone numbers?"

"There's just my home number, sir."

"Make sure we have your girlfriend's number."

"Yes, sir."

"And until further notice, entertain your mother at your place, or take her to a restaurant."

"Yes, sir."

"Good night."

"Good night, sir. Good night, Mr. Sayles."

When Collins was gone, Sayles said, "Rita?"

Barnes watched the fire.

"And who was running Van Meter? Or was he strictly a renegade?"

Whatever was burning seemed inexhaustible.

"Are you going to go renegade, John? Or are you going to tell Georgetown?"

High in the sky was a quarter moon; smoke from the fire was beginning to smudge it.

"I got to tell you this, John. There's this list, you know, of all the people who bought the Ellesse sunglasses. Susan generated the list, and turned it over to Polly, but after Susan went on the job Rita took it over from Polly, and you know what she told me today?"

Barnes waited.

"She told me there's nobody on the list who fits the description, that unless we go the route of finding out if anybody on the list—and it would mean interviewing all two hundred fifty purchasers and hoping they were telling the truth—if anybody on the list bought a pair as a gift for somebody who fits the description, then the list is a washout, a dead end, of no use at all and so on and so forth. All I'm saying, John, is it would be the easiest thing in the world, if Rita's gone rogue, if she saw one of her buddies' names on the list, to delete it."

Barnes thought about yet another thing he'd read—in the Arbus biography: a witness quoting James Joyce on the necessity that an artist practice "silence, cunning and exile."

"You want to bring Susan in, John?" Sayles said. "It's getting a little hairy out there and so on and so forth."

"Susan's safe," Barnes said. "Rita—or whoever it is—wouldn't be so careless as to whack Susan so soon after whacking Paul; that would point to an inside job. I want oversight on everything that Rita does. I want to know where she had lunch and with whom. I want to know when she took a crap and where and for how long. Twenty-four-hour oversight. Use Collins, Broughton, Pérez, Freund and Peck. Begin making up a list of alternate candidates, in the event they don't all work out, or that that's not a sufficient number."

"Rita," Sayles said. "Who would've thought it? I guess that's the point, isn't it, when you go rogue? That the people who know you and work with you and so on and so forth won't think it."

23

Henry Aaronson peered through a window that had never been washed in its lifetime at a barren patch of the Bronx. "You know the *tarrarom* this is going to cause, D?"

With the nail of his middle finger, Cool D moved fractionally the envelope in the center of the card table that, with its two folding chairs, was the room's only furniture.

"Let me get this straight, okay, D, just so I can pretend I understand it. Humor me. You have snatched this girl because why? Because she is the daughter of a woman who is in with the *shikseh* who whacked your *nuchshlepper*, Lionel, and your beloved Shiraz, *aleha ha-shalom*, and made a deal with Lorca, the *gonif*, which has left you sitting high and dry without a pot to piss in? And in exchange for this young girl's well-being and safe return to her mother's arms you are asking what? That the *shikseh* abrogate her arrangement with Lorca, the *gonif*, which would make her *trayf*, and unable to do business with anybody around town, which would leave the field open for you to make a triumphant return to the status of big hitter? Is that it in a bombshell? Did I get it right?"

Cool D picked up the letter and held it out.

Aaronson took it and looked at the address, then put it in an inside pocket. "Yes, D. All right, D. Of course, D, I will deliver this note—the Hotel Pierre I get to go to, yet—but before I do I got to know if you seriously believe that this little caper will not result in your getting whacked. Not one of your *nuchshleppers*, D. You. The *baleboss* himself. You do? You don't? You don't care?

"Talk to me, D, for God's sake, just once in your life say something to me. Shiraz, *aleha ha-shalom*, ain't here no more, D. She

155

got whacked. I'm as sorry as you are. I'm sorrier; I'm that kind of guy; any man's death diminishes me, especially a young person's, a woman with a kind heart. But we can't bring her back. You can't, I can't, the good Lord can't. So talk to me. Please. Snatching kids, D, is a terrible, terrible thing.

"Who is this girl, do you know? Who is her mother besides somebody who is in with the *shikseh* who whacked your *nuchshlepper*, Lionel, and your beloved Shiraz, *aleha ha-shalom,* and made a deal with Lorca, the *gonif*? 'In with'? What does 'in with' mean? Is she one of the *shikseh*'s sidemen—sidepersons? Is she a customer? Is she just a friend? If she's just a friend, D, then you're breaking one of the basic rules, which is do not mix business and family. D, D, will you talk to me, please?"

Cool D lifted his chin toward the door.

Aaronson folded his arms. "I'm going to be stubborn, D. I'm an *alter kocker,* I'm entitled. Plus, in this matter *I'm* your *nuchshlepper, I'm* at risk, somebody makes me for a *momzer, I'm* looking at doing points and *alter kockers* shouldn't do points, they should enjoy the fruits of their labors.

"My advice is this, D: Rather than delivering this letter to the mother of the girl you have snatched, I will speak to Lorca and explain the situation to him and inquire if perhaps there is any possibility that he would reconsider the arrangement he made with the *shikseh.* After all, it is not an arrangement that is guaranteed to make him a whole lot of friends in the community, since the *shikseh* is not a member of the community, and, as I have already mentioned to you, Lorca did not approve of the *shikseh*'s whacking Shiraz, *aleha ha-shalom.*

"If Lorca has any inclination to reconsider the relationship, then the two of you can meet and discuss matters and bury the hatchet and there is no need to continue holding the girl captive, or even mention to Lorca that a captive is what she is. If Lorca is not inclined to reconsider the relationship, then and only then would you communicate to him that you have the girl in your possession that you intend to use her to force the *shikseh* to abrogate her arrangement with him and that it would not be good for his health if he were to interfere.

156

"Either way, you would be able then to do what you really got to if you want to sleep nights, and that is whack the *shikseh*, without having to worry that it will mean a spark-up with Lorca, who has a great deal of impressive heavy artillery and a band of cutthroat sidemen at his disposal, which is more than you got, D, because you are basically a pacific fellow.

"Whatever you decide, D, I'm going to have a look at the girl so that I can testify that she is in good health and that her mental condition is as good as can be expected under the circumstances. I am not going to accept your word on this, D, because I am not a mere *nuchshlepper* and if I give my word on a matter such as this I want it to be based on the actual facts and not hearsay."

Cool D rubbed his nostrils, reset his dark glasses, and flicked his thumb at the door behind him.

"Thank you, D," Aaronson said. He patted cool D on the shoulder as he passed, and knocked on the door. It was opened by a sideman he'd never seen before. "Cool D says it's kosher."

The sideman moved out of the way and Aaronson looked at the girl and she at him. *Hello, my little* mazik. Alevai, *you will not remember that you have met me and were dandled on my lap, even, and if you do remember,* alevai *you will not say so out loud or even let it show on your pretty little face. Don't worry, my little* mazik. *I will get you out of this fucking mess. We're* mispocheh, *you and I, your mom, your dad,* alav ha-sholom.

Aaronson went back into the other room and patted Cool D on the shoulder again. "I'll be in touch, D."

24

Seeing Susan Saint Michael—who must be a narc, mustn't she?—being marched off at gunpoint after getting caught in the stable, and almost but not quite getting caught in the stable himself, had encouraged Ted Scally to rethink his strategy. It didn't take him long to conclude that it would be better to be on the outside looking in than on the inside and all knotted up in things.

He'd chosen at first to be on the inside because on the inside was where he'd spent a lot of his life: on the inside of schools, of the attic where his father locked him up when he cut school; of freight cars he hopped to run away from home, of police cars that brought him back; of packing crates and culverts he used for cover from rain and snow and sun and cops; of closets he dived in when someone's father or husband or boyfriend came home bedtimes; of more police cars and courtrooms and jails; of more courtrooms and more jails. On the inside looking out. It was kind of nice being on the outside looking in, kind of restful —the restfulness you felt at a movie (which was a sort of out-side-looking-in situation), glad you weren't up there on the screen getting your forehead trimmed with a chain saw; or at an aquarium, glad to be having the educational experience of see-ing man-eating sharks close up and glad the glass was good and thick.

Sitting out on Rachel's veranda and looking through the Palla-dian windows at the party going on inside was, come to think of it, a lot like being at an aquarium. It was one expensive tank, with some expensive fish. The rock stars and playboys and former tennis greats and baby moguls and heirs and scions and wimps were there, and so were their respective fuckers. And so were quite a few newcomers, who looked like they'd dreamed all their lives of being in this kind of company, and who dressed and talked and acted like they were the real thing, drank the same expensive booze and did the same expensive soda and rolled their eyes in the same bullshit god-isn't-this-just-the-*best*-thing way when the rush came—all of which was confusing to the real-thing fuckers, whose minds were filled just about to capacity with the names of designers and hairdressers and boutiques and restaurants and clubs and cars and island paradises and could absorb only a few stray facts from the latest *People* and *Interview* and *Vanity Fair* and *Rolling Stone* and *Vogue* and last evening's *Entertainment Tonight* and could hardly be expected to make subtle distinctions between the real thing and the new-comers, who, for all the real-thing fuckers knew, might be the real things' *best friends,* and therefore eminently fuckable.

And then there was the broad who scared the shit out of Scally. Where the hell had she come from and what was her story and was she for real or was she just so stoned and zonked and spaced and wasted that she had no idea what was real so how could anybody else?

She was wearing...Well, shit. How to describe it? Black leather pants with a waist so high it came up to just below her breasts; the pants closed with a zipper that was like a silver slash across her abdomen and belted with a wide black belt under her ribs. And a skinny black sweater with a hooded collar that she'd tucked her hair into and in addition to the collar a—a what?—a cowl of some kind of stiff, shiny fabric that nearly hid her brows and stood out in front of her face like the prow of a ship.

Or more like—what it was *really* like (Scally was a fucking armorologist, practically)—like the breaths of a frog-mouth helmet. On her hands, a pair of leather gauntlets that zipped to her elbows; on her feet, black spiked heels.

Rachel, he'd thought when he first saw her, but then he'd seen that she didn't move like Rachel, that she moved with a kind of grace that Rachel was a little short on, a kind you

159

couldn't buy, you were born with it and it had nothing to do with breeding, it was something poor people had as often as rich people, that even dumb people had—some of the dumbest fucks he'd ever known, dumb fucks who for all their dumbness could ski the shit out of a mountain or ride the shit out of a wave or sit on a horse like they were part of it or just *stand* like they were some kind of fucking god.

Then who was she? She wasn't one of the rock star- or playboy- or former tennis great- or baby mogul- or heir- or scion- or wimp-fuckers. And she wasn't one of the newcomers, wasn't one of *their* fuckers (who were getting hit on by the real thing, since *their* fuckers were all tied up with the newcomers). She wasn't smoking or snorting or toking or basing or drinking or—

Holy shit, it's her. Susan Saint Michael. It's her and will you look at that.

For Susan had pulled back the hooded collar of the skinny black sweater to reveal that she had had her hair cut like a boy's. Like Rachel's.

She's no narc, Ted, old sport, or if she ever was she's decided to see if maybe crime doesn't pay, after all, or else she's drugged, because for sure she's flying on something. Jesus, look at her. Jesus, she scared the shit out of him.

Susan scared the shit out of Kit Bolton too, so much so that drinking straight vodka and space-basing a rock sprayed with PCP and bogarting his very own joint of righteous Hawaiian reefer (to slow down the pell-mell rush just a little) wasn't doing a *thing* for him.

And Bolton was scared at the prospect of playing the game, Rachel's favorite game, a game *he'd* turned her on to, having read about it in a book about a bunch of British colonials in Kenya, or someplace, in the twenties, or maybe thirties. Or maybe it was forties. The point of turning Rachel on to the game had been that they would organize and direct and oversee it *together,* that they would share the power, the turn-on, of watching the others play. It was what they were best at, watching.

160

Like the time he and Rachel and Eric and Courtney and Monty and Bronson and Pierre and Alexandra and George and B.J. and Jennifer—the best of the Fortymost—went on a raid. They raided Nell's and the Tunnel and Madam Rosa and a benefit for AIDS or some fucking thing at the Plaza and snatched a bunch of pretty people (making it a rule that they were absolutely *not* to snatch anyone whose picture had appeared in a piece about the well-dressed social set in the fall fashion supplement of the *Times*). They drove in Bronson's Lamborghini and Pierre's 420 SL and some of the pretty people's cars to George's family place in Lloyd Harbor and gave each of the pretty people a silver spoon and sat them in front of a tray of Bolivian soda that had hardly been stepped on at all. Someone made tequila sunrises and someone put Van Halen on the stereo and the best of the Fortymost watched the pretty people dance and take their shoes off and then their clothes and fuck on the carpet and out on the terrace and in the pool. Then Eric and Courtney and George gathered up the clothes and locked them in the safe behind the portrait of George's father in the billiard room. And then everybody split up and Kit and Rachel went to the rooms on the third floor that had peepholes in their floors and watched George and Eric fuck in the master bedroom and Courtney and Alexandra and Bronson fuck in one guest bedroom and Monty and Pierre and B.J. and Jennifer fuck in another. Then he and Rachel went downstairs and rounded up the pretty people, not a few of whom weren't so pretty any longer because they were in tears and strung out, and he and Rachel fucked on the tigerskin rug in the den while they watched the pretty people watch them. And then the best of the Fortymost drove back to the city in Bronson's Lamborghini and Pierre's 420 SL and the pretty people's cars and had breakfast at Frank's. And that afternoon the Huntington town police called George's father, who called George, who was in the middle of fucking B.J. and Jennifer, and asked him what he knew about some naked people in their house who claimed their clothes and cars had been stolen and George said not a damned thing.

That had been in the old days, the good old days. Things were different now. Out of the blue, Rachel had decided that the best of the Fortymost weren't interesting anymore, were boring, in fact, and she'd gotten these new friends, half of whose names Kit didn't even know because Rachel never introduced them—not to him. She introduced them to motherfucking Nick Ivory, and since Rachel almost always had an arm through Ivory's and a leg pressed up against him, her new friends figured out without having to have a map drawn or anything that Ivory was Rachel's main squeeze and that Kit was some kind of gofer. God. Ivory. A *guitar* player.

The best of the Fortymost weren't interesting anymore and the Fortymost weren't the Fortymost anymore; they were whoever Rachel wanted them to be. The Hundredmost, the Thousandmost, the Any-Riffraff-at-All-Most.

And Scally. Where *was* Scally? Rachel wouldn't tell Kit where Scally was or why he'd gone. *If* he'd gone. And this Saint Michael woman. Look at her, in Rachel's Claude Montana threads, threads she'd taken him along to buy at a shop on the French side of Saint Martin, threads he'd fucked her in that night, bending her over the balcony rail of their villa, stripping off the leather pants but leaving on the sweater and the gauntlets and the pleated ciré scarf collar, threads he'd put on himself a time or two, once to fuck Rachel on the terrace of B.J.'s apartment (or was it Jennifer's?), once to fuck Bronson in the back seat of Bronson's Lamborghini. Rachel had bought the threads because they turned Kit on—that's what she'd said; but you didn't have to be a goddamn brain surgeon to know that she bought them because she knew they'd turn on Nick Ivory, Nick Ivory with his toys, Nick Ivory with his motherfucking armor.

So what was this Saint Michael woman doing in Rachel's threads—his threads—and with her hair cut like Rachel's, and what was Rachel trying to tell him by putting this Saint Michael woman next to him in the game?

The game was called Pass the Orange, and it was the same game kids play at birthday parties—with a difference. You tuck an orange between your chin and shoulder or chest and try to

162

pass it to the next player next to you without using your hands or arms; if the orange drops, the player or players who drop it are out; the last player left is the winner. The difference, Rachel being Rachel, was that instead of an orange they used a Galway crystal Christmas tree ornament; if a player or players dropped it, it broke, and instead of the player or players being out, they had to perform a task assigned to them. By Rachel.

Rachel began, using her chin to roll the crystal ornament off a table in the center of the living room, then catching it cleverly against her chest and holding it there with her chin. She passed it to Nick Ivory, who rubbed his thighs against Rachel's and rolled his eyes lewdly at her as he took it.

Nick Ivory passed it to a brunette in a strapless Calvin Klein who squealed at the first brush of his chin against her cheek because he hadn't shaved in days, à la mode. She nearly dropped the crystal ornament when Nick Ivory let go but managed to trap it between her chin and the bodice of her dress. She passed it to a man in a white dinner jacket, blue jeans and monogrammed Dunhill slippers, who passed it to a man in a Kenzo evening jacket, who dropped it. It broke.

Rachel laughed and applauded.

"Now, nothing too difficult, Rachel, darling," the man in the Kenzo said. "It's my first time."

"Nothing too difficult," Rachel said, looking into the air above his head as if at a chart of difficulty. "Nothing too difficult. . . . Do you have your car here, Bri?"

"Yes, of course."

"The Auburn?"

"Of course."

"Get in the Auburn. . . ."

"Yes?"

"Make a left at my driveway onto Flying Point. . . ."

"Yes?"

"Go about fifty yards. . . ."

"Yes?"

"Don't go too fast, but not too slow, either. . . ."

Bri was giggling with anticipation. "Yes?"

"There's a stone wall on the right. The road curves so that the wall's right in front of you at that point. . . ."

"Y-Yes?"

"Drive into it," Rachel said.

Bri laughed. The newcomers, especially, weren't sure whether to laugh or not.

"We'll come watch, of course," Rachel said.

"Don't be absurd, Rachel."

She wasn't being; but she granted a temporary reprieve. "We'll do it later, after we've played a little more. Sit *down,* Bri. You're out."

The game went on, for there was a boxful of crystal ornaments. Another one broke and Rachel ruled that the man and woman who'd bobbled it between them were both culpable and that their penalty was to wrestle on the rug until one of them had pinned the other. There was a beat, after which the woman, a size five, tossed champagne from her tulip glass in the face of the man, who was over six feet tall, and while he clawed at his eyes kneed him in the crotch and when he bent over gasping shoved him onto the floor and straddled him and pinned him.

The wrestlers sat down alongside Bri, laughing as couples do on TV game shows after they've won a prize by sharing with some of the rest of the nation a humiliating secret. That they hadn't protested their task made Bri look even more anxious.

The game went on. A tall blond woman in an Oscar de la Renta dropped a crystal ornament and Rachel told her to lie down on the broken glass and masturbate, using a silver candlestick as a dildo. She did, and pretended to come, and the game went on.

Two men, one a Don Johnson clone, the other in a tux and Dunhill slippers, dropped a crystal ornament between them and Rachel told them to fuck each other's dates or girlfriends or wives or whatever they were. They did, and the men came within seconds of each other, and the game went on.

Rachel handed a crystal ornament to a man in a white tennis sweater and white flannel pants, who flipped it with the casualness of a man who'd devoted a lot of his life to ball games to a

164

man in madras patch pants and a navy Lacoste shirt, who caught it as casually, as if this were a routine they did at lots of parties, then tossed it over his shoulder into the cold fireplace. It broke. Rachel ruled that they should be penalized for flouting the rules and told them to fuck each other. The man in white told her to fuck herself and Rachel laughed and went to him and lifted the hem of her Scaasi dress and put a finger inside herself and then put it to his lips, and everyone applauded—everyone but Bri, who wished he'd told Rachel to fuck herself, and Susan, who went to Rachel and took her by the wrist and lifted Rachel's hand to her mouth and sucked on that finger, a gesture everyone applauded. Everyone but Bri.

25

Playact, bullshit, pretend, Susan had said to herself yesterday or the day before or last week or last month or whenever it had been as Rachel and Nick Ivory nudged her along the road from the stable up to the house, cocking an eye now and then at their brand-new MAC-10s like children admiring new shoes.

The sun was rising, burning away the night fog, and Susan had thought about making a run for the dunes, for the cover of what fog was left. And then what? And why? She didn't have a plan, for she hadn't expected to be discovered. Why hadn't she?

In the copse alongside the house, Rachel had got in front of Susan and stopped and shot a hip and rested the butt of her machine gun against it: *Rambette.* "Well?"

"Yes. Luv," Nick Ivory said. "Well. Indeed."

Playact, bullshit, pretend. "I couldn't sleep. I was reading. I heard the Jeep. Things going on behind my back make me nervous."

Rachel laughed too giddily. "You were already in the stable when I got there, Susan. *Is* that your name—Susan? I heard you in the hayloft; I saw how you'd fiddled with the combination. I went to get Nick and you were *still* in there. That's beyond curiosity, Susan. That's snooping."

Scally. Unless it was Kit. Why would it be Kit? It had to be Scally and Susan hadn't even suspected—that was how royally she'd fucked up, how inattentive she'd been. Stable or no stable, why hadn't she smelled that rangy outlaw smell of his—Joe Cook's smell—that was starting to grow on her? Since her first sight of Scally, and especially since their first kiss—their only kiss—her fantasy had been that they would go through this

166

thing together and come out of it together and ride off into the sunset. Together. It had the deficiencies and impracticalities of every fantasy and quite a few particular ones of its own, but it had sustained her, for being out to play had meant being altogether alone. And now he was out to play for reasons of his own and all she had to do to get Rachel and Nick off her back was tell them that. But she couldn't. If she was in over her head, Scally might be the only one who would help her. If he happened to be on her wavelength.

Nick Ivory put an arm around her. "Are you. A narc. Susan?"

Susan should have felt comfortable with the suspicion; as with being loved, it gave her permission to be unpredictable, erratic. But she was off kilter. She had to playact, bullshit and pretend without seeming to, and she'd already seriously underestimated her audience—and overestimated herself. "I thought you checked me out, Nick. Or was putting your nose down my dress the extent of it?"

Ivory took a pistol from the pocket of his sport jacket. "Found this. In your closet. Speaking of dresses. Is it yours?"

Susan sighed. "No, Nick. Somebody planted it there."

"How'd you get it on the plane?" Rachel said.

She was good. Scally'd thought her a fuck-up, but she kept after things. "I got it in New York."

"Where?"

"Where'd you get the MAC-tens?"

Rachel cocked her head. "How do you know that's what they are?"

"Narc school," Susan said.

"You wouldn't be. So bloody flip. If you knew what 'appened. To the last narc. Who came sniffing round."

Susan pointed a finger at Rachel. "The next time you propose doing business with someone, warn them you get off on whacking narcs."

"There was just one," Rachel said.

Susan slapped her.

Nick hit Susan in the back of the head with the butt of his MAC-10. When she woke she had a headache, a haircut and a Thorazine habit.

The headache was nothing major, Rachel assured her; a doctor friend of Rachel's—one of her best private customers, in fact—had found no concussion, just a contusion consistent with a fall from a horse onto rocky ground, which was what Rachel told the doctor Susan had taken.

The haircut—a major haircut, carried out by Rachel's very own East Hampton hairdresser (another customer)—was intended, Rachel said, to make it clear to Susan and to anyone else who cared to notice whose side Susan was on.

The habit, Rachel assured her, was nothing major, just a pill every few hours, enough to keep Susan sedated, not enough to keep her from killing Kit Bolton.

"You see, Susan," Rachel said as she helped Susan dress for the party, "we just don't trust you enough to keep on with this relationship without getting some kind of... guarantee from you."

"I told you. There's more money coming from California."

"No, Susan. It's not money we want. We'd like a different sort of commitment. At the party tonight you'll be Kit's date. Get him alone somewhere—it's up to you where and how—and get rid of him."

On the outside looking in, Scally watched Rachel take another Christmas tree ornament out of the box on the table in the middle of the room and hand it to Susan Saint Michael, who had taken off that scary collar and hood—but not the gloves, no, sir, not the fucking gloves. Susan tucked the ornament under her chin and passed it to Kit Bolton—or tried to, for Bolton was coming down off something very high and shaking like a crazy man and the Christmas tree ornament bounced on his chest for what seemed like five fucking minutes, then fell on the floor and broke all to pieces, just like the other ornaments, and Bolton looked like he was going to break into pieces too, for there was Rachel pointing and saying something and there was Nick Ivory taking Bolton by the elbow with one hand and Susan by the elbow with the other and trying to bring them together, looking

168

as if he were trying—so heavy and limp was Susan and shaking so much was Kit—as if he were trying to smash two heavy cymbals together underwater in the expensive aquarium with its expensive fish. Or some fucking thing.

And then a bunch of rock stars and playboys and former tennis greats and baby moguls and heirs and scions and wimps and newcomers lifted Susan and Bolton up on their shoulders and carried them toward the stairs while their respective fuckers clapped their hands and jumped up and down and yelled and screamed and carried on like they were Dallas Cowboy cheerleaders or something.

And then Bolton somehow got down and broke free and ran down the stairs and headed for one of the Palladian doors to the patio and just broke the plane of the goal, as they say in sports broadcasting, before the posse jumped him and hauled him back inside and, at Nick Ivory's suggestion, started helping Bolton—cramming him—into a suit of armor, the suit that had lately been reclining on a chaise in the den, strumming an electric guitar, one of Nick's guitars, the suit a stand-in for Nick, a suit that Scally, who was a fucking armorologist, practically, knew wasn't one of the lightweight copies that Nick had around his house but an original, and heavy.

And then there was Bolton moaning and saying no no no over and over but not really fighting because he might be coming down but he was still miles high and thoroughly outnumbered and Nick did him up expertly, even taking off Bolton's espadrilles and putting on the sabbatons, strapping on the poleyns and the body armor, seating the helmet, a visored basinet, on his head. And then there they were standing Bolton up and there was Nick, like he was guiding the one who was It in a game of Blind Man's Bluff, turning Bolton in circles, twice, three, four times, then sending him on his way.

In his pursuit of armorology, Scally had tried on that particular helmet and knew that it had been made for a man much bigger than Bolton, some Renaissance Hulk Hogan or something, and that it was a bitch to see out of in any case, for the sight was just a skinny slit, and a bitch to breathe in, for the breaths were just

169

a couple of holes punched in it, and even a budding armorologist like him hadn't been able to wear it for very long without getting claustrophobic as hell, and he'd been straight and sober and Bolton was bent and smashed. So it didn't surprise Scally when Bolton walked right into a wall, then into an end table, knocking off a lamp and breaking it, then into a coffee table, which cut his legs out from under him and sent him crashing over it, breaking it, and onto a couch, where he thought maybe he could stay put, that enough was enough, but a couple of the rock stars or play-boys or former tennis greats or baby moguls or heirs or scions or wimps or newcomers got hold of him by the pauldrons and dragged him back on his feet and spun him around and sent him on his way, right into the fireplace mantel.

The respective fuckers wanted to play too, of course, and one of the real-thing fuckers or one of the newcomer fuckers had a good idea, which was to take a coke spoon and bang on the helmet. And so all the fuckers got their coke spoons out and banged on the helmet, and the ones who used vials instead of spoons banged the vials and the ones who based or cracked it up banged their glass pipes, breaking them, some of them, but what the fuck, there was glass all over the place anyway from the fucking Christmas tree ornaments and anybody who was left found *something* to bang with, including pokers and stuff from the fireplace, and to get some peace and quiet Bolton shoved his way through them and went out the Palladian doors to the patio and lumbered and shuffled and clanked right straight into the swimming pool.

And then there was everyone and their fuckers—and even Bri, who had a stronger and stronger sense that there was going to be mercy for his Auburn after all—hurrying out to see what would happen next and there was no one left in the living room except Rachel and Susan, french kissing like they'd just in-vented it.

Rachel tasted like vodka, which didn't erase the taste of her vagina, which Susan could smell too, on Rachel's hand on

170

Susan's cheek. Rachel's body was hard and muscular; the bones of her pelvis were sharp even through the leather pants.

A part of Susan floated somewhere up near the ceiling and looked down at the rest of her and wondered what she was doing, wearing a bad guy's clothes, her hair cut like a bad guy's by a bad guy's hairdresser, her hands on the ass and her tongue in the mouth of the bad guy who fucked her husband and got him to go rogue, then whacked him, helping the bad guys whack another bad guy.

And the rest of her looked up out of the corner of her eye at the part of her floating there and gave her a look like it was all right, that she was just on the job, that this what what *men* did on the job, wasn't it?—fucked the bad guys. And anyway, she wasn't helping bad guys whack another bad guy. And anyway, she was wrecked.

The part of her up near the ceiling said, *I can see that*. And the rest of her said, *Help me*.

Susan and Rachel finally broke apart and Rachel took Susan by the wrist and led her outside and they slipped through the crowd and stood at the edge of the pool and watched Bolton drown, and watched all the others watch too, and Susan saw that for a lot of people, watching a drowning man wasn't something that sustained their interest for long, for they were drifting away from the pool and getting fresh drinks and taking fresh snorts and toots and hits, and by the time no more bubbles came out of the helmet on Bolton's head even Rachel had gone away and was puffing on a glass pipe Nick Ivory had handed her and the only people watching were Susan and the man in madras patch pants and the navy Lacoste shirt.

"Help him," Susan said, but the man just looked at Susan, for she hadn't really said anything at all, just in her mind. And what she'd said in her mind was *Help me*.

And Susan knew that even though the man in madras patch pants and the navy Lacoste shirt hadn't said anything he would help her, for the man was John Barnes.

26

There were precedents, there was a chapter in the book, there was lore about what to do when the bad guys started killing each other in your presence, even in fun:

Let them.

Period.

Collins—the man in the white tennis sweater and white flannels and Barnes's ticket to these proceedings by virtue of his good looks, his wardrobe, his mother's Roll-Royce Silver Cloud and his prep school mate whose younger sister had dated one of the Fortymost and had been able to find out where he was spending the weekend—Collins knew the precedents, the book, the lore, but was having trouble keeping them from being subsumed by the lurid reality. The aftertaste of Rachel's vaginal juices, planted on his lips by their secretor, didn't make it any easier.

"Uh, sir, should I, uh...?" Collins made a pathetic gesture toward the sunken Bolton, of interest at the moment only to an amphibious virgin who had stripped off her clothes and dived down to the bottom of the pool, where she did an erotic hula not in the hope of resuscitating poor Kit but to keep from bobbing to the surface.

"Bring the car around to the front," Barnes said. "I'll be a few minutes."

"But, sir—"

"*Now,* Fred."

Collins stared, for his given name was Jack. Then he remembered that more than one game was being played here. "Right. I'll get the car. Tom."

Barnes stood very still for a moment, making sure of his breathing. It was easy to lose your breath—not to mention your life—around agents who were stunned, like Collins, and stoned, as it seemed Susan was.

There were precedents, there was a chapter in the book, there was lore about narcs who got high by accident because they smoked something or drank something or ate something they didn't know was spiked. They were usually funny stories—stories about people taking their clothes off and not knowing why or how to get them back on; about people tap-dancing on tabletops and singing songs they didn't know they knew the words to, sometimes in languages they didn't speak; about people falling asleep in public places, their faces in plates of spaghetti or puddles in gutters; about people being nice to people they didn't like or spurning people they did like. Funny war stories, to be told around the shop, to new recruits, even to spouses.

There were precedents, there was a chapter in the book, there was lore about narcs who got high because it was either get high or get dead; about narcs who got high because they *had* to know what it was like to get high; they couldn't be on the job without knowing. Sometimes they were funny stories, sometimes cautionary; they all had happy endings.

There were no precedents, there was no chapter in the book, there was no lore about narcs who got high because the bad guys got them high; or because it was get high or get dead; or because they knew what it was like and they knew they liked it; or because they couldn't stand the smell of the cesspool they wallowed in and the feel of the shit they caressed and the sound of the lies they concocted—who got high and then couldn't come down, so they walked off rooftops or bridges, or rolled out car doors in the fast lanes of freeways, or drove into abutments or across medians into other fast lanes, or whacked their families and then ate their guns; or who did none of those things, but just dropped off the face of the earth into windowless apartments with mattresses on the floor and dark oozing basements where butane lighters flared intermittently, like fireflys. There were no stories like that because there were no listeners because the only prospective listeners would have refused to listen—lest they be jinxed.

Tom. What foolishness. And what a world-class mess. And to think that it was from Joanna's bed—his bed; their bed—that Barnes had been called to sort it all out.

He had phoned Joanna to say that if she and Sally weren't going out to Fire Island in August as planned there was someone from the shop who would be interested in renting the house. (The someone was he, for he wanted a place to put Marie-Christine the homeless French virgin. Barnes had found her in tears on a bench in Washington Square Park while out on his morning run. She had come home the night before [Barnes thought: he could fake a conversation but his comprehension was rusty], to find the American *mec* who had lured her across the Atlantic in bed with a woman with blue hair. Barnes brought her home and made her breakfast and she spread jelly on him and licked it off and now he couldn't get rid of her.)

"Of course we're going," Joanna had said. "Sally can hardly wait."

"Isn't she getting a little old for the beach?"

"What an absurd notion. And anyway, Sally was conceived in Fair Harbor; it has a special resonance for her."

"Was that necessary?"

"Was what necessary?"

"Rubbing it in that once upon a time we had some good times."

"We did have some good times. Is it rubbing it in to remember them?"

"Not if that's all you're doing."

"Not if what's all I'm doing?"

"Christ, Joanna."

"I really don't know what you mean. What do you *want*, John? Why did you call?"

"I don't *want* anything. I called to find out if you're going to Fair fucking Harbor."

"I am."

"So you said."

" . . . "

" . . . "

"How are you otherwise, John? What're your vacation plans?"

"I'm too busy to take a vacation."

"Ah. And you want me to feel guilty that I'm not."

"You're *never* too busy; you're in public relations."

"Was *that* necessary?"

" . . . "

" . . . "

"And how're you, Joanna? *Other*wise?"

"Good. I'm good. I'm damned good."

"Oh?"

"How do I account for that—is that what that 'Oh?' implies?"

"That's what you infer."

"Fuck you, John."

"Ditto."

" . . . "

" . . . "

"Are you free for a drink?" Joanna said.

". . . Where's Sally?"

"Sleeping over at a friend's. I *was* a little surprised, actually—not displeased, but surprised—that Sally's looking forward so much to Fire Island. I had thought she might be too old for the beach, that her innocent summers were a thing of the past. You see, Sally's discovered boys. It's too bad—"

"Too bad her father isn't a better male role model?"

"I wasn't going to say that."

"What were you going to say?"

"It's too bad you aren't around to see Sally every day; this is one of the most interesting periods of her life."

". . . I wouldn't mind a drink."

"Come up."

"Wouldn't you rather meet somewhere—at Marvin Gardens, say?"

"I hate Marvin Gardens. Come up."

"Will you tell the doorman not to shoot to kill?" Barnes said, and Joanna laughed.

Barnes told Marie-Christine the homeless French virgin, who'd been in the bathtub all the while, looking at *Us,* that he was *désolé* but he had to *retourne au bureau.*

Joanna had not only told the doorman not to shoot to kill, she'd given him a note to give to Barnes—a note telling him to go across the street to the liquor store and get some champagne. They made love four times, which was absurd, it was ridiculous, it happened only in wishful pornography.

And there would have been a fifth time—the fifth time was already under way—if Barnes's beeper hadn't gone off, if he hadn't called the duty officer, who told him to call Sayles, who told him he wasn't going to believe this, but Carolyn Van Meter, Paul's and Susan's daughter, Carrie they call her, had gotten herself snatched by Cool D in a bid to renovate his reputation as a big hitter—snatched not because Cool D knew her mother was a narc but because he knew her mother was running with a broad who whacked one of Cool D's sidemen and who made a deal with Cool D's main supplier and so on and so forth. Someone was going to have to invade Susan's fairy tale, it looked like, to get word to her, and was Barnes thinking what Sayles was thinking, which was that the only way Cool D or anyone else could know Carolyn Van Meter was the daughter of Susan Saint Michael was for someone conveniently located to have told him so?

"So nothing's changed," Joanna said as Barnes dressed. "You still dance when the beeper says dance."

Barnes looked at a book on the table by her bed—his bed, their bed: *Sex-Based Discrimination: Text, cases and material.*

"That's a casebook for one of my courses."

"What kind of courses?"

"Law school courses, clearly."

"Clearly. But some adult education thing, right? Not the real thing?"

176

"The real thing, yes. Starting in the fall at NYU. I've just been doing some reading in advance."

"What about your job?"

"I'll do both."

And do the Jane Fonda Challenge before breakfast and teach at Smokenders at lunch and swim a mile after work and weekends write a novel; bake three-grain bread and make *sopa azteca* and lentil dal and sautéed chicken with a puree of twelve cloves of garlic; write some *Hers* columns and study auto mechanics and Ancient Greek and kendo; paint a mural on the living room wall (a triptych: Judith with the head of Holofernes on the left; Salome with the head of John the Baptist on the right; Joanna with the balls of Barnes in the middle); train for a triathlon; start a madrigal society and a writing workshop and a women's group; teach Sally weaving and BASIC and juggling and that the boys she was developing an interest in would grow up to be men, which was to say scumfuckingbags.

"Well. . . . Have a good summer."

"So cool all of a sudden, John. Just because I'm going to law school?"

"Just . . . because."

"What would you like me to do—or to have done? Sit home reading Danielle Steel? Make meat and potatoes every night? Wear a nightie to bed?"

"What would be so bad about that? What would have been so bad?"

After a long moment, Joanna dragged *Sex-Based Discrimination: Text, cases and material* off the table and opened it on her lap—as proof against any more lust as much as to study; she reached down behind her pillow and got out a bag of knitting and went back to work on what looked like a man's sweater, navy with a broad bold yellow horizontal stripe. Whoever the prospective wearer was, he couldn't fuck Joanna the way Barnes had just fucked her—fucked her brains out, fucked her to a fare-thee-well, fucked her . . . well, not unconscious, Joanna didn't *do* unconscious, but almost. And that was all that mattered—that and how well you played the bongos.

177

"Susan Saint Michael?" Barnes said.

Should she deny it? What was he doing here? And that young man he'd been with, looking like a twenties tennis player— she'd seen him around the shop too, hadn't she? Conway or Collins or... Yes. Collins. They were here to help her, clearly, but the question was how did they know she needed help. Unless.... No. Scally? No.

Rachel, who'd been bent over a coffee table cutting lines with a razor blade, sat up and draped an arm over Susan's shoulder. "And who're you?"

"Haynes," Barnes said. "Thomas Haynes."

There it was—just like in the book: *Reverse Perils: Communicating with Agents Out to Play.* It was a short chapter: the medium was discretionary; the message was always the same. Too Hot. T.H. Thomas Haynes, or whatever.

"And 'oo. Invited you. Mister 'Aynes?" Nick Ivory was on the other side of Susan, and had a hand on her thigh. They were going to be a threesome, Susan guessed.

"I represent Mister Williamson," Barnes said.

"'Oo's 'e?" Ivory said.

"He'd like to meet with both you ladies."

"'Oo in his right mind. Wouldn't?" Ivory said. "Which doesn't tell me. 'Oo the fuck. 'E is."

"My car's out front," Barnes said. "My driver will bring you back, of course."

Rachel gave him a look that said, *What, and miss a party?*

She leaned over to snort a line through a pipette.

Barnes hauled her to her feet and slapped her.

Ivory tried to heft himself up out of the soft leather sofa, but Barnes kicked him in the face.

Rachel slapped Barnes.

Barnes took his .38 from his ankle holster and put the barrel in Rachel's nostril. "Snort this, cunt."

And he blew her head off.

No. But that was what Susan momentarily thought—thought it and thought something else, something worse, something she couldn't have articulated, for it wasn't really a thought, just a....

Rachel thought her head was blown off too—though she felt nothing—and so did Barnes himself, though he knew he hadn't pulled the trigger. They all thought it momentarily—all but Nick Ivory, who was unconscious; then they realized, bit by bit, piece by piece, that the explosion had come not from Barnes's gun but from a gun fired on the patio—fired again and again and again.

Glass broke. People screamed. Barnes skimmed along a wall to what was left of a window and took a peek and saw a crazy cowboy with a MAC-10 and a determined look in his eye, bent on killing not the celebrants—he was too carefully aiming too high—but the house, screaming all the while, "Orrrrnelll-laaaaa," like someone who'd seen too many *Rambo* movies. When Barnes looked back, the women were gone.

27

"Make a right, Collins."

"Right is east, sir."

"A right."

Collins made the right off Flying Point onto 27, but didn't make the connection. "Won't she be gong west?"

"Eventually," Barnes said.

At the wheel of Rachel's Jeep, Susan went east through Water Mill into Bridgehampton. She couldn't see headlights in the rearview mirror, but she could feel the pursuit—the pursuit of her mentor in the art of flight. She went around the flagpole at the east end of Bridgehampton and headed back west, pulling into a parking space across from the Kandy Kitchen when she saw headlights break like surf on the rim of the rise ahead. "Get down," she said to Rachel, and made a note to herself to mention back at the shop that fear was an antidote to Thorazine— though she couldn't have said, were she back at the shop, what she was afraid of.

And Rachel, who was finding she liked being told what to do, did as she was told.

"I feel like a fool, sir, that I didn't see what she was driving."

"Can you go a little faster, Collins?"

"It sounded like something with a lot of horsepower, though, sir."

"That's why I'd like you to go a little faster."

"I hope I'll get a chance to make up for this, sir."

"For now, just keep going—a little faster."

Susan turned north on Butter Lane and took it to Scuttle Hole. She took Scuttle Hole west to Head of the Pond to Lower Seven Ponds to David Whites Lane to the bypass by the Omni.

"This is fun," Rachel said.

"You're a cunt," Susan said. "Your friend Haynes is the man."

"He's not my friend."

"He was at your party."

"I never saw him before. A narc?"

"You're fucked, Rachel."

Rachel was fucked and Susan was afraid. Of what? She knew this much, though it wasn't much and made no sense: She was afraid to understand why it was so interesting to her that John Barnes had tossed a Galway crystal Christmas ornament over his shoulder and drawn his pistol from his ankle holster.

In Wainscott, Barnes said, "Turn around. Get on the Sunrise to the LIE."

"Why do you assume she's still moving, sir?" Collins said. "Still moving instead of holing up in some side road? She's had plenty of opportunities."

"Never stay put, Collins, if you're on the receiving end of a pursuit like this. If you're standing still you can be dropped on, broadsided, tunneled under."

"Well, that's the other thing, sir. Why is she running, exactly?"

"Go a little faster."

On the LIE, almost altogether sober now but still not knowing why it was so interesting to her that John Barnes had tossed a Galway crystal Christmas ornament over his shoulder and drawn his pistol from his ankle holster, Susan said, "Tell me about the narc you whacked."

181

"Why?"

"Because you're fucked, goddamnn it, Rachel, and I'm trying to undo some of the mess you've made. Tell me about him."

"His name was Nelson. Charles Nelson. He was an antiques dealer. Nick and I met him at an auction. He said he could get his hands on some rare armor; he was interested in investing in our operation. Do you think Haynes called the cops?"

"No. How did you find out he was a narc?"

"Why not? Why hasn't Haynes called the cops?"

"Because he's the man. The man doesn't call the man. How did you find out he was a narc?"

"I can't tell you."

Susan stood on the brake.

Rachel slammed into the dashboard. "Jesus Christ."

"You should wear your seat belt." Susan accelerated, knocking Rachel off balance, then stopped hard again. She reached across Rachel to open the door and pushed Rachel out. She accelerated for two tenths of a mile, then coasted to a stop, turning the lights out as she rolled. There wasn't a car on the road going in either direction; it was that kind of night.

Rachel caught up to her, breathing hard, and got in. "You're crazy."

Susan started up fast again, driving Rachel back in her seat.

"Sir?"

"Yes."

"She's awfully good, isn't she, sir? She had, at most, a twenty-second start on us and we haven't laid eyes on her."

She was a silent, cunning exile. "She knows the roads."

"*How* does she know the roads, sir? I mean, she didn't know that the job was going to bring her to this part of the world, did she?"

At some point, she knew it," Barnes said. "At that point, she learned the roads. It's recommended, Collins."

"Yes, sir."

*   *   *

"You awake, Rachel?"

"Yes."

"Found out how?" Susan said. "That Nelson was a narc."

Rachel stretched. "I still think you're the narc."

Susan tapped on the brake. "This is Queens County now, Rach. Civilization. Strolling down the middle of the LIE isn't something you want to be found doing in these parts—not in that dress. There'll be a chain-reaction accident, the cops'll want to know how you misplaced your car and what your name is and where you live and they won't understand why you don't want to tell them and when you do tell them—because you know that sooner or later they're going to find out anyway—they won't understand why you don't want them to take you home, so they *will* take you home and they'll be just overwhelmingly officiously curious about the body in the armor in the swimming pool, which it's highly unlikely that anyone's taken the time or the trouble to clean up—if they even remember it's there."

Rachel spoke through a moue. "Right after I made my first big buy I was contacted by someone who said I couldn't do business in New York without her say-so."

Susan accelerated. "Was that the expression she used—say-so?"

Rachel laughed. "You're supposed to say, 'Her?'"

"Was it?"

"I think so. Why?"

It's old-fashioned, that's why. "How old was she?"

"I never met her."

"How old did she sound?"

"Not young, not old."

"Did she have an accent?"

"Doesn't everybody?"

"What were her terms?"

"A flat fee, at first; a percentage if the business got bigger."

"In exchange for?"

"Protection."

183

"From?"

"Competition."

"What put her in a position to guarantee that?"

"She didn't say."

"Did you ask?"

"Fuck you, Susan."

"Did she tell you Nelson was a narc?"

"Maybe."

"Did she tell you I wasn't?"

Rachel smiled. "I asked her to check you out with people in California. But that doesn't mean you're not a narc. Not to me. A good narc would have a background that would stand up to checking."

"And Nelson's didn't? He wasn't a good narc?"

"I really don't know. She decided to tell me, that's all."

"And you whacked him?"

"Yes."

Don't look at her, Susan. Don't say anything, don't do anything. Just drive.

"I want to meet her," Susan finally said.

"I don't think that's possible."

"What's not possible is working with you any longer. They don't get any hotter than you, Rachel."

"What're you going to do?" Rachel said.

"Send you to a cool place," Susan said.

"Want me to drive for a while, Collins?"

"No, sir. I'm fine. Thank you. . . . She hasn't gone rogue, sir, has she?"

"No."

"But she didn't want to take receipt of the peril, did she?"

Barnes looked at Collins for the first time in a long time. "You're good, Collins."

"Thank you, sir."

"No, she didn't want to take receipt of the peril."

"Do you think she already knew its content?"

"No. There's no way she could."

"But she must've concluded you were attempting a delivery."

"Yes."

"Then..."

"Go ahead, Collins. It's important."

"Then she must have felt that by taking receipt she'd be jeopardizing some aspect of her operation or in some way inhibiting her ability to function."

"Exactly."

"How ironic—and how sad—that the message is that her daughter's being held hostage."

"Yes."

"...Sir?"

"Yes?"

"If the agent had taken receipt, and if she and the Phillips woman had accepted the notion of a meeting with the big hitter, what would you have done then?"

"You mean because I *don't* represent the big hitter?"

"Yes."

"I'd've stalled, concocted some procedural obstacle. The point was to deliver the peril and to get the agent up from in deep until the matter of her daughter could be dealt with."

"And what will you do now, in regard to the matter of her daughter?"

"We'll have to go in and get her. You'll be involved, Collins, closely involved."

"Thank you, sir. I haven't said so, sir, and I don't suppose I really must tell you, but the Phillips woman, sir, is the woman I saw with Agent Van Meter—with Charles Nelson, that is—at the fairy tale apartment on East End Avenue."

Barnes nodded. "Right. Jovan Island Gardenia."

28

Red Sayles had a pillow over his head again, the way he'd had a pillow over his head when he thought some scosh was pounding on his door and yelling about Martians and so on and so forth.

Only that time he'd put the pillow over his head, and this time some scosh had; some scosh who was in his room, not pounding on the door; some scosh who was whispering in his ear, not yelling about Martians; some scosh who knew how to make a person think he was dying without actually killing him.

And so on and so forth.

Not some scosh. She. He knew the scosh who'd put the pillow over his head wasn't just some scosh, it was a she. And here's how he knew: even though he had a pillow over his head he was very aware that *his* scosh was sticking out of his pajamas; and very aware that every time he pulled down the tails of his pajama tops to cover up his scosh, the scosh who'd put the pillow over his head pulled the tails back up; and very aware that he was putting more effort into covering up his scosh than into getting the pillow off his head; and very aware that as much as he didn't like having a scosh, he didn't think about it all that much ex*cept* when there was a woman around, in which case having a scosh was *all* he thought about and he was sure that that was all she was thinking about too. So even though the scosh who'd put the pillow over his head didn't smell like a woman that he could smell or feel like a woman that he could feel or act like a woman that he could sense or talk or walk or look like a woman (which he had no idea about because he couldn't hear her or see her), he just knew that the scosh was a woman because that's how a woman's mind worked.

And so on and so forth.

"Rita?" he said, only it sounded like *Ree-er?*

"Shhh," the woman whispered. "Be real quiet."

Not a whisper you could put a name to. Anonymous, neuter, controlled and in control—a whisper you listened up to, not wondered about whose it was.

"Listen carefully, Red. I'm not going to say it twice."

A woman who knew his nickname, which meant she was either a friend or an enemy. Good to know.

"Your legs are tied to the bedposts. I'm not going to tie your hands, but when I take the pillow off, I want you to reach up over your head and hold on to the bedstead. You'll say nothing."

Nice and simple. No hotdogging explanations about how she got his legs tied without waking him—or for that matter how she got into the house and up the stairs and into his room. No threats about what would happen if he didn't hold on to the bedstead, if he didn't keep quiet; the best threats, they told the new recruits, were the ones your own imagination menaced you with, and it was easy to think of himself lying there with his legs tied to the bedposts and his hands back over his head and his scosh sticking out and something sharp between his legs, like they'd done Shiraz, or something crawly or cold or creepy or hot or something that made funny rooting noises. Or that hissed. Or that made no sound at all, just slowly consumed his crotch.

And so on and so forth.

The woman took the pillow away and Sayles sat straight up, ready to go for her throat. But she had backed off and was ready herself—ready to smash the tip of his nose with the heel of her hand, ready to inflict a little brain damage. "Hello, Susan."

"Hello, Red. I'm sorry. One can't be too careful."

Now that he knew it was Susan, Sayles wasn't surprised; if it had been Rita, she would've inflicted a little brain damage. He was surprised at how Susan looked—gaunt and angry and with her cropped hair a little deranged.

"Barnes invaded my fairy tale," Susan said. "Why?"

If it had been Rita, he would've been reluctant to tell her, for she would have murdered the messenger. "Cool D snatched

Carrie. She's safe. Aaronson's close to her. He's certain we can take her anytime we want. Cool D wants to make a deal with Rachel Phillips: Carrie in exchange for her backing out of her deal with Lorca."

"That makes no sense at all. Does Cool D think Carrie is Rachel's daughter?"

"Susan Saint Michael's, he thinks."

"*Red.*"

"I know, I know. That's why Barnes sent a peril. He wanted you to come in, even if it meant rolling things up. We'll get Carrie out and then worry about how to follow up. What happened? Couldn't you take delivery?"

Mother had Professional by the throat and was dragging her toward the door, but Professional convinced Mother that what they didn't know was worth the time it would take to know it. "What's been going on, Red?"

"Starting when?"

"When I went out to play."

"Chronologically?"

Susan shrugged. "What the hell."

Sayles started slowly, getting up speed. "First thing chronologically, I guess, our homeless eyewitness—his name's Hugh Morgan—isn't homeless anymore; he's dead. Right after you went out to play, he drank four bottles of Cutty, passed out, and strangled on his own vomit and so on and so forth. A buddy of Morgan's told me Morgan hated Scotch, that when he could afford something better than wine he drank vodka. He also said Morgan was afraid someone was going to kill him, someone he called the alligator man. The night Morgan DOA'd, a guy bought four bottles of Cutty in a liquor store on Park Avenue South. A PD artist did a composite of the guy, he was your basic nondescript male white—medium height, medium weight, medium complexion, medium hair, medium eyes, medium age, medium period—the kind of guy you need a medium to find, there's a million of them in the naked city.

"Second thing chronologically, I guess, is Shiraz got whacked. One of Cool D's sidemen got whacked first, that you know, right after Paul, and with the same piece, a twenty-two, and then after that the woman who whacked Paul made a deal with Lorca that she would take major soda deliveries off his hands on a regular basis. Then Shiraz got whacked—by Lorca it looked like, to get the jump on Cool D before he could whack one of Lorca's people to get back at Lorca for making the deal with the woman and so on and so forth. But Lorca told Aaronson he didn't have anything to do with whacking Shiraz, especially what with the way she *was* whacked, which was that she was stabbed with a sword, or some long, sharp instrument, in the, uh, vaginal area.

"Third thing chronologically, I guess, is the cabbie Needleman, who was driving Paul when Paul got whacked, he got whacked in his cab, in the high West Twenties. His fare box was gone, it looked like a holdup, except it was a professional-type hit, with a thirty-eight, one shot in the back of the head. Buffalo Bill Aldrich, the NYPD chief of D's—you know him, right?— thought we'd hung the cabbie Needleman out to dry. But we didn't hang him out to dry, because the disinformation we vended to the media didn't mention the cabbie's name, so the only people who knew Needleman was the cabbie and therefore a witness were Aldrich's guys and our guys and the scoshes who were at the meeting we had after Paul got whacked and Needleman himself, who was an owner-operator, meaning he didn't work out of a garage where he might've shot his mouth off and so on and so forth.

"Fourth thing chronologically, I guess, is the doorman in the building where Paul had his pad on the side spotted one of the young guys who'd been going up to Paul's apartment, guys we thought meant maybe Paul was, uh, you know. There was a cop handy and the doorman fingered the guy and it finally worked its way around to us and it turned out the guy was Jack Collins, our Jack Collins, Barnes recruited him, Collins being from Yale and so on and so forth and Barnes too. And all of a sudden it looked like maybe Paul didn't go rogue, like he was looking for someone who did, someone conveniently located, which was what he told Collins and four other of the young guys in the shop—Broughton, Pérez, Freund and Peck were the others—

189

told them and told them he'd handpicked them to help him find out who. Their main job was to visit his pad, to give credibility to Paul's fairy tale, which was that he was an antiques dealer, a, uh, homosexual.

"Fifth thing chronologically, I guess, is Carrie got snatched, which brings you up to date and which I know you know means Cool D must be on speaking terms with the someone conveniently located who went rogue, otherwise how else would he know whose daughter Carrie is? And the sixty-four-thousand-dollar question: Is he on more than speaking terms and along with who else if anyone and what're they playing for besides for keeps?"

Three dead, one snatched, one turned-coat turned right side out again—maybe—one sixty-four-thousand-dollar question. Not much had been happening, not much at all. Poor Shiraz, for they would have made sure she suffered maximally; that was the way they were—Rachel, Nick, the late Kit. Morgan, the homeless eyewitness, the cabbie Needleman—they would not have suffered; *their* killer was too proficient. "Is there anything else, Red?"

"Like what, Suze?"

"Anything at all. Anything strange. Anything that doesn't fit. Anything. Come on, Red, we're after someone conveniently located who went rogue."

"Well, I'd have to say that my best guess right now is it's a good chance it must be Rita."

"Oh?"

"The list of all the people who bought the Ellesse sunglasses, the list you generated, you put Polly on it, but after you went out to play, before anyone was formally named to take over your slot, Rita took over running Polly, and Rita claimed there was no one on the list who fit the description, that unless we went the route of finding out if anyone on the list—and it would mean interviewing all two hundred fifty purchasers and hoping they were telling the truth—if anyone on the list bought a pair as a gift for someone who fit the description, then the list was a washout, a dead end, of no use at all and so on and so forth. All I'm saying,

Susan, is it would've been the easiest thing in the world, if Rita was the one conveniently located who went rogue, if she saw one of her buddies' names on the list, to delete it."

"Has there been any attempt to find if there's a deleted name still in some computer's memory."

Sayles shrugged. "Computers aren't my area, Suze. And you've got to understand that it's only recently that I've been operating on the theory that someone conveniently located went rogue, which means that I can't just walk up to everyone conveniently located and ask for verification of every piece of work they've done lately, because one of them—I hope it's only one—is going to be the someone conveniently located who went rogue."

"Is there anything else?" Susan said.

Sayles thought. "Well..."

"What?"

"It probably doesn't mean anything."

"Red."

"It's probably just..."

"*Red.*"

"Look—all I'm saying is this: When it comes out that someone conveniently located went rogue, people're going to ask how it could be that nobody noticed for however long it was that nobody noticed, and I think part of the answer is that Barnes has been preoccupied with his, uh, marital situation, splitting up with Joanna, moving out, getting his own place and so on and so forth. Aldrich, for instance, called me here at home to tell me about the cabbie Needleman. He'd tried to reach Barnes, but he couldn't; he'd called the duty officer, the duty officer beeped Barnes every three minutes as per SPO, Barnes didn't respond.

"I mean, look, I can tell just by watching Barnes around the shop, in the elevator, in the lobby, at lunch, that he's checking out with renewed interest, so to speak, the various possibilities that're presenting themselves, but he's still feeling, you know, guilt and remorse and so on and so forth and he probably thinks it's best if he doesn't put all his eggs in one basket just yet, he should spread it around a little, go out with a bunch of different women, but he doesn't want it to seem like he's being, you know, promiscuous, which is what it might seem if he called up the duty officer every night with a different venue if you know what I'm saying, so sometimes he takes a chance and lets himself be out of pocket for a while, which I'm not trying to justify, but sometimes you have to look at the human side of the situation and so on and so forth." Sayles couldn't see Susan's face and he was glad, for he knew it would be full of doubt. "People're going to ask how it could be that nobody noticed that someone conveniently located went rogue, that's all I'm saying, and I'm saying part of the answer is that Barnes has been preoccupied with his marital situation and so on and so forth."

"What does alligator man mean to you?" Susan said.

Sayles shrugged. "Someone with a face like an alligator, I guess. I mean, like the elephant Man and so on and so forth."

"And why is it so interesting to me that Barnes tossed a Galway crystal Christmas ornament over his shoulder and drew his pistol from his ankle holster?"

Sayles laughed. "You got me there, Suze. I don't know *what* the fuck you're talking about."

Susan plucked at the knot in one of the cords that held his legs. "Get dressed. Is there anything to eat in the house?"

"You've met my mom, Suze. There's everything to eat; the only question is how big an army do you want to feed and for how long?"

"You and I're going to wrap this up ourselves, Red. No Barnes, no Rita, no Aaronson, no no one." Susan untied the knot and started on the other. "How is your mother?"

"Fine. She's fine. She's good." And she was clearly going to sleep through all this, which was going to be a big disappointment, for he wasn't going to be able to say through the door that no, Mom, he wasn't talking to anyone, and no, Mom, there wasn't anyone in his room, and know that she knew that he was lying, that he had a woman in his room. A woman. In his room. In her house. Her son, Martin. Finally.

29

How I Spent My Summer Vacation

BY CAROLYN VAN METER

God, I mean it was just like totally weird, okay?

Like the day we cut school—me and Jen and Matt and Philip and Jamal—and were on the 'nade smoking when all of a sudden there's my mother, okay, saying, "Come home with me, Carolyn," in this like totally zomboid you-are-in-the-deepest-shit voice. *I* think it's 'cause she found out Jen called the headmaster's office and pretended to be all our moms and said we were sick and 'cause I'm smoking and 'cause Matt and Jamal are skinheads and Philip has an orange asterisk. So I say it's cool, Mom, we're studying Shakespeare in English, okay, we came down here to like rehearse. And she says, "Your father's dead."

It reminded me of this rad horror flick I saw with Jen—not this summer, *last* summer—about these girls who're getting ready to go to a dance or a party, and they don't know the whole entire rest of the human race has been changed into zombies, and their father looks out the window and says, "The good news is your dates're here. The bad news is they're dead." And that's what it was like, okay? It was like my mother was saying, *The good news is you're not in deep shit 'cause you cut school or 'cause you're smoking or 'cause your friends're skinheads or have an orange asterisk. The bad news is your father's dead.*

Then my mother says she's going to be a narc again, and I say, "Well, what if you get killed too?" and she says, "This is something I have to do, Carolyn." Whenever she uses my name like

193

that it's like saying, "Don't ask, okay?" And I say, "'Revenge at first though sweet, bitter ere long back on itself recoils,'" which is like totally amazing 'cause it's from *Paradise Lost,* and how many things like that that you know do you ever get a chance to *say?* And she says, "There's a war going on in this country and the bad guys're winning," so it's like she's going to, you know, rid the entire world of drugs and everything, and while she's doing it, I get to stay with Grandma and Grandpa at their totally pale house and go to their totally pale club with the totally pale pool, which I would rather be gagged with a Cuisinart than do, okay?

And that's why I tried the drugs, okay? I mean, I was hurt, I was unhappy, I felt, like, you know, deserted, abandoned. I didn't try them right away. I mean, it wasn't like I was some kind of, you know, born junkie, just waiting for the chance to shoot up or anything, okay? What happened was me and Jen went to this club, okay, and we met these boys, okay, and they were maybe semi-awesome, and they had this apartment and this stuff they said was crack, but I don't think it was, I think it was Peruvian rock. Dad told me about it once, it's something that looks like crack but it's not. Soap is another thing that looks like crack. Roasted peanuts are another thing. Ounce men sell stuff like it to dweebs who think it's crack.

Anyway, Jen smoked the stuff in a pipe, okay, and I never did ask her what it tasted like but it smelled like Philip's socks, and she got totally weirded out and started making out with this guy and the other guy wanted to make out with me but I didn't want to, okay? Jen said it's 'cause I have narc genes, but that wasn't the reason, okay? The reason was 'cause I didn't want to make out in front of Jen and the other guy and I didn't like this guy all that much, okay, he wasn't semi-awesome as it turned out.

So then it's the Fourth of July, okay, Mom's birthday, okay, and I can't wish her happy birthday 'cause I don't know where she is, just like I used to not know where Dad was and neither did Mom and it used to neg her out totally. Grandma said I should think special birthday wish thoughts to Mom and she'd get them like, you know, through the airwaves. I tried it but I didn't like it, it didn't make me feel good the way I feel on somebody else's birth-

194

day, seeing them happy and excited and getting stuff and being the center of attention. So when me and Jen went to New York to see the fireworks, I didn't come back. I know now that Mom called me, and know she wasn't supposed to and she shouldn't have done it, and even if I had been home I don't think it would've made me feel very good, okay, 'cause I was in this like totally weirded-out state and I probably just would've had a fight with her or something, you know, kept asking her where she was and when she was coming home and all that—all the things I wasn't supposed to ask her—and I would've just gotten more negged out and I would've run away from Grandma's and Grandpa's anyway.

Jen had this friend who knew this woman named Lee-lee-*ahn*. That's not how you spell it, but it's how she said it, like she was French, except she wasn't French she was from Brooklyn, just like me and Jen. Lee-lee-*ahn* sold drugs to kids in her apartment and they were supposed to be safe and everything, not stepped on with all kinds of strange shit and not so pure they would kill you if you just did a little bit, either. I didn't like her, Lee-lee-*ahn*, 'cause of the way she said her name—I mean, her name's *Lill*ian, right?—and 'cause of the way she dressed, like, you know, a girl, and 'cause she listened to K-Rock, which I like but I really don't think grownups should listen to, okay?

Jen told Lee-lee-*ahn* that Dad was a narc. She told her it 'cause Lee-lee-*ahn* asked us what we wanted to, like, you know, buy and Jen said like, well, you know, what do you recom*mend* and I told Jen she couldn't do that, Lee-lee-*ahn* couldn't, she couldn't recom*mend* anything, we had to tell her what we wanted, otherwise it'd be, like, you know, entrapment, and Jen told Lee-lee-*ahn* that Dad's a narc, that's how I knew things like that, and I told Lee-lee-*ahn* that Dad wasn't a narc anymore, he was dead, okay? And Lee-lee-*ahn* said, "You poor thing."

She gave us Ecstasy, Lee-lee-*ahn*, for the wholesale price. She said it wasn't bad to take 'cause otherwise you'd've heard bad things about it. I didn't say it, but I remembered something Dad once said when somebody said something like that about some drug—that it wasn't bad to take because they'd never heard anything bad about it—and Dad said nobody'd ever heard any-

195

thing bad about the Manson family, either, before they, you know, killed all those people.

I don't know how long I stayed at Lee-lee-*ahn*'s. I don't remember if Jennifer was there the whole time or just part of the time. I don't know how I got there, but the next place I was in this room in this slum like, and there were these men who weren't mean, exactly, but they weren't nice, exactly, either. I figured what must have happened was Lee-lee-*ahn* told them Dad was a narc. I figured what must have happened was they kidnapped me 'cause they thought that even though Dad was dead, they could make a deal with other narcs, make them do something the men wanted them to do, or stop doing something the men wanted them to stop doing.

Mr. Aaronson was there too—Mr. Aaronson who worked with Dad and used to come to dinner at our house maybe once a year—not at Thanksgiving or Christmas or anything like that, but some other time, like, you know Labor Day or Memorial Day or something, or maybe the Fourth of July, Mom's birthday. He came in the room once. He didn't say anything to me or anything, and I knew from the way he looked at me that he didn't want me to say anything to him or anything. I knew from the way he looked at me that there'd be big trouble if I did.

Then Mom came, with this way rad haircut, I mean like totally cut off, like Annie Lennox, with her gun. There was a man who was usually the guard inside the room I was in, and Mom shot him in the forehead, and lots of brains and blood and stuff came out the back of his head and got all over the wall. Mom hugged me and asked me if I was okay and I said I was and she took me out to another room where Mr. Sayles was, and the man who was usually the guard outside the room I was in was lying on his face on the floor, and there was blood all around him too.

Then Mom and Mr. Sayles took me outside and we got in a car and Mr. Sayles drove and Mom made me lie on the back seat with my head in her lap and I couldn't see where we were going or anything and I fell asleep for I think a long time 'cause when I woke up it was getting light and Mom said I could sit up and we were in the country and then we came to this place with a great big house and some other houses around it and a big lawn and lots of trees and stuff, and Grandma and Grandpa were there, and Mom said everyone would be safe there and I guess it was what they call a safe house. And Mom said she'd be back as soon as she could, that she had to wrap it up.

Before she left, though, she said, "Some of us, me included, thought your father was a bad man, that he'd been corrupted by the people he rubbed up against on the job. We call it going rogue. But Daddy didn't go rogue; he just pretended to because he wanted to find out if someone else had, someone he'd worked with for a long time, someone he couldn't just come out and accuse, someone he had to build a strong case against." I said not Mr. Aaronson? and she said no, not Mr. Aaronson, Mr. Aaronson was pretending too—that was his job.

Then she said, "The people who trust us, who love us, who expect us to keep our promises, are the easiest ones to betray; they may be the *only* ones we can betray. People betray their countries, their families, their friends, their colleagues, for money, for power, for other reasons, I suppose. Some of them, I think, do it because they can't take the pressure of being trusted. I don't mean pressure; I mean responsibility. Some people can't take the responsi-*bil*ity of being trusted and loved and ... and ... re*lied* on. It's easier to cheat, maybe, than to play fair, because a cheater makes all the rules, a cheater always wins. Do you remember that book you used to like when you were little—*The Adventures of Stanley Kane?* There's a pig in it who keeps saying, 'I win, I win,' whatever happens in whatever game they're playing, and Stanley Kane asks him how come he always wins, and the pig says the rules are the pig always wins, and Stanley Kane says who makes up the rules, and the pig says he does.

I mean, if that's not totally weird—to see you mother with her hair cut like Annie Lennox shoot somebody in the head, okay, and see brains and blood and stuff come out the back of his head and go all over the wall, and then to have her talk to you about a storybook you read when you were, like, you know, four.

30

For Scally, this was *fun,* man: trotting down to the stable and opening the old year-backward lock and crowbarring open one of those wooden boxes and picking out one of those fierce, black, ugly guns and a couple of belts of ammo, strapping on the belts like Rambo and trotting back up to the house and even though you'd never shot anything but a BB gun in your life, being basically a pacific guy and hating loud noises, turning the west wall of Rachel's place into Swiss cheese.

Being a pacific guy, you aimed well above head level and didn't even break all that much glass, except for a few windows you were sure nobody was standing in front of, but you sent the rock stars and playboys and former tennis greats and baby moguls and heirs and scions and wimps and newcomers and their respective fuckers running every which way. Running and screaming and leaping into their 560's and XKE's and Excaliburs and Clouds and Corniches and Boxers and 928's and the occasional Caddy or Town Car or stretch and a white '57 Chevy with a black rag top driven by an awfully pretty blond girl you never saw before and kind of wish you had, when you were on the outside looking in.

The ones who didn't stall out smashed into someone or backed into someone else or turned into someone *else,* then tore ass for the main gate and scraped through two at a time if necessary like life was some kind of goddamn demolition derby and went left and right and straight even if it meant left into something or right into something or straight into something. And (this is the funny part—well, just one of several funny parts) Bri—remember Bri?—Bri got the Auburn away from the house without stalling out or smashing into someone or backing into someone else or turning into someone *else*, made it through the main gate without a scratch even though somebody in a Quatroporte was trying to get through at the same time, turned left and not into something, went along Flying Point to where there's the stone wall on the right, went to where the road curves so the wall's right in front of you, lost it, drove splat into the wall, just like Rachel told him he was going to have to for dropping the fucking Christmas tree ornament.

You didn't know right away about Bri, of course, 'cause after you turned the west wall into Swiss cheese you went inside, holding the gun propped against your hip Rambo-style, and looked to see who was still around if anybody, hiding under chairs or in closets or whatever, and there wasn't anybody that you saw right off and in fact the only person other than you was Kit Bolton, down at the bottom of the pool, and it was fitting that it was just you and him 'cause he was wearing that fucking armor and you're a fucking armorologist practically.

And you thought for a second or two about maybe jumping in the pool and hauling him out but there was no point 'cause he was long dead and all you'd have gotten is wet and you'd have had to dry off and all that and the cops might have come by then 'cause for sure even though the neighborhood wasn't exactly what you'd called densely populated, somebody must have heard the shooting and the screaming and yelling and the sound of the cars smashing into one another and called the cops and if they'd found you hauling Bolton out of the pool they probably wouldn't have accepted your explanations that you didn't have anything to do with his being dead, you'd only felt this sort of connection with him, him wearing that armor and you being an armorologist practically.

And there must have been *some*body still around 'cause there was one car left outside the house—a white 'Vette, '81 or '82, with red leather interior, the windshield on the passenger's side shattered by some asshole shooting a machine gun or something but the damage offset by the key's being in the ignition. And you got the key and opened the trunk and tossed in the gun and slipped behind the wheel and started her up and drove out through the main gate and down Flying Point and that's when you saw Bri's Auburn, and Bri still behind the wheel, not unconscious but staring at nothing out the windshield, which was shattered even worse than yours somehow.

And you took Wickapogue to Old Town to Meeting House to Jobs Lane to Hill Street to Moses Lane to 39 to the Sunrise, congratulating yourself on taking the trouble to learn the roads just in case the shit hit the fan, and imagine your surprise when you found yourself right on the tail of Rachel's goddamn Jeep, Rachel in the passenger's seat and Susan Saint Michael, still wearing those leather gloves, at the wheel. And you said to yourself that if this were a movie you wouldn't believe it, but it wasn't a movie, it was life, so you'd better believe it, better believe that they must have taken some evasive action to make sure nobody was following them. And since you hadn't been following them, they weren't spooked by your driving behind them for a while. You followed them off the Sunrise at the Manorville exit and when they made a left to get on the LIE you faked going straight, like anyone would ever want to go to Manorville, then killed your lights and made the left onto the LIE and it was weird, there were *no* cars at all, just them and you, and you just kind of glided along behind them like *The Spirit of St. Louis* or something.

Then this weird thing when she stopped, Susan, in the middle of the road and Rachel came flying out the passenger door like she was booted out and Susan took off like a drag racer. Rachel didn't know what to do at first and looked around like she might hitch a ride, but there was no one to hitch a ride from (she couldn't see you, who'd stopped too, white as the 'Vette was, 'cause there was no moon or anything and no lights on that part of the LIE and the only reason you could see her was your eyes were more used to the dark and she had that pale, pale skin and blond hair), so she started walking and you drove along slow after her and after a while there was the Jeep with its lights out sitting on the side of the road and Rachel walked up to it and got in.

Suffolk, Nassau, Queens, and you were listening to a Bruce special on NEW-FM, where Rock lives, which meant that there is a

God 'cause otherwise you'd have been asleep at the wheel, singing along, loud, singing "Incident on 57th Street" and "Dancing in the Dark" and "4th of July, Asbury Park" and "Badlands" and "Racing in the Street" and "The River" and "Born in the USA" and "Backstreets" and "Jungleland" and "Jersey Girl" and "Santa Clause Is Coming to Town" and "For You" and "Darkness on the Edge of Town" and "Glory Days" and "Cadillac Ranch" and "Jolé Blon," you and Bruce harmonizing on the last one with Gary U.S. Bonds.

Then all of a sudden, blinka-blinka-blinka, she was getting off, Susan, getting on the southbound Van Wyck, going to Kennedy, not to a long-term parking lot, to a short-term, American Airlines. And Susan and Rachel sashayed into the terminal like they owned it, like they were going into a movie theater, and you thought umm, umm, *umm,* what should I do, and you decided to take a chance on the long-term lot, if you ever needed the car there it'd be and if you didn't, fuck it, it wasn't your car. So you parked it and locked it up, leaving the gun in the trunk, of course, and strolled into the terminal and the first thing you did was hop into a gift shop and buy yourself a hat, anything at all, a nonofficial Mets hat, it turned out, white with blue and red trim, so you could walk around in semidisguise and not have to worry about being spotted before you spotted them.

Which you did, at the ticket counter, carrying a couple of cheap-looking bags they hadn't gone in with, meaning they'd just bought them and probably some clothes and now that you mention it, they'd already changed, 'cause they came in Susan wearing leather and Rachel hardly anything and now they were in kind of dowdy-looking threads, the kind you saw in airport shops and always asked yourself who would wear such a thing and here was your answer: ladies on the lam. Well, lady singular, 'cause Susan wasn't traveling, just Rachel. Going to Miami. In August. Did that tell you anything—like maybe she wanted to be somewhere where she wouldn't run into anybody she knew?

It was a pretty subdued leave-taking. No more huggy-kissy. Susan did most of the talking, the kind of talking she did to you back in Spruce—straight from the shoulder, direct, no bullshit.

Rachel looked a little scared, a little worried, a little like she wished maybe she hadn't let somebody drown in her swimming pool; she also looked a little embarrassed to be wearing such dowdy-looking threads, and kept her eyes down just in case there was a reasonably good-looking guy or something among all the assholes in the pastel golf slacks and pastel golf shirts and pastel golf jackets who might be wondering what a looker like her was doing in threads like that, pastel polyester and all.

That was another thing: she was sitting out there, Rachel, where any asshole in pastel golf slacks and a pastel golf shirt and a pastel golf jacket could get a look at her, not in some VIP lounge. And the reason for that was she wasn't traveling first class, she was traveling steerage with the rest of the peons, like she didn't want to attract any attention, make any fuss, do anything memorable, not even toss her name around. You knew about the name 'cause when you got up to the ticket counter and bought your ticket and they asked you where you wanted to sit and you said next to your business colleague, Miss Phillips, they queried the old computer and told you sorry, sir, but there was no Miss Phillips ticketed on this flight, which meant she was using a *nom de lam.*

And so were you, Mr. Dalton Hammersleigh, who you didn't know whether he was a rock star or a playboy or a former tennis great or a baby mogul or a heir or a scion or a wimp or a newcomer but he was for sure an asshole for leaving his wallet with all his credit cards and six hundred bills under the front seat of his 'Vette. And since it was another forty-five till launch time, you had both the opportunity and the wherewithal to make a few haberdashery purchases yourself: a pair of yellow golf slacks and a turquoise golf shirt and a lime-green golf jacket and a shoulder bag to put your jeans and stuff in and you were such a convincing asshole that you could sit right across from Rachel, practically, and not even worry about her making you, and all you had to worry about was that you didn't accidentally, unintentionally select a seat right next to hers, as it would have been hard to keep her from making you on a trip of such length, but it turned out you had nothing to worry about because she was in the front of the coach section, by the window, and you were as far away as you could get, on the other side of the plane, in the rear, by the other window, with the smokers and the actuaries, who knew that was the place to be in the event of an unscheduled landing in a hard place.

31

"Sir?"

Barnes fell down and down and down from out of a dream of being in bed, in the studio apartment on Ninth Street that smelled of Balducci's, with the cowgirl slut virgin, the lesbian virgin in black, Marie-Christine the homeless French virgin, and Joanna. Then not in bed with them but on a mat that covered the floor of not the studio apartment but a large windowless room, like a... a wrestling room.

Wrestling. There were times when the recollection that he had been consumed by a passion for wrestling struck Barnes with the force of an accusation that he felt like flatly denying. Or perhaps laughing at: *wrest*ling? Hah. But he had wrestled— with passion—through four years of prep school and half his freshman year in college, at which point he had been moved to weigh wrestling against three brand-new consuming passions —drinking, smoking and fucking—and had found wrestling wanting. For a time, to give wrestling the fair shake he thought a long-consuming passion deserved, he had tried to wrestle *and* to drink, smoke and fuck ("Careful you don't get nicotine stains on the mat, Barnes," the coach would say at the beginning of every practice—*every* practice. "On your back again, Barnes? Don't you get enough of that at *night?*" "Careful taking Barnes down, fellows. Don't want to break that bottle in his hip pocket"), but it was no contest. After wrestling—in practice or in a meet; win, lose or draw—he hurt; after drinking, smoking and fucking he felt... blessed.

"Careful you don't get nicotine stains on the mat, Barnes," the coach had said at the beginning of what turned out to be

Barnes's last practice, and Barnes had said, "Fuck you, Coach," and the coach had said, "Turn in your gear, you cocksucker," and Barnes had said, "Eat shit, scumbag," and had done a bump and grind as he pulled off his shoes and socks and his practice suit and tights and jock and made a pile of them in the center of a practice ring and topped the mound off with his ear protectors and his mouthpiece and gave the coach the finger and went to the locker room to dress and hitched a ride downtown and went to a bar near the train station where he drank and smoked and picked up a virgin secretary from Connecticut Mutual whom he fucked in her apartment over an appliance repair shop in Cranford.

Years later, when a Georgetown recruiter asked Barnes why, given his fine interscholastic record, he hadn't wrestled on the varsity in college, he'd said his class load and the demands of a part-time job in the Law School library hadn't left him any time —not even for a consuming passion. The recruiter—was he still at Georgetown? if so, Barnes, when he'd bucked his way to Director, would fire him—hadn't thought to ask the coach to verify Barnes's version.

There had been a coach in the dream, come to think of it—or a very interested spectator whose face filled the glass wall that was one of the room's boundaries, not as in the wrestling room but as in a squash court: Rita. She'd been calling out instructions or encouragement to the cowgirl slut virgin, the lesbian virgin in black, Marie-Christine the homeless French virgin and Joanna, each of whom pulled hard on one of Barnes's limbs.

"Sir?"

"Yes, Collins?"

"It's six-thirty, sir, and still no activity."

Barnes looked at his watch—it was a minute slower than Collins's—and out the window of Collins's Volvo (retrieved from the garage of Collins's mother's apartment house on Gracie Square when they'd returned the Silver Cloud) on Thirty-sixth Street between Park and Madison, where he and Collins had spent the night. The street, the street on which Rita Arroyo lived, was in a neighborhood Barnes didn't have a sense of: it wasn't Kips Bay; it wasn't Murray Hill. Or maybe it was considered the heart of Murray Hill, or of Kips Bay; but that was the point: it didn't *feel* like the heart of anything, or even the outskirts.

The Morgan Library was right here and around the corner was Altman's, and other than that Barnes didn't know anything that was around here except that somewhere around here he had had one of the most perfect moments of his life—maybe *the* most perfect moment. It was nineteen sixty-one, the summer after that freshman year, and after spending a dutiful week in Lake Forest with his parents, he had come to New York to be the houseguest of an old college buddy of his father's and to work in the mailroom of the old college buddy's ad agency (Barnes's social class's version of digging ditches or pumping gas), and (at the top of Barnes's agenda, if nowhere on his parents') to learn real smoking, real drinking and real fucking at the feet of New York's world-class smokers, drinkers and fuckers.

And one hot Saturday afternoon, going in to the office to help cope with some deadline emergency, flush from a morning fuck with a virgin stewardess he'd met and smoked and drunk with and fucked the night before, walking down Madison Avenue somewhere around here, Barnes saw Jackie Robinson. He wore a light gray business suit and carried a briefcase; he walked—in his trademark pigeon-toed way—with two other men in business suits, one of whom was talking animatedly while Jackie Robinson and the other listened. Jackie Robinson looked up at young John Barnes approaching, saw that young John Barnes recognized him, and understood full well—this was the perfect part—*his* obligation to honor the contract that was in force here, to do some barter, to acknowledge that he who had discerned a star was in his way a star himself. Jackie Robinson nodded at young John Barnes and said in his trademark high-pitched voice, "Hi. How you doing?" then looked away again and picked up the thread of the conversation he'd let momentarily go.

Jackie Robinson.

"Sir?"

"Yes, Collins?"

"I've been doing some thinking, sir, about Agent Van Meter's peril. Not Susan Van Meter's, but her husband's."

"How do you know he sent a peril, Collins?"

"It's the scuttlebutt, sir."

"And what's your estimate of the credibility of the scuttlebutt?"

"It's low, sir, and I'd ignore it if I hadn't seen the agent both when out to play and around the shop. I observed certain differences—the wristwatch, the glasses, the hair. But if you'll deny that he sent a peril, I'll withdraw my speculation and apologize for being out of line in formulating it."

Barnes heard that it was a future contrary-to-fact condition and smiled. 'You're good, Collins."

Collins nodded once—his thanks and his concurrence. "He seemed to be telling us to be vigilant for someone who's left-handed, gay, wears contact lenses, and combs his hair straight back.'

"Sound like anyone you know?" Barnes said. "Anyone conveniently located?"

"Agent Arroyo often wears her hair pulled back."

Barnes laughed. "Except when she wears it loose. And she's not left-handed."

"No, sir. I'm aware of that, sir."

"I'm left-handed, Collins."

"I'm aware of that too, sir."

"Of course you are, Collins. You're aware of every conveniently located left-hander on the eighty-ninth-floor—and not a few in Georgetown. What else are you aware of, Jack? And what do you make of it?"

Collins seemed to glow at being addressed by his given name. "Well, sir, I know you recall what I said previously—that I believed Agent Van Meter's fairy tale homosexuality was devised for the benefit of the Phillips woman, that it was intended to preclude intimacy. That may have been true—it very likely was —but I think that there's another element to it. I think it was intended to point us—the recipients of the peril, that is—toward a woman."

207

"A rather imprecise point, Jack," Barnes said. "So that we would look for a woman, Van Meter pretended to be a fag?"

Collins made a sound of polite amusement, but his voice stayed cool, almost cold. "An unequivocal point—the agent's adopting a fairy tale transvestism, say—would've been so blatant that the individual being pointed at would've taken steps to eradicate the peril before it could acquire any readers. I've been studying some of your cases, sir; the imprecise peril is a salient feature of your handwriting. And of course everyone knows that Agent Van Meter was your pupil."

"A prize pupil," Barnes said.

"Yes, sir."

"As was his wife."

"Yes, sir."

"And as was Agent Arroyo."

"Yes, sir."

"Let's go upstairs, Jack. It's time."

"Yes, sir."

32

"I shouldn't *krechtz,* Suzie, you being an *almona,* a widow and all. But you did *what?* Sprang Carrie and whacked 'two of' Cool D's sidemen? If that's so, then you may have made a serious *bulba,* a fuck-up."

Susan, being a widow and all, pouted. Aaronson got up out of his big leather swivel chair and came from behind his big oak desk to console her. But she got past him and sat in the chair herself and leaned back and smiled. "What kind of *bulba,* Henry?"

Aaronson pretended that it didn't matter to him that she'd taken his seat, and his edge. "Don't misunderstand: I am delighted that your daughter, the *mazik,* is safe, and I have no personal fondness for the sidemen you say you whacked. I am not even particularly upset at the absence of authorization; sometimes you do what you got to do when you got to do it, regardless of the availability of the brass. What is disturbing to me, Suzie, is the fundamental misunderstanding of the situation that your actions betray.

"For instance, in speaking of Cool D's sidemen, it is no longer accurate to say 'two of'; one says the two and only, Suzie, on account of Cool D, although once upon a time a big *macher,* is now just another nobody, who has watched the bottom fall out of his immediate world, leaving him with no longer two of many sidemen, but *only* two sidemen, the remainder of his once-upon-a-time sizable contingent having departed in the wake of D's *nuchshlepper,* Lionel, getting whacked by the *shikseh* who whacked Paul, *alav ha-sholom,* or with the same piece at any rate, and D's beloved Shiraz, *aleha ha-shalom,* also getting whacked, as I am sure you have heard even though you have been in deep, and probably also heard the MO, which was horrible.

"Suzie, having been on the job and having some experience, you should know this: an individual such as Cool D at this point in time is about this far away from going on sale at rock-bottom prices. His outlook on the present is that it does not offer him much to sustain or please him; he sees *bubkes* in his future— not even *bubkes, makkes;* the only thing he has that's worth anything to him or anybody else is his past—some names, some dates, some memorabilia. Someone contacts him, says you could use a friend, D, here are a few yards with which to make ends meet, in exchange for which and in response to things that we will ask you, you will tell us certain things that are of interest to us, and in addition to which and on your own initiative, you will tell us certain things that based on your long experience in this particular field of endeavor you will deem to be of interest to us—without our even having to ask.

"What I'm saying, Suzie, is that everything you see here—the office, the furnishings, the books and such, the address, you come right down to it, the location, the part of town, the particular neighborhood—all of it represents the careful construction over a number of years of a fairy tale of considerable distinction, one that I think it is fair to say has outlasted if not outshone any erected during that same period of time by any individual either directly or indirectly connected with the New York shop, a fairy tale that you, by such actions as removing from the custody of even onetime hitters even people who happen to be your daughter—I was closely monitoring the situation, Suzie; I was not about to allow your daughter to come to harm—such as whacking the sidemen of even onetime hitters; such as even fucking *being* here, you are royally fucking up and threatening to undo."

Susan looked up from picking with a thumbnail at the edge of the desktop. "Are you finished, Henry?"

Finished was what Aaronson felt like—not finished as in *done for,* but as in *over with, past.* With her shorn head, Susan looked like a teenaged androgyne. But it wasn't her youthfulness that told him that something—an era, a time, *his* time—had come to an end (and, in fact, Susan didn't look particularly fresh; she was strung out, overextended); it was the indifference in her eyes. She knew who he was, but who he was was of no interest to her; he was a tool to be used in some task and if he wasn't the right tool he would be discarded for one that was. He was finished. "Yeah," he said. *"Mechuleh."*

The Hudson looked like bile. The houseboat was lifeless, all its blinds drawn.

"A *meshuggeneh* idea you coming here, Suzie," Aaronson said. *"Alevai,* he'll make nice."

"Knock," Susan said.

Aaronson knocked in code and Cool D cracked open the door, his Beretta held up under his chin.

Susan stood where he could see her plainly. "I'm Susan Saint Michael. I sprang the girl and whacked your sidemen."

Aaronson got a shoulder in front of her and waved his hands. "Make nice, D. We just want to talk to you. I told her I thought it was a *meshuggeneh* idea."

Susan took Aaronson by the elbow and turned him away from the door. "Wait in the park, Henry."

"Uh, Suzie—no offense, D; I know you'll make nice—but I think that's an even more *meshuggeneh* idea. Look at all the trouble Reagan got into that time in Iceland, meeting face-to-face with whatshisname. You always need a third party on hand to, you know, explain some of the more complicated issues, make coffee and stuff."

"Be a *mensh,* Henry," Cool D said, "and wait in the park." He stepped aside to let Susan in the door, then closed it in Aaronson's face.

Aaronson stared at the door for a long time, then went up to wait in the park.

Cool D pulled out a bentwood dining chair for Susan. *"Would* you care for coffee?"

She smiled. "Please."

From the kitchen, Cool D said, "Some of the most extravagantly weird shit I've ever seen is going down."

She sat. "It won't seem so weird when it's over."

"Meaning things never do?"

"Meaning there's a logic to it that you can't see yet."

Cool D brought two mugs to the table. "Milk and sugar?"

"Nothing, thanks."

Cool D sat.

"I was sorry to hear about Shiraz," Susan said. "Rachel Phillips, the woman who probably whacked her, and certainly whacked your sideman Lionel, also whacked my husband—the girl's, Carrie's father."

Cool D held his mug in both hands and blew on it. "The bitch who whacked Lionel whacked the man. You're saying your husband was the man?"

Susan nodded.

"And you?"

Susan nodded.

D took a delicate sip. "Some weird shit, sitting down to coffee with the man."

Susan smiled.

"Some weird shit because Susan Saint Michael's not the man; she's a hitter. She's tight with the bitch who whacked Lionel, who's sucking up to Lorca."

"Which is why you snatched Carrie," Susan said. "Because Rachel Phillips has been walking all over you and you thought snatching the daughter of someone tight with her would be a way back at her. Or did you really think that, D? It doesn't sound like something a hitter with his head on straight would think. It sounds like amateur night."

"Where's Rachel Phillips right now?" D said, too indifferently.

"Who told you Carrie was Susan Saint Michael's daughter?" Susan said, "Who told you Susan Saint Michael was tight with Rachel Phillips? Who told you Rachel Phillips's name?"

"She here in town?"

"Who, D?"

"Is Henry the man too?"

"There's no man anymore, D, no hitters, no them, no us. It's all one big stew and we're all in it and a lot of us're going to sink and a few of us're going to swim. No one's going to make it

212

alone, so the trick's going to be to choose your friends carefully and watch your ass at all times. . . . Who?"

After a long time, Cool D said, "A woman."

"Who's given you useful information before?"

"Yeah. A lot."

"In exchange for what?"

"A little pressure here on somebody or other, a little help there moving this or that."

"How does she contact you?"

"She calls here or calls my apartment and asks for a contribution to the Police Athletic League. If it's safe and convenient, I say I'll give a hundred dollars and after an hour I go to a booth on Riverside Drive or one on Morningside Drive near my apartment and wait for her call. If I say I'm sorry, I can't afford a donation, she calls me the next day."

"And how do you contact her?"

"I call a number connected to an answering machine. There's no outgoing message on the machine; it just beeps. She calls me back and we go through the bit with the PAL and the phone booths."

Susan took out a pad and pencil and set them in front of him.

He wrote down the number and tore the slip of paper from the pad, but kept it in his hand. "For this do I get Rachel Phillips?"

"No. I get her."

Cool D snorted. "What *do* I get?"

"Someone inside my organization's running Rachel. I have a pretty good idea the same individual's running the woman who calls you about the PAL. So you're being diddled on both sides, D, and what you'll get is you'll have a better idea whom to trust."

"That won't bring back Shiraz," D said.

"That won't bring back Shiraz."

D folded the slip in two and handed it to Susan.

She put it in her pocket, along with the pad and pencil "Thanks."

"Sorry about your husband."

"Yeah."

"Be square."

"Thanks."

213

"Tell Henry, uh, adios, I guess."
"Yeah."
"Who'd've thought it?"
"So long, D."

33

"Say good night, Gracie," Susan said, and aimed her thirty-eight at Grace Lewis's face.

Grace closed her front door enough to unhook the chain, then opened it and walked with her back to Susan, Sayles and Aaronson to the center of her vast loft, bright even at twilight.

"Nice place." Susan holstered the gun and strolled after Grace, her hands in the hip pockets of her jeans. "Nice name, I thought that day in the back of the limo. Nice voice, nice body, nice face, nice clothes. Nice occupation, I thought, having no reason to think at the time that you weren't a marine biologist. You've met Mister Sayles, and this is Mister Aaronson.

"Say *shalom*, Henry, to Grace Lewis, née Foley, formerly of the San Francisco shop. Grace hung up her badge back in eighty-three, got married, tried to have some kids. Things didn't take and the marriage came apart—I don't mean to sound catty, Grace; I'm just trying to give these gentlemen the picture—and Grace let her boss, Vic Verona, know she wanted to go back on the job. There were no openings at the moment, but coincidentally, Vic had just gotten off the phone with his old marine buddy Paul Van Meter, who was looking for someone with experience but with an unmakeable face—unmakeable here in the East, that is—to do a job for him—a job off the books. When Paul got killed, Grace had to take a fall. She's out on bail at the moment."

"Charmed," Aaronson said.

Grace crossed her arms.

"Let's run through this quickly," Susan said. "The boyfriend, Kenny, was recruited too, probably also from the West Coast, but you're not sure from exactly where because you'd never seen him before, yes?"

215

A nod.

"The sailboat was an off-the-books loan from Suffolk County Narcotics, probably—seized from a hitter. The so-called Kenny's so-called parents with the house on Shelter Island were—what? —a retired Suffolk cop and his wife? Some ex-storyteller from the New York shop and his? A couple of patriots who couldn't turn down an appeal to help the good guys trick the bad guys? You don't know and it doesn't really matter. Nor does it matter who used to live in this place—some dealer to the downtown art and soda crowd, or one of his clientele.

"All that matters is that you and Kenny trolled a bar in Hampton Bays until Kit Bolton swam in and you told him how much you liked sailing and making money and he suggested you acquaint yourselves with the joys of smuggling. You and Kenny would stop in Hampton Bays on Friday night for groceries and a heavy manila envelope; you'd rendezvous on Saturday night, Sunday morning, with cigarettes or cabin cruisers with no names, no home ports, just two or three or four Hispanics with ski masks who'd give you ten or fifteen wrapped and sealed bales in exchange for your envelope; you'd spend the night at so-called Kenny's so-called parents' and take the first ferry to Greenport Monday morning; at the gas station near the bridge, someone would unload the van, you'd drive out with your share in another envelope in the back under the carpeting. All that went down, yes, Grace?"

A nod.

"What didn't go down is you didn't drive in one Monday without Kenny; and you weren't followed by someone in a red compact who was waiting downstairs when you got home and knew you liked a piece of mint in your iced tea and wanted you to work for him and make you eat soda or horse when you said you wouldn't; and there was no doctor in Brooklyn and you didn't fuck Kit Bolton or any of his friends or the so-called Charles; and you didn't have an accident on the LIE, you staged one—you and Kenny, who didn't freak out and go to Florida when he heard about the so-called Charles, because the so-called Charles was running you both in an operation to find someone conveniently located who went rogue. And what a piece of bad luck, Grace, to stage an accident and get busted and then find out that that same day the author of your fairy tale was out getting killed.

"But God, you're good, Grace, because I believed every bit of it, and so did Mister Sayles, and everybody else who heard it, and you're so good that you kept on taking the fall, you never whined or complained or whimpered even after you heard that Paul—that Charles—was dead, because you knew that if you did, you ran the risk of whining or complaining or whimpering to the someone conveniently located who went rogue. You should get a medal or something, Grace. You should get ten medals. Who went your bail? The so-called Kenny?"

She shook her head. "The rule was that either of us should roll up our end of it if there was a malfunction."

"Kit, then?"

A nod.

"Kit's dead."

Grace turned. "You?"

"No. His so-called friends. He was *in*conveniently located. And so are you, Grace. Stay indoors until you hear from us. No deliveries, no meter readers, no strangers. Stay away from windows. Someone conveniently located may figure out what we figured out and on the chance we haven't already figured it may want to shut you permanently up. There'll be baby-sitters on your doorstep round the clock. If you want to communicate with us, CQ with your bathroom light switch. Questions?"

Grace shook her head.

"I have one," Susan said. "Charles Fuller Nelson. Does it mean anything to you? Does it stand for anything, or is it just a name?"

Grace shook her head.

Susan went to Grace and put her right hand on her left cheek. "I know it's been tough on you waiting for things to work themselves out. I'm sorry I've been a little brusque, but I'm sure you can understand that I'm as upset to find out you were working with my husband behind my back as I was when I thought you were fucking him." She slapped Grace hard. "Bitch. . . . Let's go, gentlemen."

Tears welled up in Grace's eyes, but she chewed her lip and didn't weep.

Aldrich kept both hands on the composite drawing while turning it to show to Susan, as if he weren't entirely satisfied with it, didn't want to be held accountable for it. "This is what the artist came up with, based on what the liquor store owner said about the guy who bought the Cutty Sark the night the homeless guy Morgan died. The liquor store owner noticed that the guy who bought the Cutty Sark was left-handed."

Gently but inflexibly, Susan slid the portrait out from under Aldrich's fingertips. "His shirt, is it woven or knit?"

Aldrich tipped back his head and looked at the drawing through his half-glasses. "Woven or knit? I don't know if it's woven or knit. I know it's short-sleeved. The guy who bought the Cutty Sark was carrying some kind of coat over his arm. The liquor store owner couldn't describe it, except it was like a sport coat. But I don't know if the shirt's woven or knit."

"Was there an insignia on the shirt—an animal, a design?"

"I don't know. The liquor store owner didn't say."

Susan pulled the phone across Aldrich's desk and put it in front of him. "Call him and ask."

Susan went out into the hall and drank cup after cup of water from the cooler until she saw through the glass partition that Aldrich had hung up the phone. She came back in and shut the door and stood over Aldrich's desk. "Yes?"

"The liquor store owner's not sure," Aldrich said, "but he thinks there was something on the guy who bought the Cutty Sark's shirt, one of those little animals or something. You got anything against telling me what any of this has got to do with anything?"

But Susan was already heading out the door.

"She always like that?" Aldrich said.

"Like what?" Sayles said.

"You know, jumpy."

"Have a nice day, Chief," Aaronson said.

"You smartass fed fucks are doing it again, aren't you?" Aldrich said.

*　　　*　　　*

Aaronson drove. Sayles rode shotgun. Susan sat in the back.

"Charles Fuller Nelson," Susan said.

"Who, Suze?" Sayles said. "Oh, yeah—Paul's fairy tale name."

"It's a strange name," Susan said. "Old-fashioned. Ever see *Citizen Kane?*"

"Sure, yeah. You've seen it, haven't you, Henry?"

Aaronson shook his head. "I've been out to play for the last fifty, sixty years. Haven't had much time to go to the movies."

"The protagonist's name was Charles Foster Kane," Susan said. "He was pompous, arrogant, vainglorious. But if Paul was pointing us to someone, the name's just confusing. The shop, Georgetown —they're full of pompous, arrogant, vainglorious people."

"To me," Sayles said, "the name sounds like that actor who's not really an actor, he's just on game shows, like *Hollywood Squares*. Charles Nelson Reilly. My mother loves Charles Nelson Reilly. She loves *Family Feud* and *Sale of the Century* and *The Price is Right* and *Hundred Thousand Dollar Pyramid* and *Wheel of Fortune* and so on and so forth, but most of all she loves *Hollywood Squares* when Charles Nelson Reilly is on it. You know who I'm talking about, Henry?"

"No. No, I don't," Aaronson said. "I've been out to play. We don't watch much television when we're out to play."

"Tell me about the alligator man, Red," Susan said.

"Who? Oh, yeah. Morgan, the homeless eyewitness. Like I told you, I went looking for Morgan to follow up on the sunglass thing, but I did it too late, he'd had his four bottles of Cutty by the time I got there and so on and so forth. One of Morgan's buddies said Morgan was afraid someone was going to kill him, someone Morgan called the alligator man. I asked Barnes if he wanted me to follow up on it and he said he thought it was a dead end."

"Were those his words?"

"I'm not sure if they were his words. I'd have to think about it. I had two separate phone conversations with Barnes about Morgan. The first time I called Barnes at the shop from the street and told him Morgan was dead and asked if I should try to make anything out of Morgan's buddy saying Morgan didn't drink Scotch. Barnes

219

said he thought it was a dead end, so those were his words, yeah, as far as that was concerned. I also told Barnes that Morgan's buddy said Morgan was afraid somebody was going to kill him and Barnes said again he thought it was a dead end—in those words. I also told Barnes that Morgan's buddy said Morgan called the guy he was afraid of the alligator man, and Barnes said come back to the shop, which is just another way of saying it's a dead end, isn't it? And anyway, why aren't we looking for Rita, Susan?"

"What about the second time?" Susan said.

"The second time I called from the shop to a restaurant where Barnes was having lunch. I called to tell him Aldrich called and said his scoshes found out where Morgan bought his booze, that he never bought any Cutty, that the night Morgan died a guy came in the store and bought four fifths of Cutty, a guy the owner never saw before, never saw again, the guy whose picture we just looked at and so on and so forth. And you're thinking what, Susan—that Morgan called the guy he was afraid of alligator man because he wore those, you know, preppy shirts with the alligators on them?"

"Crocodiles. René Lacoste"—Susan made her voice pompous, arrogant, vainglorious—"the great French tennis player, was called *le Crocodile,* so doesn't logic dictate that the shirts that bear his name also bear as their insignia not an alligator, as most of humanity would have it, but a crocodile? . . . That's from a lecture I received on preppy haberdashery by John Barnes, who should know."

Sayles snorted. "John can be a ballbreaker at times about things like that."

They were quiet for a while. Then Aaronson said, "The time you called Barnes at a restaurant, Red, was the restaurant Trees?"

"Matter of fact, it was. Why?"

"'Cause I was eating lunch with him when you called, that's why. When Barnes said 'Meet me at Trees,' I thought he was saying 't'ree's,' like, you know, 'Two's company, t'ree's a crowd.'"

"What were you two doing at Trees?" Susan said.

"Eating lunch, talking shoptalk. It was right after Shiraz got whacked, *aleha ha-shalom,* he wanted to know more about it, about the spark-up between Cool D and Lorca. He left early, after Red called. I don't know how I knew it was Red, I just did. He didn't tell me it was you, Red, he just said he had to go back to the office. He left by the back way."

Susan sat forward, her arms on the seat. "Why?"

Aaronson shrugged. "I don't know, he just did. He took the phone call, came back to the table, left some money to pay the tab, asked the waiter if there was a back way out."

"Where was the phone?" Susan said.

"Bar."

"Was there anyone at the bar?"

"A bartender and one customer."

"A man?"

"Yup."

"Describe him."

"Mid to late thirties, five ten, one seventy, tanned skin, short brown hair parted on the right, a brush mustache, light blue shirt with a white collar and white cuffs, maroon paisley tie, tan poplin double-breasted suit, maroon pocket square, navy polka dot suspenders, brown kiltie loafers, beige socks, a copper bracelet on his right wrist, a watch on his left—gold or gold-plated case, smooth brown leather strap, white face, black classic numerals: a Movado, maybe."

Sayles laughed. "You didn't get a very good look at him, did you, Henry?"

"Didn't need to," Aaronson said. "I already knew him. So did Barnes."

Susan and Sayles waited.

"Alan Madden," Aaronson said.

221

34

Miami Beach.

Far fucking out.

Not the big mother hotel part, the old part, the run-down, hung down, funky part, the part that wasn't so far gone that it couldn't have a renaissance—or even a Renaissance—if people were so inclined. But being people, being money-hungry bad-assed land-grabbers, what they were more inclined to do was bulldoze it and pave it over and build more big mother hotels and high-rise condos and fuck the senior citizens and the niggers and the *Marielitos* and make way for the heavy hitters and the heavy hitter fuckers (and for that matter for the rock stars and playboys and former tennis greats and baby moguls and heirs and scions and wimps and newcomers and their respective fuckers) and their cabin cruisers and their wheels.

But so far, none of that. So far, they've just fixed up a couple of funky old hotels, three- and four-story, one of which was where they made some Sinatra movie a hundred years ago. Nice places, art deco and all, or so everybody says, though you don't know art deco from Art Gecko—the name (the damn clever name, you thought) you gave the lizard that lives in your room on the third floor of one of the hotels (not the one where they made the Sinatra movie; the one across the street, the one that has an alley behind it that you're pretty sure was the alley Don Johnson was standing in on the album cover of the record he made around the time he went from wearing light-colored clothes to wearing dark-colored clothes—not the worst record in musical history and not likely to be, as long as Barry Manilow was still turning them out, but certainly a, uh, indulgence).

Summertime and the living is easy. Up at five to beat the heat, a run on the beach down to Government Cut and back, some yoga in the little park in front of the hotel, upstairs for a shower, dress in shorts and flip-flops and an I Heart Miami Beach T-shirt 'cause it's already starting to be hot as a bitch and slip on your Wayfarers and stroll over to Washington Avenue to get a paper and eat breakfast at Jerome's.

Jerome's isn't the name of the place, but you think of it as Jerome's 'cause the counterman's name is Jerome and he's the only one around at that hour and he makes decent-to-good scrambled eggs, which—let's face it—is an art. Jerome says he's an actor and he even has a framed eight-by-ten glossy up behind the counter, but the fact is Jerome is a stone psycho killer (of the thin-as-a-snake variety, the fat-as-a-pig variety being the only other variety) if ever you have seen one.

You confirm this by asking Jerome if he knows where you can get a gun and he doesn't say why or the fuck're you asking him for or anything, he just says how much do you want to spend. Being basically a pacific guy and hating loud noises, you don't know all that much about guns, but you do know that if you spend twenty-nine ninety-five or thereabouts you will get a gun that will explode in your face when you pull the trigger or even if you don't. Furthermore, you still have about four hundred of the six hundred bills that Dalton Hammersleigh, the asshole, left in his wallet under the front seat of his 'Vette, along with the key in the ignition—still have it not 'cause you've been scrimping but 'cause you've been mostly using the credit cards Dalton Hammersleigh also left in his wallet, the asshole. Therefore, you tell stone psycho killer Jerome that you will spend as much as a yard and a half, and he tells you for a yard and a half he can get you a Smith & Wesson .38-caliber double-action revolver, which you like the sound of 'cause you may not have made much of your life, but you have learned to appreciate brand names.

After breakfast you stroll over to Flamingo Park and sit in the shade of a bougainvillea or some fucking thing and read the paper—not the *Miami Herald* or the *Miami Beach Mortician* or whatever it's called but the *New York Times*, which you get out of a

223

vending machine on the corner of Washington and Espanola and which you figure is more likely than the *Miami Herald* or the *Miami Beach Mortician* to have news of Kit Bolton drowning in Rachel Phillips's swimming pool in Southampton, Suffolk County, Long Island, New York, while wearing a visored basinet helmet and a bunch of other shit that you've already forgotten the names of 'cause your heart was never in armorology in the first place.

And there's no such news, which can mean only one thing, which is that even with everybody running and screaming and leaping in their wheels and stalling out or smashing into someone or backing into someone else or turning into someone else, then tear-assing for the main gate and scraping through two at a time and going left and right and straight even if it meant left into something or right into something or straight into something—even with all that, *someone* did a pretty thorough job of housecleaning and lip-sealing.

If that's the case, why the fuck is Rachel turning into a junkie five-to-eight-trick-a-night hooker?

Oh, that's right—you forgot to mention that you and Rachel are neighbors these days, what with her living at the hotel right next to yours (not the one where they made a Sinatra movie, either; the one on the other side) and occupying a room that from your window you can see almost everything that goes on inside even without using binoculars. Stone psycho killer Jerome got the binoculars for you at a store he says his friend, Leon, works at in the Lincoln Road Mall for he says a double saw. A double saw would be a bargain, 'cause you went in the store and checked the binoculars out and they cost a yard, but you think stone psycho killer Jerome kept the double saw and lifted the binoculars 'cause no Leon works in that store, Arabs do.

Rachel doesn't get up till noon or so, so you get to finish reading the paper without rushing and sometimes you watch the little Jewish guys with barrel chests and arms like gorillas play handball for a while and then you go back to your hotel—it's starting to get so hot now it's hard to breathe—and take a little nap and then it's time to see what Rachel's up to.

The same old shit. Every day, like clockwork, she wakes up, makes a cup of coffee in the coffeemaker in her room just like the one in your room, sits at the window (not the window you can see through but the window looking out over the ocean; she's got a corner room, with cross-ventilation and an ocean view) and looks out over the water, drinks maybe half the cup, then does two lines of soda, masturbates, using just her hand, no vibrator or anything, coming like it's work almost (you can hear her sometimes, if the wind's from the south, unh, unh, *unnnnnh*), and takes a shower. (What being a five-to-eight-trick-a-night hooker and still wanting or needing to masturbate every morning means you don't even want to think about.)

Rachel dries her hair with a comb sitting by the window, looking at a magazine or sometimes a book, and then she has a room service lunch (you know that 'cause she gets up and goes away from the window and in just a couple of seconds she's back with a tray of sandwiches and stuff and a pitcher of iced tea or something) and after lunch she takes a nap or reads or watches TV or something—you can't tell and you don't really give a shit 'cause it's what Rachel does at night that interests you and anyway it's time to go to the dog track.

You walk down Ocean or sometimes Collins, giving a wide berth to the *Marielitos*, to the Kennel Club and you don't go in the main gate, you go around the back 'cause you're not here to watch a bunch of greyhounds chase a toy rabbit, you're here to try and get to first base with Darby. You're a sucker for women with names like Darby, especially when they have straight blond hair that they pin up in a kind of loose bun in the back but you know comes down to their asses and wear blue jeans and bush shirts and desert boots and say *Wayne Gretzky* and *vitiated* in the same sentence, which she did the night you met her, coming out of the movie theater in the Lincoln Road Mall where she'd just seen *Tin Men*.

You were at the ticket window and said any good? and she said go for it, which is an expression you hate but you could tell she hates it too and was just saying it 'cause it didn't matter what she said to some jerk who was hitting on her. You said you didn't think you would go for it because you'd fallen for her and she rolled her eyes and walked down the mall toward Collins and you followed after her and convinced her that letting you buy her an ice cream cone at Denny's wouldn't constitute any kind of legal contract between you or anything. You sat on a planter or some fucking thing and talked till every store on the mall closed, talked about things you'd never talked to any woman about before. Like hockey, which was when she said Wayne Gretzky is not the greatest hockey player ever 'cause hockey is the sport most vitiated by expansion, having twenty-one teams where there used to be six. She wouldn't let you take her home, she took a cab, but before she did she said she wasn't going to fuck you till she knew a hell of a lot more about you than it was clear to her you were willing to tell—not that she told you how she knew so much about hockey, just for example, and wouldn't even answer when you asked if she was Canadian, though you don't think she is 'cause she doesn't say *oot* and *aboot*.

She's a dog handler, Darby, and without saying the races're fixed she told you to save your money. You don't mind 'cause you're not a betting man, but you'd bet the ranch if it'd get you to first base with Darby. As it is, you don't know whether you're halfway to first with her, or not even out of the batter's box, or still in the on-deck circle, or down in the dugout.

On the one hand, somehow, for some reason you can't possibly imagine and she won't tell you, she knows stone psycho killer Jerome, and when you made the mistake of letting slip that you know him too she gave you a look like *you* were a stone psycho killer and stood as much chance of getting to first base with her as you did of being President. On the other hand, one day after the races she slipped a hand in a hip pocket of your jeans and let you slip yours in a hip pocket of hers and walked with you that way along Collins and showed you something you'd never noticed, around Seventh or Eighth or Ninth Street, a store, a *bodega,* with a homemade sign on it that she said was her favorite sign in the whole world, sometimes it makes her happier than she's ever been and sometimes it makes her sadder, and it says

BEER

SODA

SADWISHES

and anybody who would share something with you that was that important to them must be going to let you get to first base, don't you think?

What Rachel does at night:

In a word, she dresses like a junkie five-to-eight-trick-a-night hooker and works the big mother hotels farther up the beach, which is even more pathetic than it sounds 'cause remember this is summertime and the living may be easy for you but in the hotel biz it's the off-season 'cause the only time you can go on the beach without getting microwaved is before the sun comes up or after it goes down, which makes it hard to get a tan (the reason people come to Miami Beach in the first place) and the town is one big vacancy—*chambres à louer,* as Darby says, liking to spice up her conversation with a French phrase now and then, having lived in France for a time but under what circumstances she won't tell you (which means it was with a guy).

Traveling salesmen, lounge lizards, off-duty cops, airline pilots, airline *stewards,* fifth-rate nightclub comics, bass players in the fifth-rate bands that back the fifth-rate singers who open for the fifth-rate comics, mobsters, slumming millionaires, thin-as-a-snake and fat-as-a-pig stone psycho killers, Cuban hitters, Haitian ounce men, Arab arms dealers, jockeys, caddies, chauffeurs—these are Rachel's customers: half a yard a poke, for a yard Rachel gets all the way undressed.

You know the rates 'cause you asked stone psycho killer Jerome to ask Rachel's pimp, Warren the ratfuck with a face like a Clearasil test strip, who is another old friend of stone psycho killer Jerome's (which raises some unsettling questions about what Darby handled before she handled dogs at the Kennel Club). Stone psycho killer Jerome thinks Rachel is your old girlfriend from someplace like Stark or Apalachicola or Valdosta who ran out on you and came to fabulous Miami Beach to make her fame and fortune, otherwise why would you be spying on her with binoculars and asking her rates? He thinks that when you have rubbed your face enough in Rachel being a junkie five-to-eight-trick-a-night hooker you're going to whack Warren the ratfuck with your Smith & Wesson .38-caliber double-action revolver and whack Rachel too and then yourself. It is a measure of the kind of friend stone psycho killer Jerome is to Warren the ratfuck that he doesn't tell him that his days may be numbered, the reason being that if you do whack Warren the ratfuck and Rachel and yourself, Jerome will undoubtedly cop the Smith & Wesson .38-caliber double-action revolver and be up a yard and a half.

Little does stone psycho killer Jerome know how much you're enjoying watching Rachel be a junkie five-to-eight-trick-a-night hooker; enjoying watching her stagger around in her red stiletto heels and black net stockings and black Egyptian-style wig and her red Chantilly lace camisole and matching elbow-length gloves and black leather miniskirt; enjoying watching Warren the ratfuck glom her and slap her around and yell at her; enjoying seeing the track marks on her arm when the gloves slip down, which they have a way of doing when you're so zonked you don't care what you look like, meaning the soda she snorts for breakfast is just the first course in a day devoted to serious pharmacology; enjoying following her into the drugstore in the Lincoln Road Mall and watching her try to remember where they keep the Preparation H 'cause that's what she and the other junkie hookers use to shrink the track marks; enjoying seeing the bloodlessness of her face when she comes out into the microwave sun after turning a matinee trick, or seeing the fear that comes into her eyes when some greaseball flicks his finger at her and puts his hand on her ass and slobbers something in her ear and she has to look like it's the funniest thing she's ever heard, or the sexiest; enjoying walking right up to her sometimes like you're checking her out, knowing she won't recognize you 'cause you look different with the tan you're getting even though the sun's like a microwave and with your Wayfarers and your shorts and your I Heart Miami Beach

T-shirt or your baggy white painter's pants and Hawaiian shirt that you wear sometimes and your crew cut that you got 'cause it's too hot to have long hair—checking her out, looking her up and down, then making a face like you may be a guy who has to pay for it but you're not so hard up that you need a junkie five-to-eight-trick-a-night hooker.

35

"Alan Madden?"

"Yes?"

"Keep the nice smile on your face and get in the back of the red Plymouth."

"Or what?" Madden said. "You shoot me in the kneecaps and I spend the rest of my life on crutches wondering who *was* that woman?"

"The red Plymouth."

"I have a luncheon appointment. Would you mind if I just stepped inside the Russian Tea Room and left a message for my guest?"

"I canceled your lunch for you, Alan. Get in the red Plymouth or I'll shoot your balls off."

Madden laughed and got in. Susan got in after him. "Let's go to the park, Henry."

"Well, hello, Henry," Madden said. "It's been ages."

"Alan."

Madden shifted to look at Susan. "And I remember now— you're Susan Van Meter."

Aaronson went east on Fifty-seventh, north on Sixth.

"You do due diligence work these days, Alan," Susan said. "Your clients are law firms whose clients are corporations that're targets of unfriendly acquisition attempts. Your job is to abort those attempts by finding out things about the raiders that they'd rather you didn't—undisclosed litigation, sweetheart arrangements, connections with organized crime. You talk to former employees whose severance was less than amicable, to competitors, to suppliers, to customers. You're not above using paid informants, clandestine photography, graphological analysis—probably, even, the odd burglary. The target company lets it be known that unless the raider desists, it has a moral obligation to reveal what you've found out. Ideally, arrangements can be made."

"I dig up old shit, yes," Madden said, "for people to rub in other people's faces."

"And do it very successfully, is the point," Susan said. "A-town-house-on-Saint-Luke's-Place-a-house-in-Sag-Harbor-another-in-Barbados-a-Benz-and-a-supercharged-Blazer-with-halo-gen-lights-on-the-roof-and-a-winch-on-the-front-bumper successfully."

A Dixieland band played at the foot of the Mall. "I've done well, yes," Madden said. "And this little drive is to remind me how transient it all is, how unhappy my clients would be to hear that there's a blot on *my* escutcheon."

"You were fired from a top-security government job because you're a homosexual, Alan—let's not fog up the car. In light of recent dispatches from the medical front, yours isn't the world's favorite sexual preference—never mind Wall Street's. It didn't make a ripple at the time; we intend to splash it all over the fronts of at least the business pages."

"Unless?"

"Unless you tell us what you said to John Barnes at Trees."

"Then that *was* you, Henry," Madden said. "I don't see well from a distance these days without my glasses and I didn't think it would do to make a closer inspection."

"Be good, Alan. Just answer the question."

Conservatory Pond on the right. On the left, the Lake. "I said, in effect, 'Remember me?'"

"And?" Susan said.

"He said he didn't."

"And then?"

"And then he went back to his table."

"In fact, Alan, he went out the back door."

"Did he? The client I was meeting showed up just then and we were seated in another part of the restaurant."

"Why did he, Alan?"

231

"I have no idea."

"Why do you think?"

"I think I shouldn't say anything further without the advice of counsel."

Susan laughed. "Alan, we left due process back in front of Carnegie Hall. You were a first-class operative—everyone was agreed on that. Just pretend we're playing scenario: a chance meeting generates a flight response. Use your Benz-and-Blazer-with-a-winch-on-the-bumper mind and make a fucking guess why."

Past the Metropolitan Museum, down the aisle of trees alongside the reservoir. Bicyclists swarmed past them, their chains sizzling. Madden turned his head to look right at Susan. "It's not a guess."

She waited.

Madden looked forward again. "When I asked Barnes if he remembered me, I didn't mean from the shop. I looked different in those days. I was different; I was trying to be different from what I was. Henry ran my group and was our intermediary with the eighty-ninth floor. I knew who Barnes was, of course, but I didn't see him weekly or even monthly. I had no basis on which to form an opinion about his personality."

"You said it wasn't a guess, Alan; now you're talking about opinions."

Madden worked on a rejoinder, then let it pass. "I didn't know when I was around the shop that Barnes was gay. I didn't find out until—Jesus, Henry!"

Aaronson had spun around to look at Madden, sitting behind him. The car headed for the guardrail. A taxi swerved around it, horn braying. Aaronson looked back at the road and got going straight again. He drove up the hill alongside the North Meadow and turned into the service road connecting the East and West drives. He stopped and turned the engine off.

No one spoke for a long time. The only sounds were bats on balls in the Meadow and cars on the drive and birds in the trees and planes overhead and sirens on the perimeter streets and the clicking of the car's metal as it relaxed.

"We used to belong to the same club, Barnes and I," Madden finally said. "A club, essentially, for gays who don't join clubs for gays. It's rather like one of those supereccentric British clubs where talking is discouraged if not prohibited, where members sit for days with newspapers in their laps before anyone realizes they're dead, not napping. Some very important people are members. There's some sexual contact among members, but that's not why people belong. They belong to... to belong. I resigned when my business began flourishing, for fear I'd run into one of my clients. Barnes may still be a member, for all I know....

"Why did I talk to him at Trees?" Madden shrugged. "I'd just broken up with someone I'd been seeing for a long time. I guess I was feeling sorry for myself. I thought... Well, Barnes and I have quite a bit in common, don't we? Maybe we could make some connection. It's absurd. I thought it for only a moment; the thought was gone by the time I got the words out of my mouth."

Another long time passed. Then Susan said, "Thank you, Alan. Where shall we drop you?"

"I'll get out here. I could use a walk."

Susan opened her door and got out and held the door for Madden. He didn't look at her when he spoke. "The winch is for a sailboat—a little thing—a Dyer—and for uprooting some stumps at the place out on the island. The halogen lights're for show. We're just like everybody else, you know." He walked toward the East Drive and crossed it and took a path leading south. Susan went to the verge of the service road and poked at the grass with a toe.

Aaronson got out of the car and stretched. The car phone rang and he leaned in the window and answered it. "Yeah?... What? ... What does that mean?... Yeah, I'll tell her." He hung up and stood straight and shrugged at Susan.

"What?"

"That was Grace Lewis. She said to tell you 'wrestling.' She said you'd know what it means."

Susan nodded.

"You *do* know what it means?"

233

Susan nodded.

"You going to tell me what it means?"

"Charles Fuller Nelson. Full nelson. Wrestling."

Aaronson shrugged. "Yeah? So what does that mean?"

The phone rang again.

"Enough already. This phone, it's like a mobile *yenta*."

Susan leaned in the car and answered it. "Yes?"

"Red, Susan. Are you ready for this?"

Susan waited.

"Aldrich just called. Rita's dead. In her apartment. Shot in the head. A thirty-eight. A professional whack. Dead a couple of days. With her, and also whacked, was Jack Collins. A porter found them after a neighbor complained about the smell. The apartment door was unlocked. The building's got a doorman, but there's a service entrance with a pickable lock. Collins had a set of picks in his pocket. Jesus, Susan. What the fuck and so on and so forth? And on top of everything, no one knows where Barnes is. He's been out of pocket since he went looking for you out on the island."

"Is Polly in Research?"

"I don't know. Who the fuck cares?"

"Hold her for Aldrich. The charge is conspiracy to murder."

"Polly? Murder who?"

"Have someone in Research do a lost-data search on that El-lesse sunglasses list. It ought to turn up Rachel Phillips's name. Tell Aldrich to tell his ballistics people to run the thirty-eight that killed Rita and Collins against the one that killed Needleman."

"The cabbie Needleman?"

"Yes."

"Murder who? Polly conspired to murder who?"

Susan sighed. "Paul, for one."

"Conspired with who?"

"Go get Polly. She may run, or she may get whacked. Like the others."

"Just tell me, Suze, are we still looking for someone conveniently located who went rogue or what?"

"A conveniently located left-handed bisexual who combs his hair straight back, wears contact lenses and Lacoste shirts, and who wrestled in high school or college."

"Wrestled?"

"Go get Polly, Red."

36

In the Palm Court of the Plaza, Barnes sat where he could watch a virgin with well-developed calves read the *Wall Street Journal* and drink a cappuccino. He ordered an iced espresso and told the waiter that he was the Mr. Nelson for whom a Miss Henry would be asking.

"I'm Helen Henry," the virgin said, folding her newspaper. She got up from her table and smiled at the waiter when he came to ferry her coffee cup across the room. She was Alcott and Andrews on the outside—linen suit, silk blouse, floppy bow tie —but something about the way she slalomed through the tables said that underneath she was Victoria's Secret—if she wore anything at all. Her calves were what Barnes thought of as French —Frencher than the calves of Marie-Christine the homeless French virgin, about whom he hadn't thought in days: Was she still living in his apartment? Did she miss him? How sharply had his Director-bucker stock tumbled when she answered his phone and told Georgetown she had *aucune idée* where he was?

Helen Henry gave Barnes a cool hand when he stood to greet her and looked him over without abashment before sitting down. (He was dressed all in black—black boat-neck cotton sweater, black cotton pants, black rope-soled espadrilles with no socks— an outfit the waiter had puckered his mouth at disapprovingly, finding it too louche for the surroundings.) "I expected someone older, grayer, less attractive. I'm delighted, of course, from a marketing standpoint, for I must say the prospect of meeting a—how did you put it on the phone?—'a federal narcotics agent with stories to tell' hardly induced fantasies of the best-seller list. I imagine Nelson's not your real name. If you're not wedded to it, I'm confident we can do better."

236

Barnes's expectation, formed from a newspaper article head-lined PUBLISHING'S NEW POWERHOUSE and illustrated by a file photograph many years out of date, had been of a strict librarian. Face to face, she had a whiskey voice, but on the phone it had sounded stern and cold. "It's a name to be discarded. I'm traveling light."

"Meaning you're being pursued?"

"My absence has people concerned. Before a full-scale search effort's made, they'll have to determine precisely the extent of the damage."

"And what have you got, exactly?"

"'Got'?"

"Files, records. Microfilm. Whatever."

He liked the caesura before *microfilm,* the little shrug that admitted she knew she'd seen too many movies. "It's all in here." Barnes tapped his forehead. "Everything."

She tossed her head at that assertion. Like the heroines on the covers of romance novels, she had dark ringlets that fell around her shoulders. "Everything you know, you mean. Everything that passed through your little niche."

"Everything. I'm the boss."

She gave his clothes a looking-over again. *"The* boss?"

"Of the New York office."

"Which must be a large office."

"Yes."

"And a very active one."

"Yes."

"One whose activities are constantly being meddled in by your superiors in Washington."

"Oh, yes."

She cocked her head and squinted into the middle distance of profit and loss. "That sort of Washington exposé, I must say — even one written from a New York perspective — is more appealing than a book exclusively about the plumbing of the narcotics business."

"I wasn't thinking exposé, exactly, and I certainly wasn't thinking plumbing," Barnes said. "I was thinking of something maybe a little more personal."

237

She frowned and leaned toward him, a move that afforded an opportunity to see what was under that blouse—or what wasn't. "How do you mean?"

"A book about me."

"*Just* about you?"

"I've done some controversial things."

"I'm sure."

"Unpopular things."

She smiled, sure of that too.

"The book would be a kind of... apologia." Her frown said she didn't know the word, that she imagined mawkish, unmarketable self-pity; so he added, "A defense. A justification."

A further tilt toward him; her top button had somehow come undone and she was all décolletage now. "What have you done, exactly?"

"I killed four people."

She pretended to pout. "Only four?"

"Recently."

"Drug dealers?"

"No. Two were agents; two were witnesses to the death of another agent, who was killed at my instigation. A fifth killing was also carried out at my instructions."

The slightest of shudders, until an explanation occurred to her. "Agents who were defectors, or whatever you call them?"

"We call them rogues."

"Rogues. It would be nice to use that word in the title somehow."

"I was the rogue," Barnes said. "I am the rogue."

She cocked her head and said with the singsong of a child who's certain she's being teased, "Killed them how?"

"I shot the agents in the backs of their heads, as I shot one of the witnesses, a taxi driver. The other witness, a derelict, I force-fed Scotch until he choked to death on his vomit. The agent I ordered killed was shot; the fifth victim was stabbed in the genitals with a sword."

She leaned away and looked at him sideways. "You're not serious. You *are* serious."

"Yes."

"Why?"

"I can't interest you by being frivolous. Can I?" He leaned forward to look down her blouse.

She clutched the placket. "I *meant,* why did you kill them?"

Barnes sat back and crossed his legs. "What's more interesting, at this point, is why're you still sitting here? Why aren't you out in the lobby, out in the street, screaming for help?"

"I guess. . . . "

"You don't believe me."

"No"—with fervor. "No, I do believe you."

"But—or and—you want to fuck me."

She set her jaw, but blushed. "How did you get my name?"

"Let's go upstairs to my suite. We'll be more comfortable."

"You said you read the piece in the *Times* about my recent successes."

"And about your bicoastal marriage. How does that work?"

"My husband's in the movie business."

Barnes laughed at her literalness. "Is his cock three thousand miles long?"

She sniffed. "Is yours?"

"No." He took out his wallet and put some money on the table and pushed his chair back. "Let's go."

She had both hands at her throat now. "I will scream."

"John."

"Let's go."

"*John!*"

Helen Henry sensed that the call was for him, and swiveled to see the woman standing at the entrance to the Palm Court. Hair cut like a boy's, dressed in jeans and boots and a work shirt and a blazer, she looked like a woman who knew what she was doing. "Help me, please," Helen Henry said.

"Move away from her, John," Susan said.

"I'm disappointed in you, Susan," Barnes said. "You should've taken me down minutes ago."

"Move away from her."

Barnes put his hand on Helen Henry's shoulder.

"Oh, no. Please God, no."

"It'll be all right, miss," Susan said. "What's your name?"

"H-Helen."

"It'll be all right, Helen. I promise. Just do what I say."

"Susan, you're really fucking this up." But he had fucked up, for though the room had been nearly empty, it hadn't been entirely empty, as it was now; he hadn't noticed the waiters clearing customers out and blocking new ones from coming in. Silence, cunning, exile: he'd lost his touch, his moves, his sense of where he was.

"Helen?"

"Y-Yes?"

"Get up, Helen. Leave your briefcase, your pocketbook; don't worry about them. Get up, push your chair in, move to your left. Do you know where your left is, Helen?"

Helen Henry flicked her left hand, like an uncertain schoolchild.

Susan smiled. "It wouldn't be surprising if you didn't. . . . Okay, Helen, do it now. Slowly. John, keep your left hand where I can see it—on the tabletop. You carry in an ankle holster. Seeing you draw at Rachel's was the first time I ever registered that you're left-handed. I've never noticed you writing anything. I guess you get to where you've gotten by writing down as few things as possible. I've had meals with you, so why I never noticed your handedness there I don't know. Maybe you ate sandwiches. Get up, Helen."

Helen Henry looked at Barnes, at Susan, at Barnes. She stood suddenly, nearly upsetting the table. She banged from chair to chair until she was out of the Court and into helping hands.

Barnes considered using the momentary distraction to draw his .38, but Susan never took her eyes off him. "It was at Rachel's, even before I saw you draw, that I made the connection between the shirts you're so fond of and poor Hugh Morgan's alligator man. That was why I wouldn't take delivery. The hair —well, you have different hair from Paul's, so that part of his peril didn't read very well. The contact lenses were a surprise. You're so vain, you didn't want anyone to know you needed glasses. Not even Joanna knew. Joanna's quite upset about the messages you left for Sally. She didn't play them for her and she has no intention of doing so. She feels, quite rightly, that it's she who's owed the explanation. How foolish to leave a phone number, John. And it was foolish to be a member of Alan Madden's club and to deal with Cool D over the phone. You're a classic case of a crook who wants to be caught."

Barnes laughed. "And yours is the classic bluff. You're talking far too much, Susan. It's only in the movies that the good guys tell the bad guys how they figured it out. Where's your backup? You don't go solo after a rogue. Where're you carrying? In your bag? Never carry in your bag."

"You kept the wrestling a secret too. You were ashamed of it, weren't you? It puts you in the same bag with the phonies on television. You wish you'd done a more glamorous sport. Tennis or rowing. Paul rowed, for the A.C. I remember how you used to pooh-pooh it, but with a kind of envy. You wish you'd been with a more glamorous outfit—the bureau, the company. It was easy to betray us because of your contempt for us. You're a snob."

It was that simple. He had wrestled because he had been undisciplined at tennis, because he had not been tall enough for rowing. And how easy it had been to betray wrestling for smoking, drinking and fucking. For tennis, for rowing, he would've turned his back on smoking, drinking and fucking. Especially for rowing. Collins had rowed. How dismayed he had been to discover that Collins had rowed, had been what Barnes had only daydreamed that he might be. And then he remembered that he had recruited Collins because he had rowed, because he had been what Barnes had only daydreamed that he might be: Collins had rowed six on a crew that won the Easterns and lost to Washington by a deck in the IRA's; Collins had done a year of graduate work in England and stroked the crew that had been Head of the River at the Cambridge Lents and Mays. Head of the River at the Cambridge Lents and Mays: there was nothing so fine-sounding as that for a wrestler to achieve. There was nothing so fine-sounding as that to be achieved anywhere.

And just as Barnes had wrestled because he was undisci-

241

plined at tennis and not tall enough for rowing, so he had joined the shop because he was not straight enough for this agency, a little too straight for that, not brilliant enough for another. And just as it had been easy to betray wrestling for smoking, drinking and fucking, so it had been easy to betray the shop for money, drugs and sex, for that's what it had come down to, that's how simple it was.

Barnes wagged a thumb in the direction of Helen Henry's exit. "Helen's a book editor. Very successful. There was a piece about her in the *Times*. I thought why wait till I'm captured and tried and convicted to tell my story? Why not get a jump on things, tell it while it's still fresh? She was very interested. She was interested in me too. It's a thing that happens between me and women, Susan. I'll go to my grave regretting that it never happened between me and you."

"We've got Polly, John," Susan said. "What did you promise her that she would go and ruin her life? You son-of-a-bitch."

For an instant he thought she meant Polly the nicotine-caffeine-cocaine triathlete illegal-alien-of-a-sort record-pirate virgin from Hoboken. Then he remembered that he'd had an accomplice—Polly the computer specialist virgin who liked him to use a necktie or a belt to tie her wrists in the small of her back, then be in her from behind. He'd promised her nothing but what he'd given her—lunch-hour fucks in a Battery Park City apartment rented for the purpose, a week a year on some warm island and all the cocaine she could inhale.

"And never letting Rachel know that I was a narc." Susan shook her head sadly. "You son-of-a-bitch.... *That's* the thing that happens between you and women—between you and everyone: they trust you and you deceive them. You son-of-a-bitch."

There was a hubbub in the lobby now and Barnes knew that cops were arriving, summoned by the management, no doubt, being kept at bay for the moment by Sayles or someone—whomever Susan was working with. But only for the moment. Soon there would be too many of them to keep corralled—which might mean some salutary (from his point of view) confusion. It was time for a serious lie to stir things up, to make her go for her gun. "Of course, Paul and I were lovers, so I fucked you indirectly."

She didn't bite. She didn't even nibble. She just waited.

Barnes laughed. "How do you think Paul knew all my secrets? Even Joanna didn't know all my secrets."

"Save it, John. Save it for your book."

That's what Collins had said. More or less. *Save it, you scumbag.* No interest whatsoever—even after watching Barnes whack Rita, even after making final sense out of Van Meter's peril—no interest in knowing why someone conveniently located would go rogue. Barnes had told him anyway:

Because none of it matters—being conveniently located, being successful, being smarter than the bad guys, being Head of the River at the Cambridge Lents and Mays. All that matters is saying hello to Jackie Robinson, how well you play the bongos, and whether you can dance all night.

He'd told him and then he'd whacked him.

It wasn't going to make much of a book, was it, if that was the best he could do for an explanation. He'd have to reread *Othello,* and see what made Iago tick. Maybe he'd find a title in *Othello;* he didn't have a title now. He didn't need to be a publishing powerhouse with French calves to know *Someone Conveniently Located Who Went Rogue* was not a very good title.

Oh, hell. Fuck the book. Besides, who would play him in the movie? A star wouldn't play someone who went rogue. It would have to be someone a little bent, someone the audience wouldn't buy the starlet virgins sleeping with.

And who would play Susan? It was really Susan's movie, wasn't it? Jane Fonda. Sigourney Weaver. Susan wasn't as beautiful as either of them, but he still wished he'd fucked her. He wished he'd fucked Paul too—and Collins, before he whacked him. And Rita, even Rita. And Helen Henry the publishing powerhouse with French calves, of course.

That was about it. He'd pretty much fucked everyone else he wanted to.

It's Susan's movie. Let her get the glory in the end and the last motherfucking word.

243

And Barnes went for the .38 in his ankle holster and Susan went for the .38 in the holster in the small of her back and she outdrew him and shot him in the left elbow, shattering it, which was the thing he hated about women—that at a time like that, when the SOP said shoot to kill, they could have the thought that if they did, you'd be dead, beyond pain, beyond suffering, that you'd be Head of the River at the Cambridge Lents and Mays, and what they wanted was that you suffer, so they shot you in the elbow, or the kneecap, or the balls.

37

"Hi."

Ted Scally took his Wayfarers down out of his hair and put them on before opening his eyes. "Hi."

"Mind if I sit?"

"That end of the bench'll be in the sun in about five minutes."

"That's about all the time I have." Susan sat and watched an old-timers' handball game. "It's a wonder they can play in this heat."

"You going to be here long?"

"No."

"Long enough to, you know, have a drink or dinner or something?"

"No."

"Lunch maybe? Brunch?" Some of the dudes he'd done points with should hear him—inviting a woman to brunch.

"No."

"Too bad. It's nice to see you."

"It's nice to see you."

"First time in Miami?"

"Yes. It's pretty, what I've seen of it. Dramatic. But so hot."

"*Are* you a narc, or what?"

"Yes."

"That night at Rachel's, with people kissing each other and walking into swimming pools and shooting off guns and driving off every which way, I kind of lost track of whether I thought so or not. I guess you came to collect Rachel."

Susan nodded. "How did you know she was down here?"

"Just by pure dumb luck that night, I ended up behind you guys on the Sunrise and followed you to Kennedy. I'd never been

245

here, either, so I decided to come on down. You're too late, by the way. Rachel got busted last night."

"Those were my people," Susan said.

"Hunh. I'd've thought you'd want to be in on it, after all the work you did."

"Rachel killed my husband. He was a narc too. My bosses're afraid I might accidentally shoot her in the crotch."

Scally smiled, then winced. "That's tough—about your husband. So Carrie's your daughter?"

For a fraction of a second, Susan wanted to take her gun out of her bag and blow his head off, for she'd clearly fucked up one more time that she wasn't aware of. "How do you know about Carrie?"

"I listened on the extension at Rachel's place in town the night you called her. July Fourth."

"Why did you listen?"

"I wondered who you were calling."

"You never told Rachel?"

He just gave her his what-do-I-look-like-a-stone-psycho-killer? look. "So the woman named Bob is who?"

"My mother-in-law."

Families: they could twist on and on in every direction, couldn't they? Would he ever have one that did, even just a little, even in just one direction? "How'd you know I was here?"

"I watched the bust last night, and spotted you. Where'd you disappear to anyway? After the night you were in the stable, I mean."

Scally sighed. "You knew I was in the stable, hunh?"

Susan smiled. "Yes."

"I just figured it'd be better for me to be on the outside looking in, instead of inside and all knotted up in it. I'm not exactly Mister Clean, though. How come you don't bust me?"

"There's no point. You never got in my way and arguably you helped me. The driving you did, well, we'll just pretend you were unwitting. . . . We picked Nick Ivory up Tuesday in Seattle, trying to get on a flight to Tokyo. He'll face some kind of charge in Kit Bolton's death and he's already started singing that Rachel killed Ornella."

He hadn't read about it, but then he'd stopped reading the *New York Times;* he read the *Miami Herald* and the *Miami Beach Mortician,* read mostly the job listings and the apartments for rent, read them but didn't do anything about them because he wasn't quite sure yet if doing something about them was the thing to do until he knew for sure whether it meant anything that Darby knew stone psycho killer Jerome. "Nice of him."

"They're nice people. I was getting a little worried about all the time you were spending with Nick, playing with his toys. I guess you were just doing research."

"Armorology," Scally said. He thought about telling her about the 'Vette he'd technically stolen and about the various purchases he'd made with the cash and the plastic; and about the gun and sundry items stone psycho killer Jerome helped him get. And then he thought again, because all he'd be doing was showing off in some way that he didn't really understand because it wasn't really his way; and he knew he didn't really want her to think he was a car thief and someone who shopped with other people's plastic and a would-be stone psycho killer and maybe he had done some felonious things in his time but most of them he'd done because he'd been so goddamn miserable about Ornella's dying. "I met a nice lady down here. Her name's Darby. She works at the Kennel Club.

Susan turned her head and gave him a long look. "I'm happy for you, Ted. If you're happy. You don't look too happy."

Scally shrugged. "I don't know. How do you know if somebody's right for you? I mean, if they take you for a walk and show you a homemade sign that instead of saying beer soda sandwiches says beer soda *sad*wishes, is that more important than it turning out they know somebody you just happen to know is a stone psycho killer?"

Susan didn't think long about it. "Yes, it's more important."

He laughed. "Sounds funny, hearing you call me Ted."

"Sounded funny saying it."

"Is Susan your real name or your narc name?"

"My real name. Susan Van Meter."

247

"They teach you in narc school about people like Rachel?"

"No. Not really."

"Did you think when you sent her down here she'd go off the deep end?"

Susan shook her head. "You'll be reading in the papers about the arrest of somebody important who was the real kingpin of Rachel's operation. I needed Rachel out of the way for a few days while I went after him. I figured even if she got restless, being out of her element, and came back to New York, I'd know where to find her. Did she start hooking right away?"

"Like she'd been waiting all her life for the chance."

"Maybe she had been. It's just as well, isn't it?"

"How do you mean?"

"I mean it fascinated you, so you just sat and watched. If you hadn't, you might've killed her. I had you followed last night and searched your room this morning when you went out for breakfast. If you paid a lot for the gun I'll give you some money."

He shook his head. "You've been a kind of momma to me through this whole thing, haven't you?"

She smiled. "I guess maybe I chose that role to make sure I wouldn't get any closer than that."

"Our famous kiss," Scally said.

"Our famous kiss." Susan got up and fanned at her face. "This end's officially unbearable."

Scally stretched out his legs and put his Wayfarers up in his hair and folded his arms. "I've got a couple of more minutes here before I have to move. I've never lived anywhere where there wasn't snow or you could drive to it in a couple of hours."

"Maybe you'll take up water skiing."

He smiled. "Maybe."

Susan backed away. "Good luck, Ted."

"You, too, Susan. I hope...."

She stopped. "What?"

"I don't know. It's none of my business and I don't mean to take away your right to mourn, but if you wind up with somebody, I hope it's somebody you like."

"Thanks."

"Not some rock star or playboy or former tennis great or baby mogul or heir or scion or wimp."

Susan laughed and waved and turned and walked straight into the sun.